MW00714690

THE LAND'S LONG REACH

We gratefully acknowledge the support of the Canada Council for the Arts and the Ontario Arts Council for our publishing program. We also acknowledge the financial support of the Government of Canada.

Cover artwork: Mary Riter Hamilton, "Mount St. Éloi," Library and Archives Canada, reproduction copy number C-101318.
Cover design: Val Fullard

The Land's Long Reach is a work of fiction. All the characters and situations portrayed in this book are fictitious and any resemblance to persons living or dead is purely coincidental.

Library and Archives Canada Cataloguing in Publication

Mills-Milde, Valerie, 1960-, author
     The land's long reach / Valerie Mills-Milde.

(Inanna poetry & fiction series)
Issued in print and electronic formats.
ISBN 978-1-77133-509-6 (softcover).— ISBN 978-1-77133-510-2 (epub).—
ISBN 978-1-77133-511-9 (Kindle).— ISBN 978-1-77133-512-6 (pdf)

     I. Title. II. Series: Inanna poetry and fiction series

PS8626.I4568L36 2018   C813'.6   C2018-901533-0
                                               C2018-901534-9

Printed and bound in Canada

Inanna Publications and Education Inc.
210 Founders College, York University
4700 Keele Street, Toronto, Ontario, Canada M3J 1P3
Telephone: (416) 736-5356 Fax: (416) 736-5765
Email: inanna.publications@inanna.ca   Website: www.inanna.ca

THE
LAND'S
LONG
REACH

a novel

Valerie Mills-Milde

inanna poetry & fiction series

INANNA PUBLICATIONS AND EDUCATION INC.
TORONTO, CANADA

For Donna

You have to be true to yourself but at the same time understand,
or try to, the world today in all of its manifestations.....
The artist is and always has been ahead of his time.
—Yvonne Mckague Housser, Canadian painter, 1897-1996

*R*UN. *HURRY. FASTER.* Margaret Carter is hurling herself down the footpath that leads to the still.

The path is slick with mud and melting snow and her legs are weak. Spindly cedars crowd in, and to keep from falling, she grabs a branch, wrenching her shoulder and instantly, there is an explosion of pain.

She stops and closes her eyes, tears of astonishment forming.

Damn. If Margaret says this out loud, she doesn't know it; a fever in childhood took part of her hearing. Sounds are felt as much as they are heard, and now the pain in her body is a screech, a howl.

She opens her eyes, the pain receding. *Look around,* she commands herself. *Where are you? Where?* Through the trees, a dull moon; no help with illuminating the rocks that are half-sunk in muck. *Keep going. You can't stay here.* Her feet strike hard things, the soft soles of her shoes giving little protection. No matter. Leaving the house, she had given no thought to a coat or boots.

She doesn't feel the chill tonight although the air is heavy. Rotting logs and leaves. Earth and wood smoke. The smell of the mash, sickening even after years of living with it. Dizzy now, her stomach heaving. *Don't stop. Go on.* Her mind spins and then slows, a picture emerging, a story she once told the boys: trees that become horses and green moss that turns into saddles, soft cedar branches that transform into reins. *You climb up on the backs of these creatures and ride to the other side of the woods, where there is sunlight and clear water.* She sees the horses, their thrusting heads, their sure-footed gallop, and feels herself grow lighter, stronger.

It was after her hearing went down that Margaret began to read in earnest, devouring fairy tales, every adventure story she could find. And then the stories had come to her without the need for books. She hadn't written them down. Perhaps she should have.

Further. Go further. Just ahead, the glint of metal. The open ground around the still is stirred with footprints, a mess of broken jars, pails, empty pallets. Four stumps have been dragged close for sitting. The stream is fast and swollen with melt, a glitter on the water near the bank. Light cast by flame, the fire licking the belly of the still.

No one's here. She knew he wouldn't be. *Further now, go on.* It's a relief to be moving. The path peters out just beyond the still, but her legs seem to know the direction. And then, in front of her, the ground swims up, the trees swirling, and to steady herself, she squats, puts her head in her arms, her thighs trembling beneath her. Water drips down the back of her neck. Cool drops that trace the length of her spine, soft like a child's finger.

Run. Try. She gets up and stumbles, gets up again. She has dreamt of places that are far away, of emerald jungles, of flat-footed elephants, of ships rolling in the sea. Now somewhere here, not far, is the only thing that matters. A child. Her very own.

The stream is vanishing while all around the trees fall away. The sky is open. Sour clouds, a frail moon. Ice on the swamp, deadwood thrusting through, a dirty glitter where there is melt. A ringing in her head. No sounds. She strains to hear. *Catch breath.* Falling on her knees, her eyes scrub the ragged, muddy shoreline, her heart thrashing in her throat.

Over there. Go on. Go. Reach.

1. MAY 1914

ENA IS ON HER KNEES in her garden when Hugh drives in with the bull, the animal a wedding gift, and late, because Jamie and Ena were married last October.

Never in Ena's life has she seen a bull this close. It stands on a cart behind Hugh's team of horses, all four legs bound to the cart's rails. There is a mountainous hump where a neck should be, and rigid waves of muscle cascade down the shoulders. The body and face are a splattering of black and white, and a fawn-coloured sac hangs between its legs. The animal is wall-eyed, the skull boxy. The head is pulled forward by a taut rope that has been looped through a ring in its nose. When Ena studies the soft and exposed throat she feels a sickening tug between staring and looking away.

"Got your bull," hollers Hugh, standing, hoisting his trousers. He squares his shoulders and studies the yard, the bull letting out a long, rising bellow that breaks in a series of snorts. Hearing it from inside the barn, Billie, the border collie, starts up with her yipping.

The barn door opens and Jamie ambles out, Billie trotting behind him, her nose to his boot heels, her tongue lolling. In his hand is a tall Hawthorn staff, the instrument of persuasion he intends for the bull, and he lifts it high in a wide, graceful arc.

"Look what the cat drug in," he calls, grinning. The smile opens his face, which is narrow and gently angular. His bright hair is shaved close at the temple, the front fringe left long and swinging to one side where it grazes his cheek.

"Yup. Well, you better be talkin' about that bull and not me," answers Hugh, his voice at once playful and gruff.

Jamie silently laughs, his head nodding affably, his face taking on a shine. "Either way you want to take it. " Then: "See you brought the boy—"

Hugh has brought Blain Carter with him, a newly hired hand. Blain is related to Clem, Hugh's lead man. His gangly legs hang from the side of the wagon and his dusty boots wag loosely off his heels. He wears black suspenders and brown trousers, and a blue-checked shirt billows at his thin waist; pale shinbones flash above his brown socks.

"You gonna get down, Blain?" Hugh frowns at the boy, his head jerking toward the bullpen. "You help Jamie set the ramp. Then you be ready with the gate on that pen. And to give a hand with the lead, case we need you."

Ena looks at the bull. It is so heavily muscled she wonders if it can walk. Her gaze shifts to Blain who jumps from the wagon and scratches energetically behind one of his red-tipped ears. His expression looks easy and smoothed over, as if he conceals some secret feeling—wariness or doubt. He is considering the ramp, the effort it will take to lift it.

In April, Ena had been at the home farm visiting with Hugh's wife, Sarah. Glancing out the parlour window, she'd seen Blain aimlessly shovelling manure in the yard. Part way through the job he'd simply stopped working and studied the sky, a dreamy look floating across his features. Despite a cutting north wind, he wore no coat.

Later, as they drove home, she asked Jamie who the boy was that Hugh had working for him—the boy seemed lost, she said, and he wasn't properly clothed.

Jamie gazed at her, curiosity in the look. It wasn't like Ena to ask about other people. She seldom ventured into other people's lives. The clamour of other people's feelings disturbed her, the thrust of their disappointments, their desires.

"You must mean Blain. He's Clem and Annie's nephew. Lost his mum a few weeks back. You likely read about it in the paper, Ena—Margaret Carter was her name. She got turned around in their bush and went through some ice."

Ena had recalled an article in the *Sound Times* from several weeks past, a story about the remains of a woman, discovered somewhere in the southern part of the Bruce Peninsula, the body found floating in a half-frozen swamp. The woman had been face down, as though she were little more than dross or jetsam. Apart from her name, the article gave next to nothing about her.

"You knew her...?"

"Margaret used to help Mom with keeping house. I think she was deaf or close to it. Always talking a little too much, shouting to push the words out so people would hear her. Got on Mom's nerves some," he'd chuckled kindly with the memory, "but she was a cheerful enough girl."

Ena watches Blain and Jamie drag the ramp for the bull, Jamie bearing most of the weight. Next to the bull, Blain is utterly frail looking, something about him like a plant uprooted. After the ramp is secured, he walks the length of the wagon, the slight sway of his back giving him a rocking gait, just short of swagger. He circles the wagon twice, a mindless energy in his legs, his hands jammed into his pockets. Occasionally he lifts his feet as if to ease them, his gaze moving between the arc of the fields, and the garden where Ena kneels, her brown dress pooled over her thighs. Their eyes meet and for a moment they each become as still as stones. And then the intensity of the boy's gaze breaks, his features melting into a lazy smile. He turns his head toward Billie who stalks around the horses' giant hooves, sniffing the ground, whining. Blain lifts his knuckles to his head and rubs, the gesture already familiar.

From the wagon, Hugh takes off his hat and tosses it, the brim catching the boy at the point of his shoulder. "Blain, is that dog more interesting than this damn bull?"

Blain is suddenly wide-eyed, looking up at Hugh. "There's a dog over at Jackson's Corner that took off," he says. It sounds like nonsense, each word tumbling over the next. "Gone for months and no one knew where. Then one day he showed up, sitting next to the barn and missing an ear—"

"Blain, you gonna talk all day about dogs or are you ready to move that bull." Hugh is scowling, his chin pushed out, his eyes buried beneath his brows.

"No. Not a bit. I'm ready, Mr. McFarland."

"Glad to hear it. Now, you gotta check again and make sure that ramp's really secure."

When Blain moves off, Hugh throws his coat onto the driver's bench of the wagon and rolls back his sleeves. His forearms are amber-coloured, like Jamie's. A sigh rises from him, his palm thumping his chest twice, as if to dislodge some small scrap of irritation. Reaching into his back pocket, he pulls out a pair of thick black gloves.

Blain hops on the ramp, jumps up and down, and then fingers the knotted ropes that Jamie has tied at the corners. "It's real good, Mr. McFarland," he says, nodding as if to assure himself. He leaps from the ramp and saunters to the fence.

Hugh and Jamie talk, Hugh still up on the wagon with the bull, Jamie on the ground with Billie. The McFarland brothers have light hair, although Hugh's is ashier. While Jamie is long-boned and fluid, Hugh's shape is a collection of hard mounds, thrusting lines, a handsome enough man except for the wayward eye—the left one—which veers badly outward, not staying fixed but perpetually struggling to come back into line.

A single cloud floats across the sun, its shadow more dramatic because of the absence of others. In a moment the sun shows again, more brilliant than it was before. Ena blinks and adjusts her sight, her focus keenly fixed on the men, the boy, and the animal. Earlier that morning, Jamie had told Ena it can be a big job, moving a bull, and anything can happen. Now, seeing the rope-bound bull and the men so close to it chatting idly in the sun, it seems to Ena that the moment will go on forever. The bull will stay tied to the wagon, the boy will be always leaning against the fencepost, Jamie and Hugh will share stories, trade news of their neighbours, rib one another, talk about the market price of their crops.

The sun is climbing the sky, the heat pressing on her back. The spring has almost passed she thinks, eagerness mounting in her belly. She turns to the garden and scoops black earth into her hand. Holding it to her nose, she breathes, the smell making her think about stone and iron and rotted leaves. Today she will put in her peas, although Jamie had warned her it was too early to plant. In May, this close to Georgian Bay, she might wake up to a frost.

Although Ena knows almost nothing about gardens, she looks at the loosened ground, imagining the possibility of rows of tender green shoots: peas, cabbage, beans, and potatoes. One entire row *just* for tomatoes, she decides. Ena feels the sharp anticipation of a harvest—her first. Two weeks before, she had taken a spade and dug around the edges of the overgrown plot, and then turned the heavy soil with a fork. She's grown stronger since coming to the farm; when she looks at herself in the mirror she doesn't see a woman but rather a boy—her centre of gravity seated in her powerful thighs and calves. Her deep-set eyes shine back at her, the colour of Indian tea.

Watching her work, Hugh, who had been helping Jamie with the ploughing, had given her an encouraging wink. The very next day, he surprised her with a full wagon of rotted manure. "This will kick up whatever you got growing," he grinned over the rise of his shoulder as he shovelled clumps of manure from the cart. He'd stood and watched her for a few minutes, curiosity and amusement in his face.

"You got any questions about how to *plant* a garden?"

Ena had shaken her head *no* and Hugh let out a long round-sounding laugh. "You afraid of words or are words afraid of you, Ena?"

Ena had stared at the uneven soil for a moment. "Fear's got nothing to do with it," she said, raising her gaze to him.

He'd looked back at her quizzically and shrugged. "Best leave you to it, then."

She liked Hugh but the sheer force of him was a distraction. What she wanted was to enter into the puzzle of the garden on her own. She'd applied all the strength she had into preparing the plot and after it was done, her body was alive with pain, her back throbbing, her calves tight. When she thinks of the ache, she savours the memory.

She looks away from the garden now and lets her eyes travel the newly furrowed fields that stretch behind the grey barn and end in a line of dense bush. To the east of the barn is an ancient orchard, the trees stooped, the limbs tangled and broken. These are Russet trees and their apples, if they still produce any, will be nutty and dry. Perfect for baking. Next spring she will learn how to prune them.

The house rises, sober and plain behind her, a single gothic window above a narrow porch, a peaked roof, no gables or fret-work. It sits at the centre of the farm, and the land flows away from it in all directions.

JAMIE FIRST BROUGHT HER HERE the summer before they married. He had slowed the horse gradually and turned into a lane that was bristling with thorn and golden rod.

"A fine sort of place," he joked, nodding at the forlorn house, "for a family of rabbits. What do you think, Ena? Is it fit for people?" His eyes narrowed as they moved slowly over the ragged fields. "Not as many acres as the home farm. This one belonged to Uncle Ross." He pushed his hands into his pockets and smiled, suddenly shy with her. There was an appeal in the look. "Ross was old—he'd let things go before he died. People can't go on caring for things by themselves. We're dividing land now. The family, I mean. I'll take this farm over. Hugh's working the bigger one—Dad's farm. "

He'd gazed into the west, where summer thunderclouds were building, large overblown heads of grey-white glowering in the distance. Turning, he drew her in close, and then lowering his head, he kissed her, stroking the hollow of her cheek with his thumb.

"We could make something of the place, Ena. You and me."

She had circled him with her arms. They stood like that on the tilting porch, hardly noticing that the rain had started.

ENA LETS THE EARTH FALL through her open fingers. The sensation of it leaving her causes a ruffling in her chest, a strange weightlessness and she puts both palms down against the feeling, the heels of her hand pressed deeply, assuredly, into the cold ground. She pushes herself up to a stand.

The day is clear, the light almost too sharp, and she throws an arm across her eyes and studies the men's progress with the bull. Blain is standing to the side of one of the enormous horses, his hand on its halter, his eyes on Hugh who is undoing a rope from one of the bull's bony legs.

"Not too fast, Hugh." Jamie walks slowly up the ramp. Hugh grunts out a response and, freeing one of the bull's legs, he moves to another leg, the muscles in his back fanning broadly as he squats.

Jamie shifts himself to the other side of the bull, his hand on its bulging side. Although she can't hear him, she knows he is talking to it, soothing it. Co-boss, co-boss, he'll croon. She's heard him do it with the six milking cows they bought earlier in the spring. Before he brought them to the farm, Jamie had made repairs to the barn—securing stalls, hanging lamps, bringing in the milking equipment. Now, with the bull, their herd is growing.

The bull's massive shoulders are hunched, its sides heaving. She can see the lolling whites of its eyes. Jamie leans back his head and calls to Hugh: "He's not easy, we should blinder him."

"No need. Tame enough. We had no trouble with loading."

The lead rope bristles between the shiny nose ring and the great wheel mounted on the floor of the wagon. Hugh bends to the wheel, turning it, and the lead rope slackens.

Jamie reluctantly takes his hand from the bull's mottled side. "I'll stay ready with the staff." Swinging his legs over the rails he jumps from the wagon. There is a grace in Jamie, a kind of languor which Hugh, teasing, calls laziness. Jamie's strength is always a surprise. He turns and looks at Blain who is now planted resolutely against the fence. His shoulders hunch up to his flared ears, and the point of his boot digs mercilessly at a ragged bit of chickweed.

"You best move away from there, closer to the pen, and get ready to help with the rope." Jamie says.

Hugh has completely freed the lead from the wheel. Holding the rope firmly in his gloved hands, he carefully steps backward and the whole time his eyes are on the bull. He stops at the bottom of the ramp and heaves the lead tight. The bull's head swings and jerks as if testing his strength.

Excited now, Billie wheels around the wagon, her head down. Small for a collie; Jamie's little shadow, she has one brown eye and one blue. Jamie glances at the dog and then studies the bull, changing his position to get a better angle.

"Don't rile him, Hugh."

But Hugh is off the ramp, tugging, his full weight against the bull. "C'mon now, silly bugger. Into the pen."

Ena sees Blain press himself further against the fence, one boot heel hooked on the lowest rail, his arms wrapped around his belly. He openly gawks at the bull but the men don't pay him any mind. They only see the animal, which, free of its footholds, quivers as though it's being bitten by flies.

"C'mon, you," Hugh shouts, widening his stance. One hand slides up the rope to add to the tension, and his bare arms swell against the bull's resistance.

Jamie is shaking his head, a bright lank of hair swinging across his face. "Holdup, Hugh! Give 'im a chance."

But Hugh has thrown himself completely against the bull. With one determined tug, he has the bull lurching down the ramp, its hooves slipping and clambering, its small black eyes rolling.

"Slow, slow," yells Jamie, and then Hugh tugs again.

There is a bellow. It draws Ena in closer to the yard. The bull seems to charge and then stumble, righting itself by leaping too soon off the ramp, lurching and then landing woodenly on four legs. It stands frozen, its tail held up in an arch.

Keeping the rope taut, Hugh walks sideways toward the pen and Jamie moves with him beside the bull, his staff ready. "Easy, easy," he croons. The bull's spindly tail flicks and its head comes down. "Hugh." Jamie circles around to where Hugh stands with the rope wound around his waist. "Secure the lead, Hugh," he says quietly. "Do it now."

There isn't time. In an explosion of earth, the bull bucks, leaps, shimmies into the wooden fence where the boy is standing. For an instant, Hugh is on his backside, and then he's up again. Ena can't see the boy. His slight frame is hidden behind the rise of the bull's neck. It's pawing the ground, its bulk grinding into the fence, its weight thrown against the lead. Ena runs a few steps and then stops, her heart jumping and thrashing. She runs closer, skirting the perimeter of the fence, staying away from where the bull has the boy pinned.

Hugh is in the grip of the struggle, the muscles in his arms now frankly straining. Ena can see the beads of sweat at the top of his brow.

"Let it go, Hugh," Jamie shouts. "Drop the damn rope and he'll run."

Hugh is about to drop the lead but then there is a new tension in it, the animal throwing itself away from him, Hugh cursing, his boot heels gouging the ground.

The boy is partly eclipsed, only an arm, the tip of one black boot visible now. The bull is too large for the yard, for the men. It blocks out everything, a heavy cloud that moves suddenly across the sun. Jamie charges at the bull with his staff, jabbing at its face and throat, and all the while, Billie snaps at its legs, dancing just below its bulbous chest, drawing it away from Blain.

Fixing its eyes on the dog, the bull snorts, its great head twisting against the rope, and then it lunges. The fence shakes as the bull releases its weight, and Hugh finds slack in the rope. He runs to the pen and ties the lead to the gate.

Jamie drops the staff and takes up the slack, and together they haul the bull toward the pen. The dog is nipping and jumping at its hindquarters, the bull breaking into an innocent trot, almost eager for enclosure, and once inside, Jamie slides the bolt closed and wraps a chain around the post.

Ena doesn't think *get water* but she finds that she is moving. A freshly filled pail sits by the barn door and she takes hold of it and runs, her skirt lifted, her free arm held out for balance.

Still upright against the fence, his body sagging, knees buckling, Blain's eyes are huge with astonishment. One of his hands moves to his chest and his mouth gapes. Holding on to the pail, Ena climbs over the fence rail but Jamie has gotten to him first. He guides the boy down onto the ground and slowly rubs his chest.

"Go easy, now."

Blain is nodding, his lips forming words but no sound comes out.

"You feel hurt anywhere?" Jamie's long fingers travel over Blain's slight frame, checking him. "There. Now you're breathing better. Anything feel like it's broke?"

With his eyes pinned to Jamie, Blain shakes his head. "No," he gasps. "Think I was just enough underneath—didn't get the brunt." He sucks in air then rushes toward more words. "Thought he'd got me—"

Grinning, Jamie taps Blain's thin chest. "Save your air."

Hugh is unconcerned and leaning against the post behind them. "Boy's still got the damn gift of gab. Guess he'll live."

Ena draws water into her palm and lets a few droplets fall over Blain's face and hair while Jamie squats next to him, his gaze fixed on the bull who now stands dully at the corner of its pen.

"Boy's going to be sore, after bearing all that weight. But everything seems to be where it should be." He looks at Hugh. "We all got lucky." He stands and leans against the fence.

"Damn bull is a mad bugger," Hugh grumbles, kicking the ground.

Jamie laughs, his hand now on Billie, his fingers rubbing her outstretched chin. "Don't think he is. This is a new place for him. Bulls don't like change. You pushed him too hard, Hugh."

Hugh glares hard at his brother. "You're soft. Too bloody soft."

Ena peers into Blain's face. She reaches out and touches his downy cheek and feels heat. His colour is seeping back.

"Should'a seen that comin'," he wheezes, shaking his head, almost smiling in wonder.

She puts more water to his lips. "Take some." He cranes his neck and drinks from her hand, lapping the water up like a puppy would. Water clings to his speckled lips. He looks up at her, and she sees him wince away a tear. Not more than fifteen, she estimates, now that she sees him this close. Hugh will want to fire him for being so careless around the bull. He might do it yet, after they have gone from here, once they are back at the home farm. Hugh should have known better than to bring a boy.

Jamie nods in the direction of the bull. "Don't ever be up against a fence or in a tight spot with a moving bull. Gotta give yourself some room, in case you need it."

Blain grins, embarrassed now but not contrite. "Don't think I'll forget—"

Looking up at the brash spring sky, Hugh starts to laugh. "The damn bull don't *like* change. Well, I don't *like* bulls." He grunts then and glares at the boy, his jaw held sideways as if he's considering something. "You're okay. Go on up with Ena. She'll fix you up. "

As Ena takes Blain's arm and walks with him up to the house, the farm seems to sigh and settle into its usual peace. For the moment, even the bull is quiet.

2.

WITH THE EARLY SUMMER HEAT, Blain keeps the bedroom window open at night, waiting for a merciful wind. The Carter house is built low, in the old style and it is surrounded by ragged brush. Inside, the air carries mildew, and dank smells invade from the swamp: decaying logs, sludge, and the unmistakable sweetness of fermenting mash. His mother used to say the smell of mash was worse than living above a barn full of hogs. Tonight, rising up through the usual funk is the cold pure smell of alcohol. The old man is pouring jars, the vapour from the still reaching Blain in his bedroom, a knife boring a hole through Blain's left temple.

Ten minutes earlier, a truck had pulled up, its predatory headlights sweeping the walls of his room, its engine sputtering. Now there are voices. Someone clears his throat and horks. Men talk, laugh, swear. There is the rattle of glass as the jars are stacked into wooden crates and the crates slid into the back of a wagon.

Blain sits on the floorboards by the side of his bed, his spine pressed against the rough wall, his shoulders curled. In the centre of his chest is a dull ache, a reminder of the weight of the bull. With the passing weeks, his bruises have faded but, in the beginning, his body was a flow of vivid colour—yellow, green, purple. He remembers how Ena McFarland had wordlessly sat him on a kitchen chair and checked him over, her eyes narrowed in concentration. Her hands, where she touched him, were firm. After, she'd taken him out to the porch and poured him a glass of strawberry cordial and water. "I got a story 'bout a man who got kill't by his own bull," he started-up, his voice wheezy and strained. Ena had not shushed him and he'd felt better, talking, even if the story was just made-up.

Instead of listening to the men outside, he'd like to go back in to his brother. Owen had taken his time tonight, falling asleep. "Tell me a story, Blain," he'd said, propping himself up on his elbow, his little spider-fingers on Blain's jaw, willing him to move it.

"Which one?" Blain's voice, lazy.

Owen shrugged. "'Bout the train robbers. The ones in the wild, wild west." It was the one he always asked for. A band of four brothers who eat and sleep under the moon, robbing trains filled with gold bullion. Sometimes, Blain adds new details—a stampede of horses or a runaway train. Blain can't think what the brothers will do with all the bullion. He has never had to finish a story. Owen is always asleep before he can.

"BLAIN! GET YOUR ASS OUT HERE and give a hand." The old man's voice is hoarse and weak, which gives the impression that he's spent. He's thin, his middle like a sinkhole, and the only bits of fat on him are under his eyes and his chin. He seems to hang off his own limbs. *Poor sad son-of-a-bitch* the men at the Queens Hotel said after Blain's mother was found, like Jack Carter is an old dog that someone should take out in the bush and shoot. Except Blain knows better. The old man's venomous strength and purpose lie coiled inside of him, like a sleeping snake.

His father would have people believe that it was him who found her, but it wasn't, it was Blain. Her arms were floating and stretched and her dress billowed in a plume, some bit of air trapped inside. Her hair had become part of the half-frozen swamp weed. All around her, the tangle of dead trees, jagged ice, and still black water, a half-choked moon looking down.

"Christ, that boy's lazy and the other one's small as a hen."
The old man sounds like he is making a joke. His voice is almost
wistful, as though it is tragic that he happens to have children.
"Go on, Jack, you don't mean that," one of the men laughs.
The men take the crates to sell, some out of backyard wood
sheds in Owen Sound, others under the cover of businesses—
liveries and cafés and hotels. There are men at the dockyards
who sell from the backs of their wagons; there are farmers
and blacksmiths and tailors who offer jars to their regular
customers, for a price.

What these men don't take, the old man sells to the Queens
Hotel in Wiarton. No prohibition there, and the proprietor of
the Queens buys Jack Carter's shine because it costs him much
less than Canadian Rye Whisky, not to mention Scottish, Irish,
or American imports; he'll still charge his patrons an arm and
a leg for it. There's an unquenchable thirst for liquor in the
county, people driving up the peninsula every day of the week
to get a taste, except for Sundays when the Queens has its
doors shut tight. The road down from Wiarton is famous for
crash sites, people, too full-up on hooch, having lost the road
and fatally swerving into swampland or bush. Motorcars and
buggies, wagons and trucks. The road's like a slaughter yard.

The old man's stuff is the most popular hooch for miles
around. He'd deny his moonshine business if questioned by
reputable men. He'd say he's a woodlot man, that he was
raised in the woods somewhere up around Thunder Bay. A
log driver, a pike-poler, he came down to work on the river
rafts for Piper Lumber, and that's how Blain's mum met him,
washing his muddy clothes in Blain's grandmother's laundry.
Blain imagines Carter as he was, dark-haired and light-footed,
dancing from log to log, strong and lithe. He bought this land
for the woodlot, but the lumber means nothing to him now.

With the ruckus outside, Blain hopes that Owen has stayed
asleep, warm and tucked up just as he left him, his nightshirt
buttoned to his chin. If he isn't, he'll soon be standing in Blain's

room, his small hand tugging at an ear, his eyes like saucers, spilling tears. *I want mum. I had a dream....* Blain will carry him back to bed, and lie beside him for a little while, Owen resting his head on Blain's chest.

Blain tips back his head and feels the certainty of the wall. His eyes close, the lights from the idling car drilling into the dark of his room. He was in town today with Hugh McFarland and Clem, loading supplies. They drove past the docks, the last of the fall lake boats just pulling out. Blain didn't know where the boat was going—Chicago maybe. He'd asked Hugh McFarland if he knew, and whether Chicago was the place to catch the trains west, to Montana, Wyoming. Had Hugh ever thought about ranching—Alberta maybe? "Ranches the size of small countries out there," Blain said. "Cattle as far as the eye could see."

"You talk a blue streak, boy."

"Just wondering if you ever thought of it," said Blain.

"Nope. I don't like cattle neither. More a crop man myself. What I want, I got right here. You ought'a quit with pipe dreams and pay attention to the work you got. Now hop out and lend Clem a hand."

It's the other McFarland brother that knows about cattle. Blain could tell the day he and Hugh McFarland had delivered the bull. There is something far away about Jamie, like he's breathing different air than other people. Like his head is up higher and he can see forever. And Ena—little and neat as an acorn. Child-sized but with dark round eyes, like Owen's.

Blain listens to the sounds of the men's grunts as they load the wagon. Before long, a cork is popped and then the sounds of grateful swigging. One of the men giggles girlishly and another starts to sing. He used to have to report to Mum what he heard the men doing—a wagon pulling up the lane, or customers sampling too much of the hooch, getting themselves into dust-ups, cursing and wrestling. Maybe it's why he's such a gabbler, all those years of yammering to Mum rubbing off.

If Blain goes out now, looking ready to help, eager even, the men will be softened up from the moonshine, too stewed to pay him much mind. He can claim he's been looking after Owen all this time. There's a chance the old man won't lay one on him later, after the men have gone and the delivery is on its way up the Peninsula to the bar outside Wiarton. He stands, the blood rushing to his head, a flash of white behind his eyes like the glare from a distant range of snow-topped mountains.

3.

ENA FEELS SHE LIVES CLEAR-EYED inside of a dream. Dust rises in clouds from their rutted lane whenever a slight breeze stirs. In June, the Archduke and his wife were shot in a city called Sarajevo, and now, at the height of summer, Ena barely thinks about their murders.

Consumed by work, she rises early to bake and to help Jamie with the milking. There are weeds to be pulled in her garden, plants to be watered. There is pickling and preserving, churning and scouring. There is work for her in the fields.

And Jamie. She has given herself over to him. At night, they bathe together and then, their skin cooling, they lie without clothes on their bed. He tickles her with a white goose feather, stroking the bottoms of her feet, her ribs, the soft parts of inner thighs, tormenting her until she laughs and hungrily wraps her arms and legs around him. They become tangled in one another while outside, in the deepening pink dusk, creatures jostle, their sounds feverish, and compelling. Then Jamie closes his eyes with a secret smile. In the morning, she's not certain that she's been asleep.

In mid-August, the threshing on both of the McFarland farms—Jamie's and Hugh's—has been finished. Hugh and his hired hands come with Hugh's team of horses to help collect the bales because Jamie has only one horse, and his wagon isn't large enough.

When Ena tries to thank Hugh, both brothers stand tongue-tied and then Hugh guffaws. "We're gonna leave you on your own next time, Ena," he jokes. "Just you and the crew."

"I don't know a thing about threshing," she says, frowning. "Or horses."

Slipping an arm around her waist, Jamie gives her an affectionate tug. "Don't take him too serious, Ena. He's pulling your leg."

Ena loosens and smiles uncertainly. She senses in Hugh's teasing a prod toward clanship. It perplexes her, leaves her feeling awkward, uncertain, as though she listens to a language she hasn't yet learned to speak.

A few hours later, while the men still work, Ena and Sarah sit together on Ena's porch, the air humming with heat. Sarah peers intently into a newspaper. Her yellow skirt is pulled above her knees and her feet are bare, the soles dusty from walking on the gritty floorboards of the porch. Placing a finger lengthwise across her mouth, she mindlessly bites the knuckle and then pulls it away. Her hands are covered in freckles, not like Ena's which under the summer sun have turned to an even brown. Sarah's hands are large, like the rest of her; deposits of coloured paint—reds and greens and blues—are caught up in the creases at her knuckles and around her nail cuticles. Evidence of her work with her canvases.

Sarah arrived sometime after the men, driving herself in the buggy. "Here," she'd said, thrusting a basket brimming with redcurrants into Ena's hands. "I picked them this morning from that terrible bush at the farm. Too hot for canning and conserving for me, Ena, but I know you'll want them."

Ena *does* want them and she'll keep them cool in the root cellar until the next day. She only lights the stove before sunrise, letting it die out as soon as the breakfast tea is made. For the rest of the day, she uses the summer kitchen. She relishes the solitude of her early mornings; the kitchen door propped open and cool air wafting in, scented steam rising from the simmering fruit, the lid on the kettle amiably rattling.

"You didn't need to thank Hugh," Sarah scowls into the paper. "It's what the McFarland's do—look after McFarland farms."

The heat is building, not a hint of breeze in the thickening air. The Grey County landscape swells with golds and greens, the colours smudging seamlessly into a soft blue sky. Ena pours pink lemonade into tall glasses, hands one to Sarah and then raises her own, turning it. The colour is lovely. She mixed the juice from the lemons with a few drops of raspberry cordial. Tasting it now, she thinks she would have preferred less sweetness, the extra sugar cloying on her tongue.

IT WAS SARAH SHE MET FIRST, before any of the other McFarland's. A November day and Sarah had been on the kitchen stoop dumping a can of water onto the lane, her red hair pulled off her high forehead with a colourful print scarf. A coil of it had loosened and blown across her mouth. She drew it slowly away and then, seeing Ena, a smile spread.

"I'm here for eggs," Ena said simply. "*Good* eggs." She'd ridden to the McFarland farm in a dairy wagon, exchanging three loaves of brown bread for the lift. The driver promised to pick her up in an hour or so when he passed by on his way back to town. The ride left her feeling windblown and, collecting herself, she smoothed down her skirt.

Looking at her, Sarah's smile widened. She set aside the can, roughly wiping her hands on a paint-streaked smock. She was fresh-looking, perhaps the same age as Ena and almost a foot taller. Her nose was narrow at the bridge and that made her wide-set eyes seem vast.

"Couldn't you get eggs at the market?" she asked, coming down the steps, her hand outstretched. "*Good enough* eggs, anyway?" There was a trace of an accent in her voice, a suggestion of English schooling. The sound of it made Ena think of old stone and portraits of the King.

"The woman I go to at the market wasn't there this week."

Sarah stopped and crossed her arms. The gesture could have

seemed combative but to Ena, at that moment, it was intensely curious.

"What do you *do* with the *good* eggs?"

"I bake, for my employer." Standing with Sarah was like being held in strong sunlight, welcome but momentarily blinding. Ena wasn't used to other people's interest in her. At the McLaren's home in town where she worked as a domestic, she preferred to go unnoticed. Strangely, she wanted to be noticed by Sarah McFarland. She kept her eyes steady on Sarah's, watching Sarah's curiosity about her move freely across her face.

A few moments later, Sarah McFarland was throwing on her coat while striding toward the barn, Ena walking fast beside her. Earlier, it had rained but a cold clean sun had broken through. There was a smell of wet earth and animals. "Watch your step," Sarah said leaning in to Ena, pointing at the churned-up ground. "The rain's made a mess of things. You haven't got the right shoes for this." Ena's head had been flooded with the largeness of the day, the brightness of it.

NOW, WITH THE AFTERNOON WEARING ON, Sarah takes a long drink from her glass and then curls her muscular legs beneath her. After a time, she lifts her eyes to Ena's—large almond-shaped eyes, grey with a flash of green, their colour changing with the light. "Listen, Ena. Listen to what our great Prime Minister is saying: '*Canada promises Great Britain troops in the war against Germany.*'" She lets out a low groan. Every day Sarah drives to town and buys the *Sound Times*. She combs through it, restless for news of Europe. Her family's letters from England are full of news—young men, friends of the family, cousins—who have already gone to France to fight. She is both anguished about the war and furious.

She goes on reading under her breath, her lips feverishly forming the words, and Ena shifts her gaze to the wagon that jostles across the fields and toward the barn. Blain sits at the edge, the white insides of his elbows rotated outward, his broken straw hat in his lap. He talks to Clem, only a few of his words recognizable over the clatter of hooves and harnesses: *that was the biggest … his tail was tied … the saw broke in two.*

"That boy tells stories," mutters Sarah not looking up, her reading interrupted by the boy's jabber. "That's about all he knows how to do."

Blain's eyes catch on Ena and his face splits into a grin. He waves and Ena raises her own hand and then folds it into herself again. For weeks, the memory of Blain slumped against the fence, chalk-faced, has stayed with her. For a few moments, struggling to breathe, he'd looked like someone poised on the edge of a cliff, contemplating whether the leap would kill or save him. Ena felt she was seeing something undeniably true in him, something usually kept hidden.

"The boy's been working most of the summer at Hugh's cousin's place, helping to build the new barn. He's only been back on our farm a couple of weeks and Hugh's already talking about letting the boy go." Sarah sounds impatient. She isn't interested in the day-to-day decisions that are made on the farm. Ena suspects that much of farm life bores her.

"Why? Why would Hugh let him go?"

"Because he makes all kinds of mistakes. I mean he's friendly enough. He's even comical at times." Sarah smiles ruefully into the paper. "But he set fire to a bale of hay with a lantern last winter. Boy's head is full of nonsense." Her eyes lift from the page, narrowing and studying Blain. "He doesn't always show up in the mornings. And then there have been shows of temper …."

Ena thinks of Blain and how furtive he seemed the day with the bull, and how blithely cheerful. She pulls her eyes away from him and studies a bug-riddled bush that pushes against the house. "He's just a boy. Of course he won't do everything right."

Sarah shrugs. "Hugh has a farm to run and he puts the farm first. I don't always agree with him. Anyway, it was Jamie who persuaded Hugh to keep Blain and so he'll stay. Truthfully, I don't think he'll work out for long."

Farm hands come and go and Ena knows this, but the uncertainty about this boy is a hum, unsettling and surprisingly sad.

Sarah has her nose buried in the paper again. "'We enthusiastically and whole heartedly take up this call...' she reads, bitterness in her tone. "I can't stand how stupid we are, sending men into that." Sarah's moods can colour a room, change the temperature.

Ena is thinking of the men in the barn loading bales, *these* men, how hot it is and how it's time she brought them some lemonade to drink. She gets up lightly from her chair and leans against the porch railing, her eyes on the barn where the men are unloading the wagon. "If it's such a mess over there, then a lot of men won't bother to go."

Sarah snaps the newspaper and then wrestles it into a diminished square. "Oh, yes, they will; they'll sign up. They think what's going on over there is just a game. *Sport.* They think they'll go over and pitch a tent, have a cookout with their pals. Parade around with a gun planted on their shoulder like it's a toy. They'll be slaughtered and we will have a party for them before they go."

Ena imagines the men across the country, volunteers who will gather like bees to a hive. The image is strange, fantastic, and impossible for her to hold on to. She looks toward the barn door where Blain stands. He leans into the doorframe, his hands on his narrow thighs, his face flushed with heat.

"I'm going to bring out something for the men," she says flatly. "It must be past three." She turns from the porch railing and places the empty glasses on a tray, grateful for a reason to walk.

EVEN WITH NEWS THAT THE COUNTRY will send troops, the war seems very far away. Europe, in Ena's mind, is the contoured map that hung on the classroom wall of the East Hill School.

Germany, France, Belgium, just shapes and colours– green, orange, blue—the borders between them faint and serpentine.

Had she learned about Bosnia in school? When she tries to imagine Bosnia no colour or shape comes, although her memory unspools a string of impressions that has nothing to do with world geography. She is back in the classroom, in a hard wooden chair: Godwin Douglas, three rows up, his orange hair, the angry hives at his neck where his woollen jacket rubbed; Miss Parker and her heavy-looking breasts; the smell of damp in the fall; the initials (so many of them) carved into the honey-coloured top of her school desk.

She kept very still in the classroom, her knees clenched, her fingers burrowing a small hole in the wool of her sweater. All around her bodies fidgeted and strained toward the schoolyard. In winter, there was always the possibility of a snowball fight, in spring a mad dash toward the river on the first warm day. She didn't want to throw herself into the noisy, eager mass of other children. Their frantic demands, their whoops, their cries felt deeply and terrifyingly like the vibrations of a bell being rung. Ena wanted to stay fixed to one point, one small place, where she could touch and smell and taste a single, perfect thing.

SHE RINSES OUT THE STICKY GLASSES and sets them in the sink. The kitchen is old and narrow, not much wider than twice the span of her outstretched arms. A small table sits at one end under the window, the large, cantankerous stove against an adjacent wall. There is a square wooden worktop, a deep tin sink; a jam cupboard stands in one corner beside the icebox, and open shelving lines one wall. Ross, a bachelor, probably hadn't cared much about this kitchen, but Ena has given it order, scrubbed and then white-washed the shelves. Setting it up had been a joy, each small decision—the placement of the flour tin, the choosing of utensils for each drawer– had brought her pleasure.

A pie sits on the worktop, the glistening pastry stretched over a mound of sugared blueberries. There are two pitchers of pink lemonade in the icebox for the men. She pulls the jugs out, and then from one of the shelves she takes down fresh glasses and places them together with the pitcher on a cloth-covered tray. She slices the pie into equal pieces, efficiently stacking the plates and forks.

When she goes outside with the tray, Sarah is walking with her bare feet in the grass, her shoes held lightly in one hand. "I want to get back while the light is still good." She looks over her shoulder at Ena, her hand held over her eyes. "I've got something up on the easel. Hugh will be busy with the men—it's easier for me to work when he's not around. He doesn't understand the painting."

Ena nods. "What are you working at?"

Sarah laughs. "*This*, I suppose." A tension comes into her strong jaw as her eyes sweep the fields. It is difficult for Sarah to paint at the farm. Hugh grunts and guffaws when he sees her at her easel. In an implicit declaration of friendship, Ena now does all the baking for Sarah and Hugh so that Sarah might find more time to paint, and Sarah provides Ena with as many eggs as she can use.

Ena sets down the tray on the step just as the loaded wagon sails past on its way down the lane. The hired-hands are leaving, going back to their home farm. She's too late with the pink lemonade. Clem, Hugh's lead man, is driving. In his late fifties, Clem is wiry, his skin scored with lines from the sun. When he turns and lifts his straw hat to Sarah and Ena, his eyes are a startling blue.

Ena plants her flat and unwavering gaze on Sarah. "You think Hugh should let Blain go." Not a question.

A fly circles Sarah's head and she swats irritably at it. Her fingers are stained, as though she has been picking blackberries, but Ena knows it is paint.

"Ena, you are like a dog with a bone. What does it matter?"

Blain is a *particular* boy, a boy who has drunk water from her palm, a boy who has watched her in her garden. Ena is staring mercilessly at Sarah.

Sarah sighs. "Of course not. I'm *sorry* for Blain." Sarah has pulled on her shoes and she hikes the hem of her skirt above her knees, swooshing the cotton fabric in an effort to cool herself. "He's lost his mother. But things like that happen. My father was a doctor, Ena. People get sick, there are accidents, particularly in the backwoods."

Ena moves off the porch and on to the dry grass. There is no cover here and the hot sun bears down ferociously.

"Hugh should give him a chance."

Sarah's eyes trace the sliver of road visible from where they stand. She lets her skirt drop and looks at Ena.

"*Yes*, Ena. That's what Jamie said too. "

The lane is empty now that the wagon and the men have gone. The cicadas have started up, a febrile chorus. Ena tastes a fine line of sweat on her upper lip, salty and private and her own. Her mind tosses up the long years of her father Michael Connelly's sickness. Old ripples of hope and worry wheel through her, the remembered tides of Michael's illness. First it was a cough, alarming and violent, overtaking Michael while he was in his dry goods store, his head turning from customers, his hand in his pocket for his handkerchief. Her mother Ellen scolded him for it, as if he were deliberately shrinking, intentionally turning away.

Sarah has been fiddling with the horse's harness and now she turns from the horse and waves her hand at Ena. "Clem thinks he can keep an eye on Blain if he's just working at our place and nowhere else from now on. That should keep him in line."

Impatient with the subject of the Carters, Sarah pulls Ena into a warm, long embrace. Then holding her at arm's length, she studies Ena's face, inch by inch. "I don't know why you're so upset about Blain. He's not on a boat to France. He's safe, at least for now." Swinging herself up to the buggy, Sarah takes hold of the reins. "Get on," she urges the horse.

Ena stands on the lane with her feet planted, sweat banding her waist, her collar, the smell of the fresh cut fields making her dizzy. It seems to her then, that the McFarland buggy is a beautiful shade of green and in the mid-afternoon brightness, it sends out shards of light, hard as fists in Ena's eyes.

4. SPRING 1915

THE WAR HADN'T ENDED at Christmas as all the politicians said it would. "Our first hundred lost. A place called Neuve-Chapelle," Sarah is saying. They are upstairs at the home farm in the room with Sarah's paintings, the room airless and scented with the pine-sharp smell of turpentine. Although Ena has been to the house many times, the door to this room has always been closed. It is the first time Sarah has shown Ena where she keeps her work.

Ena's eyes travel over the room. A thin April light streams through a single west-facing window, and beneath it stands an easel, a table covered with drawing pads, pens and ink, paints and brushes. In years past, the room had been a bedroom but the bed is gone and of the original furniture only a large wardrobe remains.

"You must know that the first contingent of Canadians has been in France for months," Sarah says, peering into the back of the wardrobe where the pictures are stacked. Ena had known but she has pushed the war far out and away.

"I know." Her finger runs over the tip of a paint brush, the bristles articulated and singular, definite to the touch. She wants to see what Sarah does with the brushes and paints and canvases, what she makes with them.

Sarah has pulled out a number of paintings and now she piles them against the wall. "I'll show you a couple of these if you like."

They squat close to one another, balancing on their haunches, their elbows jutting into their thighs. Sarah's long fingers flip impatiently through canvases, and pictures appear and disappear—feverish and startling flashes of colour. They flit through Ena's imagination like an angry flock of birds. A jousting energy lies just below Sarah's surface. It comes off of Sarah in waves and Ena feels herself flatten and smooth over as if to protect herself from it. Putting her small hand on top of Sarah's, she urges Sarah's fingers to still. Before, when she had imagined them, she'd thought of Sarah's pictures as the likeness of things: drooping flowers in a vase, a bowl of gleaming red apples—the sort of pictures she'd seen hanging in her former employer's home. They turn out to be nothing at all like those. Dropping to her knees she crawls closer to the stack and lifts up a canvas—crowing oranges and blood-hued reds. Hard blues, close to black. A surrounding dome of yellow, a radiating curve of light.

She looks at the painting closely. There is the initial shock of colour, no one thing distinguishable from another, everything a rush. She tilts her head and studies each brushstroke and then feels the surprise of recognition. Sarah has painted their farm, Ena and Jamie's, their fields and woods, but not as they appear. At the centre, a presence of dense, rich colour. Their house.

Sarah inhales sharply and gives a terse nod at the canvas. "You can have that one. I've been wanting to give it to you."

Ena looks at Sarah, perplexed by the gesture. "Don't *you* want it?"

"Pictures are meant to be seen, not stuffed into the back of wardrobes."

Ena realizes quite suddenly that none of Sarah's pictures hang on the walls in this house. In fact, she can think of only two pictures at the McFarland farm: one of Highland cows grazing in a Scottish glen and the other of forlorn and deadened snow-topped hills. It's as though Sarah's paintings have been exiled.

She frowns into the painting. "Other people must have seen

some of these, Sarah. You must have learned from someone."

Sarah nods. "Years ago, a man named Craig Murray came to the high school in Owen Sound, to teach a few of us who showed a bit of promise with drawing. He'd studied in Paris with Henri Matisse." The names mean nothing to Ena.

"I wouldn't know where to start," she says.

"You start with a blank canvas." Sarah takes up a canvas that is empty and white. Turning it over, her fingers tap the plain wood frame at the back. "These are called stretchers. They keep the canvas taut. I can make them easily myself from old egg crates. The size of the slats is about perfect. And you see how this canvas has been coated? That's called gesso—it helps the paint set properly."

Ena takes the stretched blank canvas from Sarah's hands and holds it. She tries to work out how a white-swept surface can be transformed into anything convincing. Ena knows an apple by feeling its weight, her finger finding the soft fleshy part where a bruise has settled. She knows summer by its smell—warmed earth, ripened blackberries, a freshly sliced watermelon. To convey the world through lines and colours, layers of paints, seems unimaginably difficult.

Sarah is energetically pulling out more canvases and lining them up against the papered wall. They are each different in mood and the range of colour is dizzying. As she takes a step back, Sarah's expression becomes instantly critical, her desire for better straining in the tendons of her neck. "These could be so much more, if I had better technique. I've gone as far as I can without having more instruction. "

Ena is silent, tentatively studying each piece, oddly self-conscious, imagining that her eyes had somehow stretched and she had shrunk. "They're not pretty. They're something else." She fiddles with the cuff of her blouse. "You're *in* the paintings, Sarah." She can think of no other way to say it.

Sarah takes her wrist to the back of her neck, her eyes on the wardrobe.

"I try with them, but I'm an amateur really. I'd like to paint more. I used to paint all the time but art doesn't go very well with farming."

"You didn't grow-up on a farm," says Ena.

"No, I grew-up in a town." Sarah's face is long and angled, strong in profile. "I went to visit farms with Dad on his medical calls sometimes, to keep him company. He got called out here to look in on Hugh's father after the first stroke. "

Distracted, she takes her hand from her neck and rubs at the paint on her knuckles, her gaze on the fields visible through the window. There is something tender in the expression. "Hugh and I were quite a pair—nothing in common—but we were crazy about one another. "

Sarah picks up another painting. "This one's no good." She sets it down scornfully and returns to the subject of Hugh. "Around the time Hugh and I were getting close, my mother began talking about us moving back to England. She hated it here. She'd only come for Dad. He had romantic ideas about Canada, like a lot of English people do. And then my sister got sick with some sort of wasting disease. I'm not sure it wasn't just in her head. She's a fussy thing, my sister. I think Mom wore Dad down eventually because he agreed we should go back, but by then, I didn't want to. And then Hugh's father died and it was clear Hugh was going to take over the farm. Marrying him, staying, made sense to me. *Hugh* and a family of my *own* was what I wanted." Sarah turns and looks at the canvases as though they are surprise visitors. "Now I want more. I want this too."

Soon after Christmas, her face radiant with excitement, Sarah had announced she was pregnant. Within a week she'd lost the baby. Jamie drove Ena to the McFarland farm, the cutter loaded with food, and Ena sat with Sarah in her room. Sarah talked about the emptiness in her belly and the staggering anger she felt because this was her second miscarriage in less than twelve months. There had been a hard knock on the bedroom door. Stiff-necked and drawn, Hugh walked in and awkwardly perched next to Sarah on the bed. He'd taken Sarah's face between his palms and wiped her tears with his great thumbs, and she'd wrapped her arms around him, the embrace hard and raw and fierce. Hugh gritted his teeth, as if he intended to bear the full force of Sarah's sorrow. Ena had left the room and quietly closed the door.

Now, Sarah looks keenly at Ena, her eyes glittering. "I want you to see what I am working at." She rummages in the wardrobe and pulls out another picture, placing it on the easel. There is an unexpected violence in it, a brash and messy collision of colour. Nothing is recognizable although what Ena feels, looking at it, is familiar—a mix of fascination and fear.

"There is worry in this one," she says. "Hurt."

Sarah looks at her shrewdly. "Yes, it's more to do with what's underneath."

They are pensive together, studying the painting. The room grows quiet except for the sound of their breathing, synchronized and rhythmic. The kitchen door slams shut and Ena drags her eyes from the painting, toward the fields outside, tawny-coloured and uneven with the crops taken off. The men have been working, unloading logs from a wagon. Blain drifts around the yard while Clem passes logs to Jamie, Jamie adding them to the pile by the fence. They all stop moving, Clem motioning to Blain to get up on the wagon and roll the logs toward him with his foot. Clem demonstrates the action with his boot, his leg kicking, his arms held out cockeyed at his sides like a scarecrow while Blain watches, his hat is in his hand, his knuckles scrubbing at his head.

For a few seconds Blain's lips curl in a half-smile and then his face shifts to a grin. He lifts up his own leg, waggles it at Clem, mimicking, clowning, hopping a short distance. Clem shakes his head in a broad flat line and shoos him up to the wagon and the logs. Ena sees in the way that Jamie's face tips back that he is laughing.

"What do you know about the Carters?" Ena's eyes remain with Blain Carter and the men.

Sarah stands and shakes out her skirt. She hauls the canvases into the wardrobe, three at a time, and then closes the doors. Her fingers linger on the latch.

"Jack Carter's been busy, ever since prohibition."

Ena doesn't say anything. The town has been dry for almost ten years. All kinds of backwoods businesses have sprung up since then. Now with the war, no one is paying much attention to what happens in woodlots and bush all around the county. Ena watches Blain, the eagerness to please there in every movement. He's grown taller over the last year, but he's still very thin.

"Did you know his mother?"

"Margaret? She was a Thompson before she married I think. She worked here sometimes, for Mrs. McFarland. Tiny woman, same eyes as Blain—you know—the same dreamy look that he gets. Mischievous grin, like his. She wanted them to move into town, have a life with people. She wanted the boys to have some kind of chance. I can't imagine what it was like for her, living out there with Jack. "

Ena can see an impression of Margaret in Blain, a frail but definite outline, a breeziness that would transport the mind to places the body couldn't go, a force of imagination; now, in Blain she sees a boy who doesn't want to go home.

Downstairs they find Hugh, his boots and straw hat off, his hands freshly pinked from the washhouse. He's having trouble unbuttoning his jacket, his large fingers clumsy with the buttonholes. He turns and regards Sarah, out of breath as though he has just run up from the barn. His features are strained, the one eye flitting back and forth, the other stony.

"You've been at your pictures again," he says, his tone murky, none of the usual good humour in it.

The air seems to have gone from the room. Sarah's paintings, particularly the last, has left Ena feeling startled and newly awake, her eyes keener. All around Ena are jarring fragments—incomplete tasks, ragged feelings. On the table, a crate of eggs has been partly filled, the rest of the eggs left in a basket on the floor. Dishes from lunch are haphazardly stacked by the sink and unfolded laundry hangs from the backs of kitchen chairs.

Sarah pulls herself to her full height, her eyes flashing, heat rising to her cheeks. She walks toward Hugh as though she is holding her breath. Ena hasn't understood precisely what is between Sarah and Hugh, but she feels the heat of it now.

"I wasn't painting, I was *showing* Ena."

Their bodies are only a finger-length apart, Sarah not much shorter than Hugh. Hugh's chest heaves; Ena sees the rise and fall of it through his clothes. Sarah roughly takes hold of his shirt, and then she slips the stubborn buttons from their holes.

"There. Undone." Her hands have moved to rest on Hugh's powerful forearms and when she looks into his face he grips her, his wide fingers encircling her elbows, the broad knuckles blanching.

They stay like that for a long while, not noticing Ena. Sarah lets go of his arms first.

When his hands finally drop from her, they are huge and lost with nothing to hold.

5.

THE FIELDS ARE THAWING. Ena has cooked a pan of dried apples, and now that they are soft, she uses a slotted spoon to pull them from the water and carefully slip them into a bowl. She pours in the flour and baking powder, the beaten butter, and sugar mixed with egg, lastly the buttermilk, and then she gently folds. An apple cake in spring; the scent of cinnamon and vanilla will fill the house.

After she slides the cake into the oven, she puts the ingredients away. The design of the baking powder tin hasn't changed since her father owned Connelly's Dried Goods. She helped him to sort the deliveries, reaching deep into straw-lined crates, pulling out the canned goods—peaches, tomatoes, peas. Bottles of vinegar, sacks of white beans, kidney beans, and flour. When she pulled an item from the crate, Michael had encouraged her to touch it, feel the weight, to know the texture. "Tell me what it is and what it's used for," he said, the Irish lilt of his voice, like music, circling. He'd talk to her about fly swatters and pie plates, the genius of butter churns and sewing machines, a well-crafted boot. "Hold it, Ena," he said, handing her a rubber boot, "You'll know the quality of it by feel only. Only quality goods at Connelly's." There was a warmth in his voice that found her always, no matter how flat and grey the day.

Sometimes, Ena thinks that her use for words disappeared when Michael died. She's grateful that Jamie doesn't need her to talk much (he is that sure of her). Drying her hands, Ena looks through the kitchen window to the rutted field where Jamie is walking with Billie, his long legs devouring the uneven ground. His hands are in his pockets. Every so often, Billie races ahead, stops and turns to locate him, and then she's off again. He whistles to Billie—Ena can't hear the sound but she sees the whistle in his gesture, the way he tosses his head in encouragement. He takes something from his pocket—the leather ball he carries for the dog to chase. The ball moves high and long when he throws it, and all around them the ground spreads like a black sea.

He is good with animals, she thinks, seeing him with Billie. She'd met him for the first time the day she'd gone to the McFarland farm for the eggs. He was bent low over a crib containing two bantam hens. As Sarah and Ena got closer, he stood but kept his hand on one of the birds, gently stroking its piebald feathers. To Ena, his narrow frame suggested concentration.

"They lay, but the eggs are small." He'd looked at her, smiled, and then he'd stepped in closer, his expression intently focused at her shoulder. With a single fluid motion he made as if to pull something from her ear. Unfurling his fingers, he presented her with one perfect minuscule egg.

Behind them, Sarah loudly sighed. "Don't mind him, Ena. He's playing a trick."

Astonished, Ena took the egg from his palm. Of course there had been a sleight of hand involved. The care he took in the ruse delighted her, the gentleness of it, no loud braying or joking. Looking at the egg, a smile had spread easily over her face.

"Why do you keep them?" she asked. "I didn't think farmers kept pets."

The birds' feathers were mud-coloured with specks of caramel and black. Beautiful and plain. She reached out her hand to touch a breast. These were tiny birds.

He tilted his head and regarded the birds with a quizzical

expression. "I don't know," he laughed. "I like caring for them, I guess."

Now, having reached the top of the field, Jamie is a small figure on the crest of a bare hill, the bush etched in black behind him. Billie races ahead and then turns back, stops, waits for him to catch-up. He will touch her on the head, offering her that simple assurance, and then she will be off again.

A sudden snow shower and instantly a curtain of white drops. The snow is slanted, pushed to fury by a mysterious north wind that steals down the Bruce Peninsula and across the shores of Georgian Bay. Jamie's concealment from her is jarring and it brings a memory of Michael Connelly, his hand held out to her, in his palm a crystal orb. Inside, a tiny village with half-timbered houses, a church, and cobblestone streets. She'd peered at it, longing to see more, to move closer. Suddenly, Michael shook it and the scene was engulfed in an angry swirl of white and the village instantly disappeared.

"Where did it go, Daddy?" She took the globe from him and shook it as if to clear away the snow, but that only made it worse.

He'd laughed and put the globe inside of the display case at the front of the store. "Be patient, Ena. It's still there. You just can't see."

It disturbed her, the village's vulnerability to the storm, and each time Michael shook it, she felt unsure that the village would appear again.

She searches the spot where she last saw Jamie and Billie and then finds them at the gate. The snow ceases as suddenly as it began.

6. SEPTEMBER 1915

OWEN ISN'T STACKING WOOD at the woodpile, which is where he should be when Blain gets back from the Mc-Farland's. Sliding his hands into the cavernous pockets of his pants, Blain studies the haphazard pile. Heavier logs are strewn over the ground, abandoned by Owen who, after many lifts, likely found the weight of them too much. Blain knows that Owen wouldn't have given up easily; Owen is nothing if not persistent.

Blain has spent much of the summer fencing for Hugh McFarland, pounding posts and sawing lumber. Now, his muscles form dense tight mounds on his arms and his body is sinewy. He feels himself hardening, lengthening with the benefit of steady farm work although he's still too skinny. A few months back, Blain had been both impressed and envious when Harry Stewart, just two years older than himself and a good four inches shorter, had run off and joined the 18th Battalion out of London. Harry is a burly lad, powerful through the shoulders. A farm lad from Kemble. If Blain can add some heft, some weight to his own frame, who knows where that might take him.

Standing beside the woodpile, looking for his brother, he fingers the two hard-boiled eggs he has just taken from the icebox– one for himself and one for Owen. A glass salt-shaker is in his pocket. Owen loves salt. He can't seem to get enough. Owen puts salt on the porridge Blain makes him each morning.

He shakes it onto apples picked fresh off the tree. It makes Blain smile to see him do it, the eagerness in him, the contrariness; *normal kids are partial to sweet,* their father remarks. *Kid's got potatoes sproutin' inside where there should be brains.* But Owen is smart. By the time he was six, he was reading as well as Blain, and he has a good head for figures, too.

Blain slips the eggs into his pocket and picks up one of the logs and lazily tosses it on the top of the pile, his eyes scanning the line of birch beyond the clearing. When Owen gets back from school each day he does his chores. Blain has told him he's not supposed to split the wood or handle the axe at all. He is only to keep the inside stove supplied. And before he does that, he's to see to the still. The old man gets cross with Owen if he has to go back to the pile himself for more wood.

The old man isn't around and Blain thinks for a moment that he might have taken Owen with him, although that isn't likely. He delivers wood on Thursdays and then stops in at the Queens Hotel. He won't be home until well after dark. Owen would be an inconvenience for him. A nuisance.

To shake off the quiet, Blain hums tunelessly and heads off in the direction of the creek. He doesn't like the silence that clings to the place like a thick fog and recently he's started to talk to himself, shortened sentences for the most part: *Well I'll be ...* or *don't that beat all....* Once or twice, Clem's caught him at it in the barn. "Too young for conversin' with just yourself, Blain," he said, shaking his head solemnly. Blain finds he likes the sound of his own voice, the certainty of it driving out ghosts.

The underbrush thickens as he gets closer to the creek, bugs coming up in plumes and the land falling sharply. Rocks hump out of the path, ragged and creviced. Blain doesn't mind the shadowy terrain but he worries about Owen walking here alone, his arms full with logs, his feet loose in Blain's hand-me-down boots. The sound of the creek, when it finally reaches him, is both a relief and a disturbance. It fills the hollow of the ravine, utterly takes it over with its jousting of rocks and stones. At first it drives away the silence. But after a time, the sound hammers at him and leaves him feeling like he can't get his breath. Clearing his throat, he cups his hands to the sides of his mouth. "Owen!" His voice mixes with the rush of the creek and he calls again.

He follows the path westward to the still that sits just at the water, its copper sides glinting in the spray of light. Around the site, there is a scattering of galvanized buckets and broken mason jars, old slats, and stir sticks. Wooden crates filled with empty jars and jugs are stacked and partly covered by a stained canvas sheet. The boiler is lit, embers burning bright in its stone fire pit, and the woodpile underneath the lean-to has been replenished. It looks to Blain like Owen has faithfully done his job, but he's nowhere in sight.

Blain pulls the saltshaker from his trousers and turns it between his fingers, the salt spilling over the trampled ground. It's a silly gesture, fantastical, as if by offering up salt, Owen will magically appear. Blain's inclined to fanciful notions. *Pipe dreamer,* the old man hisses when Blain starts in on one of his stories.

When Blain spun his stories to Mum, she always rewarded him with a laugh or—feigning incredulity—she would drop her jaw, open her eyes wide, and shake her head. When she grinned, her lips had to ride over the unevenness of her front teeth, the smile all the more robust for the effort.

She was barely seventeen when Blain was born, with punk hearing from an illness when she was a girl, the bone carved away at the back of her ears, soft caverns, hidden beneath her hair. The poor hearing was all the better for ignoring Carter's bull, Blain conjectures.

"Don't ever run dry on stories, Blain. They'll take you far." When Mum talked, (which was often), the words came out blunted as though she was speaking underwater, and she was loud even when she aimed to whisper.

The best thing was to make her laugh. He tries to make Ena McFarland smile. He's worked at it, ever since she'd taken him up to the house. A few times, he's caught her face change when he tells her a story, a softening coming into the corners of her mouth. Ena doesn't say much but the attention she pays is as taut as a guide rope.

He's seen her struggle with that vegetable garden of hers; something had eaten Ena's tomatoes, tunnels of black boring through to the heart of each and every fruit. Blain rounded the corner of the house and found Ena kneeling in the garden, her face streaming with tears, a heap of the ruined tomatoes beside her. She looked up at him, her expression closed over, and she had wiped her hands neatly on her skirt and stood.

They'd been sitting over the midday meal when Hugh McFarland told Ena that there was powder she could put on the tomatoes to keep off the bugs, but it was too late for that this year. Ena had looked like the tomatoes meant nothing, but Blain knew better.

"Owen!" Blain calls again.

"I'm here." Owen's voice is clear and strong for such a little boy and it comes from the direction of the swamp. Blain goes beyond the footpath and follows the creek to where it widens into sleepy islands of moss and rotting logs. The air above the swamp is alive with flying bugs. He sees Owen bent down, his spine curled, his legs splayed beneath him like a frog. His hands are cupped in front of him. When Blain gets close, Owen looks up, his dark eyes solemn.

"Got a beetle. Not like what I got before."

Blain nods. Owen has taken to collecting insects in the bush, putting them in a mason jar. He tries to feed them grass but all the insects eventually die. He's discovered if he puts them in the icebox, they die faster. After, he pins them to a piece of fabric cut from one of their mother's dresses that he's stretched in a needlework frame. It's a strange practice and sometimes Blain worries that something is wrong with Owen.

"You don't have to come to the swamp to find your bugs," he says to Owen. "You ought to stay in the bush. Not so far away. I didn't know where you got to."

Owen nods energetically, and then peers into his partly opened hands. "You wanna see, Blain? It's a green colour. All shiny."

Blain kneels down next to him. "You shouldn't come here alone."

Owen's brown eyes sweep the surface of the mottled water, as though he is looking for something. "I came here lots of times before," he says.

Blain scratches at his head and then puts his hat back on. His eyes track to where Owen's now rest. "You come here looking for her?"

Owen doesn't say yes or no. He cocks his head, as if listening. Owen doesn't mind the quiet as much a Blain does. "She knew I came," he says plainly. "She always knew where I was."

Blain stands and stretches his back. He puts his hands into his pockets and pulls out the eggs and the salt. Owen slips the jewel-like bug into the jar and puts on the lid. The purposefulness in Owen, his dedication to his bugs and beetles is both mesmerizing and disturbing to Blain. There is something in it of Ena McFarland—a willful exclusion of large and frightening things in this world.

Owen wipes his hands on his trousers and holds out his grubby palm for the egg. Blain drops it into his hand and then waits, the salt poised in his hand.

"Owen, she's gone. She don't know you come here, looking for her. I'm sorry about that." It breaks his heart to have to say it. It would be nice for Owen, in a way, if he believed she was here. But Owen isn't one for imaginary encounters. Blain looks at the swamp again, remembering how he'd found her, floating like a doll, her hair parted down the back of her head as if with a comb. He had been glad not to see her face.

Owen has peeled the egg and he reaches purposefully for the salt.

"It's a good place, Blain. Lots of live things. Under rocks and logs. You gotta look, that's all."

Blain sighs and then walks to the closest tree where he cracks the egg's shell before eating it.

7. NOVEMBER 1915

A BURNISHED FALL LINGERS, colour hovering in the bush until late October. Finally the weather closes in and the farm work slows. The dark rolls in over the fields by four-thirty, leaving the house in gloom until Ena lights the lamps.

Jamie sits in the parlour with the newspaper that, for the past few weeks, has been full of accounts of the Battle of Loos and the British losses there. Cloistered in the kitchen, Ena makes brown bread, her hands in the mix, the texture of the dough like velvet. The dough is pliant, stretchable, sure signs that it will resurrect, and she is careful to use just the heel of her hand to knead it. After touch, it is smell that guides her, her nose in the bowl, the scent of the yeast registering in a place deep behind her eyes. It *looks* right, pale but living. After the bread is risen and moulded and baked, taste will be the last test—a confirmation of what she already knows.

"Blain says last week he found old Mr. Savage wandering without his clothes in the bush at our home farm, Ena." Jamie sounds amused. "Told me and Clem that he helped the old man find his trousers and his shoes, then he took him by the hand and walked him back to his son Percy's place. Says that Savage was near dead drunk on moonshine." The pages of the newspaper rustle softly. "Clem thinks the boy probably sold the stuff to Savage in the first place. You can never know with Blain."

The idea of Blain selling moonshine has the unmistakable

ring of truth. Ena takes a sharp knife and cuts the ball of dough in two; inside it is full of fine and even bubbles, no lumps or unmixed portions. She thinks of her mother Ellen: Ellen expertly measuring with only the palm of her hand and then mixing with the lightest and swiftest touch. She must have learned how when she was just a little girl. Ena frowns at the cleanly severed dough on the worktop. She tries to conjure Ellen as she might have been, before she left Ireland—bright-eyed, resourceful. A quick study, Michael used to say smiling widely when Mrs. McLaren, Ellen's employer would breeze with satisfaction into the store singing Ellen's praises: *She provides the best every-day baking in town, we'd be simply lost without her.* But what Ena remembers is the blade-like quality of her mother, the reserved thrust.

Ellen's disappointments had been exacting. On a February night, ice-crystals on the inside corners of the windows, they had sat at the table, the evening meal over. Ellen held an envelope, a letter from home saying that her mother had died in Drogheda, the place in Ireland where she was from.

"I won't get back," Ellen said, her words hard-packed and joyless. "My brothers will be there, but not me. No money for that."

The snow had been falling for close to a week. Michael had just sold the business to McFadden, and his cheeks were sunken, his face grey, the blood vessels in his eyes all broken. The cough, when it came, was startling.

"It wouldn't change it, going back. What's a funeral anyway, Ellen?" He'd smiled sadly, imploring her. "She'd still be gone. I know it's hard, but your mother understood. Remember how she was pleased for us, that last day before we left? The beautiful lunch we had, the hours with her in the garden? Your brothers were home to see us off." His tone was cajoling, kind, but there had been something evasive in it, something of an apology that made Ena sorry for him.

"No one at home expected that we'd come back," he said,

his hands reaching for Ellen across the table.

Ellen's answering fury had been a shock. She picked up a plate from the table and hurled it at him. It hit the sideboard and instantly a slew of Blue Willow stoneware crashed to the floor. Ena remembers how she'd felt herself contract, something at her centre darkening, in that moment finally setting herself without reserve against Ellen.

"Daddy's not well."

"It's all right, Ena. I'm all right." He had kept his eyes on Ellen.

Ellen had been shaking with rage. "*Not* all right. No need to make-up stories for the girl—"

Rocking back in his chair, Michael looked up at the ceiling, his hands now jammed in his pockets. "I'm s*orry* it's turned out this way, Ellen. We couldn't have guessed—"

A solitary, stubborn tear, Ellen's blue eyes mercilessly pinned to him. "How many times did I *ask* you, years ago, when Ena was still small, to give this up? You were healthy enough to go back then." A dense silence, and then white-faced and stiff, Ellen rose from her chair.

Now, Ena paws through her early memories of her mother as if sorting through a jar of mismatched buttons. Orphaned images in which Ellen seemed stranded and somehow apart: Ellen on her way to the McLaren's, a newspaper held over her head to keep off the rain; Ellen standing stubbornly on the straw mat inside the door of Connelly Dried Goods, Michael and Ena behind the high, polished counter and Ellen's keen eyes roving over the exquisitely ordered shelves, her expression at once admiring and guarded.

And then Michael had sold the store and soon after he died, Ellen seemed to age overnight, her black hair seeding to grey, brittleness creeping into her small frame. She continued to work for the McLaren's, doing their baking, their housekeeping. At the end of the day, sitting in the kitchen on 7th Street, she and Ena ate wordlessly together, Ellen's slate-cold gaze on Ena, a pained anticipation about her, a frustrated and angry grief.

Ena felt herself incased in a solitariness that was like the shell of a beetle. It kept her separate from the others at school and Ellen was either unable or unwilling to call her out of it. And then at fourteen, Ena began to work for the McLaren's after school, taking on many of the more gruelling chores—beating carpets, bringing up buckets of coal. Ena hadn't objected. In truth, the work was a relief from her perfunctory exchanges with her mother.

Very soon after starting at the McLaren's, her favourite place became the attic, vast and yawning, the light streaking in from gaps in the roof. Lit like a barn, she thinks now, re-membering it. A single grimy window cast narrow shards of sun across the grey, planked floors. Attuned to the close air, the half-light, her breathing slowed as she sat cross-legged, her mind drawn into the objects around her, her hands running over moth-eaten carpets, a pair of rose-coloured silk curtains. There was abandoned furniture, old toys, a crate of medical books, rolls of mouldering fabric, trunks of blankets, linens, and a rack of coats, baby smocks, and toy soldiers. Each item spoke to her senses, no need for words.

There had been two children in the McLaren household: Mary, a year younger than Ena, still wearing the formless shifts of childhood. Her features, which otherwise might be pretty, were distorted by extra weight. Douglas, who was then eighteen, tall, athletic, quick to smile, had been easy for his mother to love. Mary also adored him, was beaming and breaking into hard giggles when he teased. When the mood suited, he was tender with Mary, slinging his arm over the hump of her shoulder, kissing her cheek.

Surrounded by the McLaren's outgrown and discarded ob-jects, Ena wove a story about the weight of sadness and how it could be borne. Grief blanketed her, sheltered her, but deeper still was a sharp, bright longing—an appetite that finally took shape in the McLaren's kitchen where Ena was particularly deft with the baking.

The McLaren kitchen was a perfect tidy square at the back of the otherwise sprawling house. It was not over-sized, with only one narrow worktop for Ena and Ellen to share. Lining up the ingredients on a small table beforehand, Ellen taught her that everything they needed should be within easy reach. Ellen's movements were quick, her directions terse. "Milk cold, eggs warmed to room temperature, Ena. No more than four strokes to mix or you'll toughen it." It was in these moments that Ena was aware of a certain keenness in her mother. She was a stringent teacher, not encouraging or proud the way Michael was. Nevertheless, Ena moved surely and steadily toward possibility. Simple ingredients could be brought together—coaxed, whipped, blended into something deeply satisfying.

"ENA, COME SIT WITH ME. Stop working." Jamie's voice is warm and it makes something inside ease and lengthen. "I'll find something to read to you from the paper." There is a long, sleepy pause and she wonders if he's dropped off with his feet propped up on the arm of the chair. "Oh, like this...." His tone is bright with new interest. "*Here's* a piece about a local regiment being formed," he says. "The Grey Overseas Battalion, they call it. The 147th. They'll recruit for it out of Owen Sound."

She only half-listens. Wrapping the ball of dough in one of the bread cloths, she carefully takes it to the corner of the kitchen furthest away from the window and the threat of draughts. "Why do they need another regiment?" She smooths the cloth over the bowl. "A lot of men have signed up already, with regiments from other places."

"Maybe so but the fighting's gone on longer than anyone thought. You'd be surprised, Ena, who's talking about going over. You hate to think of men in that, thinking no one's coming to help..." His words trail off and she knows he is lost in his reading.

It will be over by spring. By September at the latest. She doesn't understand what the fighting is about now. Sarah, in her lather about all the casualties, says it's a war without reason. A tussle over a few square fields, a quarrel over a black line on a map.

"Ena," he calls to her again, the newspaper apparently abandoned. His voice is light with tease, with private affection. "Let's walk down the lane together. The moon's full. A good night for a kiss."

Before she puts on her coat, she stokes the stove, its heat beating back the gathering draughts. "All right," she says, eager for him now, for that promised kiss. She'll bake the bread when they come back and then she'll fall into bed with Jamie, curling into his hollows, the warmth of him spreading to her limbs.

ONE OF THEIR COWS has a flaming udder. It kicked when she first put her hand on the teat. Now, when she touches it, the cow presses its flat black nose into the side of its stall, its ears flattened, its nostrils billowing as if trying to relieve itself of heat.

Ena has mastered many aspects of farm work, including the milking and the day-to-day care of the cows. Still there are things she doesn't know, that she can't see her way into. From the back of the barn, the bull sends out two long and sullen bellows and the cow balks, its distress testing her. Ena clenches her teeth and stares at the heavily veined udder; it looks full—distended and hard like Indian rubber.

"There's something wrong."

Jamie has finally come in from another stall. His face tilts toward the animal and she sees that he recognizes the problem right away. "Did you touch it?"

"Yes."

He nods. "Best go to the washhouse before we touch her again." He turns and smiles into her eyes. "Don't worry, Ena."

After they've washed up, she follows him back to the cow. He squats down, his hands hanging between his knees, the long fingers uncurled and patient-looking.

"An infection," he says carefully. He places his clean hands lightly but surely on the stretched and inflamed sac. "We'll make a poultice for her. She's a young healthy animal. She'll be all right."

"I'll do it," she tells Jamie firmly. "I know how." She thinks back to the endless mustard plasters she'd prepared when Michael was sick. *First mix the mustard powder with the flour,* Michael instructed. Her hands slipped through the silky mix, letting it run through her fingers, three times, four, five. *Then pour the warmed water over top.* The kettle was heavy and she had to pour the water slowly, careful it wasn't too hot. *Now the mixture has turned to paste, take the torn strips of cotton and layer them in the bowl.* The best part. The half-submerged strips would deepen in hue, taking on the colour of autumn.

"That's it, my girl. That's the way."

As he lay waiting for the poultices to begin to do their work, he'd tapped on her hand in lively silent rhythms. Smells mingled in the room—mustard, sharp and insistent, and the chalky blandness of the flour paste. And peppermint, the flavour of the tonic that the doctor had prescribed. Smells that drew out each new breath from Michael's lungs like the long-fingers of a magician.

In a few days, the cow is better, the udder softer, the angry heat dispelled. Everything is just as Jamie said.

The early winter crashes in with lashings of wind and rain, and an ancient maple at the foot of their lane loses a large limb. It was too weighted with leaves, says Jamie, and unprepared for the early weather. He harnesses Ted and hauls the jagged limb to the back of the barn where he will saw it into pieces. They can use it for firewood at least.

After he's finished with the tree limb, Jamie unhitches the horse from the wagon, leads him into the barn and Ena follows. Ted is broad-chested, not tall, but powerfully built, his eyes a rich brown, the lashes luxuriant and long. Picking up a comb, she moves closer to the horse. Ena has learned how to take care of him, how to muck out his stall, what to feed him, how to pick his feet clean. She has learned how to curry comb and brush him, and then massage him down with a cloth. The horse is always patient with her and quiet. Sometimes, when she thinks that Jamie isn't looking, afraid she might seem foolish, she strokes Ted's neck and puts her forehead flat against his, a calmness falling over her.

"I want to know how to drive him."

When they had the store, Michael had a horse and cart, but Ellen sold both after he died and then Ena had walked everywhere in town. Jamie goes to the side of Ted's stall and lifts the leather collar and harness from the long spike. They take Ted out to the yard and Jamie shows Ena each piece of equipment, letting her handle it first before placing it over Ted's broad neck and back. Finally, he hitches Ted to the buggy, the snow not deep enough for the cutter, and they sit close together on the bench, their knees beneath a heavy blanket, Jamie offering her the reins.

"He'll know what to do," he beams at her playfully. "You don't have to do much with Ted."

At first, she sits rigidly, her fingers clenching the reins, but then Ted's easy gait, his swing loosens her. They take the road south, toward the bay, and then turn along the broken shore, where the road cuts under the stone cliffs, and crooked pines grow out of crevices.

Jamie's eyes are closed, his hands making a triangle behind his head, his mouth set in a half-smile. "You like Ted," he says, one eye opening mischievously. He yawns. "I'm going to put aside some money for a truck."

Hugh already has one. A truck would make it easier for Jamie to pick up supplies in town and there are more and more motorcars driving from town each day. When they get back to the farm, Jamie unhitches Ted and slides off the harness, and then goes to fill a pail with feed. The horse whinnies when he sees him return, the pail full. A world without horses, Ena thinks. It would never have occurred to her before coming here, before Jamie, to mourn the passing of the horse.

"We won't let Ted go," she says, running her hands down the length of Ted's nose, "Even with a truck."

"No," Jamie laughs. "We won't do that."

8. DECEMBER 1915

ON HER WAY HOME from Owen Sound, Ena plans to deliver an English Christmas cake to Sarah and Hugh, and with it a large tin of assorted cookies—hermits, ginger drops, snowballs, and Scottish shortbreads. The first real snow has fallen, leaving a silvery-white blanket over the fields. Ted's pace is brisk. He tosses his head and snorts into the crystalline air. It hasn't taken Ena long to feel confident in handling him. She shifts her weight on the worn leather seat, relieved to have left Owen Sound behind her, happy to be alone on the road with the horse.

Her visit to town has been difficult to shake: the gathered throng outside of the town hall, the man with the bull horn shouting out a challenge for anyone who could, to enlist, the scene discordant and raw.

Buggies and motor cars jammed the street. Navigating the bottleneck, Ena slowed Ted and a sharp-eyed woman stepped forward; she reached up to Ena, a flyer in her hand. "You should consider what your influence is," she said. "Talk to your man and urge him to help, if he hasn't done so already." She gave Ena a terse nod and turned away, her hand already out to another woman pushing a pram, a child walking, pressed close beside her.

Ena had studied the single page. It featured a drawing of a man in a uniform:

To the Women of Canada. Do you realize that the safety of

your home and children depends on our getting more men.
NO W! *When the War is over and someone asks your husband
or your son what he did in the Great War, is he to hang his
head because you would not let him go?* It gave the address
of the newly opened recruitment center, located on the main
street of Owen Sound.

There had been something of a bully about the woman and
her leaflet, which left Ena both angry and strangely ashamed.
For a long while, she sat motionless and watched as the woman
made her way down the bustling street. The crowd at the town
hall was swelling, the man with the bull horn hammering on
and on, the sound thin and distorted, and Ena tried to com-
prehend him but in truth, only every third or fourth word was
recognizable to her. She had no wish to join in the enthusiasm
for the war but it suddenly became important to know *who*
was signing-up. Not just their names, but whether they were
in some way familiar.

She pulled the buggy out into the traffic and turned Ted
toward the main street. Immediately, she heard a riot of car
horns, the sound coarse and jarring. The recruitment center
was located halfway down the block. Slowing, she eyed a
sizeable cluster of men waiting outside the red-painted door.
They were young for the most part, but some were in their
thirties and forties, all of them chatting, stamping their legs,
and convivially sharing tobacco or a pre-rolled smoke. It was
a shock to recognize some of the faces. Boys from school.
Neighbours. Faces she had seen at the market, in the post
office, at McFadden's Dry Goods.

Now, as she pulls Ted into the McFarland lane, Blain is turning
the corner of the barn, a green wool hat pulled low over his
ears. The hat makes his forehead fold into creases, although
the rest of his face is smooth, his jaw narrow, his chin still the
round chin of a child. For a moment, he stops and studies her,
and then he ambles over. The tip of his nose is a flaming red.

Ena wordlessly gathers up the Christmas baking she has

brought for Sarah and hands him the canvas bags. "Why aren't you in school?" she asks as he takes them from her.

He grins, his smile seeming too big for him. "No school now. It's holidays. And I'm glad."

Ena smiles back. "School's not so bad."

"Maybe it weren't for you," he says, "but I hate it."

She nods her head and climbs down from the buggy. Blain looks gaunt. His trousers have holes and he doesn't wear gloves.

"So you're working for Hugh every day now?"

He shrugs and cocks his head. "More hours over Christmas 'cause Clem's takin' time at home, just 'til New Year."

She reaches out her hands to take the bags but he holds on to them. "I'll take 'em in to Sarah for you," he says.

"If you want," says Ena, "but I'm going to find her anyway."

They walk together down the lane and something opens in him, making him chatter. "I found out that a private's gonna make $1.10 per day plus all his meals. You know, that's not too bad. It's about what I make workin' here for the McFarland's." He steals a look at her and slyly grins. "Clem makes more. Maybe you could put in a good word for me, see if Mr. McFarland would raise the wage." Blain's feet are slightly turned out, and his hips sink as though he intends to stride out somewhere. He is chewing something that smells like licorice.

Ena laughs. "You need experience before he'll pay you more." She lifts her eyes to Sarah's kitchen stoop. Her pace slows. She likes the sound of his voice, yipping at her like a little fox.

"What I'd like to do is join up," he says.

She stops and stares at him. "Why? "

His eyes narrow and he is stands up straighter.

"Why not?"

"Because," she says, her voice stern, "you're not old enough. And your father and brother need you."

His face reddens. "Since Mum died, people got ideas about what I should do."

"They don't mean any harm," says Ena. "It's sad, about your mum. I'm sorry...."

He wipes his nose with the sleeve of his coat and smiles widely again. "No matter."

She sets her shoulders. "Forget this stuff about volunteering. Enough boys have gone over already. I just drove past a line-up of volunteers in town—they have more than they can use. And it's not as easy over there as people thought at first. I'll talk to Hugh about your wages."

He blinks almost coyly, his grin broadening. "Thanks." He opens the door for her, but he doesn't go in.

WHEN ENA ARRIVES HOME, she finds Jamie tossing wood into the stove. She stands behind him, her eyes on his back, her fists clenched as though she is squeezing something out of herself—concern, some unnamed worry. The dread she felt earlier in town.

Before she left the McFarland's that afternoon, Sarah told her that Craig Murray had written from Paris about the war artists there; they wanted to document everything—the causalities, the way the men lived on the battlefields, the field hospitals. It wasn't being reported properly in the papers.

"They might start taking younger boys now. Blain Carter's talking about volunteering."

Jamie nods, prodding the fledgling flames with the poker. "Lots of boys talk of it. It's an adventure for them, goin' over."

Her chest is tightening. She peers at his back. "Blain's got responsibilities to his family."

Jamie doesn't turn. "He's too young to fight anyway, Ena. Don't worry about it." She watches him as he straightens, his attention now on the door and his barn coat, and the animals waiting for their evening feed.

9. JANUARY 1916

IT SURPRISES BLAIN HOW EASY it is to lie. Almost effortless, like making up a story, some part of him ready to believe it himself. That's how convincing he is. He's had to be, living with the old man. Hugh McFarland believes that Blain is at home looking after Owen because Owen is sick.

When Blain told the lie the day before, he and Clem and Hugh had been working in Jamie McFarland's barn, mending stalls. Ena and Jamie were milking. Clem squinted over at Blain, concern crumpling his forehead. "Annie ought to have a look at him. Maybe he'll need the doctor."

"Naaah," Blain said, swatting a bent nail with the hammer. "Just gotta make sure he stays warm and in bed for a day or so."

Hugh had given a tight nod and continued with ripping out the old planks with a crowbar. "All right to miss a day," he'd said. "Just don't make a habit of it, Blain."

Sitting rigid on the milking stool, Ena stared hard, her dark eyes finding their way inside of him, inside the fabrication. It had made Blain uneasy, doubt creeping in when he should have felt complete conviction about what he now sets out to do.

This morning, after Owen left on his trek into school, Blain told the old man he'd be off to the McFarland's. He'd caught his usual ride with John Frewer, who each day, on his way into the Foundry in Green's Bay, drops Blain at the McFarland farm. In exchange, Blain provides Frewer with a few jars of the old man's hooch.

"I'll take a lift the whole way to town," he told Frewer, "and catch a ride back at the end of the shift." Now Blain rides with several foundry men in the open bed of Frewer's truck, a tarpaulin over their legs. The ride is frigid, Blain's thighs as numb as stumps and his eyelashes stick together, hoary with the steam of his breath. The men's faces are grey and tired in the thin morning light and they don't talk although several times, Blain tries to entice them with a little light conversation.

He's the first to hop out at the harbour and he watches as the men stiffly climb from the truck and make their way into the smoking foundry. A couple of them turn back to see where he's headed, but the others don't seem to care much. Blain imagines that working in the foundry isn't a job he would care for. Dirty and shut in, no windows to look out on the water or sky. And he'd have to stay here. A shiver goes through him, cold snaking its way through his belly, his teeth starting to rattle. Shoving his hands in his pockets, he walks toward the centre of town.

When he passes the Wesley Hotel, two young men in uniform push through the front doors, red-cheeked and laughing, thick as thieves. They rush past him, half-running in the direction of the harbour; new recruits, late for their early morning drills and exercises, he guesses. Abandoned warehouses and waterfront sheds had been reclaimed as training sites since the first draft of Grey volunteers enlisted in late 1914. Watching the men, he is taken-up in a heady mix of envy and admiration and now, with his shoulders hunched against the cold, he quickens his pace.

The recruitment office is operated out of a low red-brick storefront, a flag sagging from a pole in the large square window, recruiting posters pasted to the glass. One of them reads: *Here's Your Chance, It's Men We Want*. The place had been a dispensary before the military took it over. Since the New Year, each time Blain has driven into Owen Sound with Hugh McFarland, he's stolen a glance at it, and although in the first weeks of recruitment it was a busy place, this morning, too frigid for even the most eager, it's deserted.

For weeks, he's told himself a story about what signing up will mean. He has tried to make an adventure out of the war, the sort that Mum would have told, but he knows, since Flanders, that Canadian soldiers are dying in mud over there. He's frightened by the thought, but the idea of a life spent here, under the old man and his moonshine—the endless days and nights living beside that stinking swamp, is simply too terrible.

He pauses at the red door and wipes his nose on the cuff of his coat. Straightening, he rocks back on his heels to get the blood flowing to his near-frozen toes. It wouldn't be good to walk in hobbled. Volunteers get turned away for all sorts of reasons: flat feet, a cough, bad eyes. He knows he will be asked about his age. "Eighteen," he's going to say without a moment's hesitation. Finally, he squares his shoulders and thrusts out his chin. *Don't smile, Blain Carter,* he says under his breath. *Smiling makes you a boy.*

The recruiting officer behind the counter is friendly enough, a lean man, greying at the temples and with a bristling black mustache. It is so black, Blain wonders if the man puts shoe polish on it. The man takes an application from a stack on a shelf and, leaning conversationally toward Blain, he asks him a number of questions, writing down each answer in a crisp and efficient hand.

"Ever had rheumatic fever, Blain?"

"Don't know what it is."

"Any childhood illnesses? Fevers? Spots?"

Blain shakes his head.

"And trouble with your lungs. Asthmatic?"

"I work on a farm," he says. "If I got problems I never noticed 'em."

The recruitment officer smiles. "Can you read and write?"

"Sure I can."

"I'm going to hold up this book for you. Come close. Can you read the coloured section to me?"

"'The dog ran after the cat and the cat ran after the rat. The farmer—'"

"That's fine, Blain, thank you. So you don't need glasses, eh?"

Blain had never thought about wearing glasses. "Guess not."

The officer smiles warmly, knowingly at him. It is obvious he likes him and Blain hopes maybe that will be enough for him to pass. He didn't even blink when Blain told him his birthdate, but Blain had rehearsed it enough that it sounded right. The officer asks Blain to wait and disappears into the adjoining room. When he comes back through, a doctor is with him.

The doctor is a little man around fifty, spectacled, grey hairs sprouting from his nostrils, fat pouches beneath his eyes. He takes Blain to the room in the back where there are floor-to-ceiling shelves laden with bottles—blue and brown-coloured. On a small table in the centre of the room is a wash basin, a small hammer, a stethoscope, a tongue depressor. Some of the instruments are not recognizable and Blain turns his mind from imagining their uses. He pulls his eyes from the table and looks hopefully at the doctor.

Waving his hand, the doctor tells Blain to take off his shirt and trousers. A small desk is angled in the corner of the room and while Blain undresses, the doctor sits behind it, his spectacles on the end of his nose. Blain's recruitment application lies on top of the blotter.

There is no stove in the room, and standing, waiting for the examination, Blain's bare skin turns a bluish-grey. The ruddy hairs on his thighs stand up and his teeth begin to chatter. Finally the doctor looks up, his eyes taking in Blain and then he sighs. "Let's get on with it, son."

With an air of reluctance, the doctor taps and prods, runs his hands over Blain's ribs, and then gets Blain to open his mouth. He places his hands on each side of Blain's jaw and slides his fingers down the length of jaw bone, grunting, a slight clucking coming from somewhere near the back of his throat. After he is done, he stands back from Blain, his eyes just to the left of

Blain's face, his arms crossed and heavy-looking.

"That was awful short," says Blain brightly.

Ignoring him, the doctor goes and sits behind the desk again and writes something down on his application. It can't be more than three or four words.

"You're not more than sixteen," he says, not looking up. "Jaw's like a little girl's. I'm not going to pass you, son."

"Thompson jaw. My mum's. We all got 'em."

"Sorry, son. No."

As Blain walks past the recruiting officer, he gives Blain a wink. "Try again," he says. "Maybe put on some weight."

Blain flashes a smile at him and shrugs. He pulls up his woollen collar and steps out onto the street and into a saw-toothed wind. Slipping his hand into his pocket he feels the hard promise of coins—enough to buy some tea and a slice of cinnamon-sugar pie. *Fatten-up and try again*, he tells himself. The war isn't going to be over anytime soon. There are other recruitment offices in other towns. It doesn't have to be the 147 Grey Overseas.

10. MARCH 1916

THEY HAVE BEEN UP half the night with a labouring cow. Rain mixed with snow splatters the window. Ena anxiously inspects a covered bowl of yeast she'd earlier set by the stove. When she lifts the cloth, the mixture looks flat, dispirited. Stale yeast, she thinks, disappointed. Tired this morning, she'd looked forward to slipping into the ritual of bread baking, knowing it would revive her.

After breakfast and ready for chores, Jamie slides on his coat and then pushes his feet into his barn boots. He goes to the woodshed door, hesitates. "I've something to tell you, Ena." She is still brushing the crumbs from the tablecloth, stacking their plates in the sink.

"I'm going to go in for the medical."

Ena's hands simply stop.

Her first thought swoops down, hard and practical, rooted in refusal. "You won't. You can't leave a farm, Jamie."

"There'll be help for the farm," he says gently. He tilts his head and studies the door. "There'll be Hugh."

"You don't mean it." Her words are sudden and battering, something in them of Ellen. They astonish her with their ferocity. "You didn't ask me. It's a selfish thing for you to do."

He is gazing directly at her now, urging her to understand. "I don't *want* to go. A lot of fellows that went over probably didn't, but they went anyway. Mathew Rolly signed up and his dad's got trouble with his hips—can barely walk to the end of his lane, let alone run a farm. Matt's brother-in-law's going to have to pitch in while Matt's away. Same as here."

She doesn't care what Mathew Rolly does or how his family will manage. She stares at Jamie, wordless and stunned.

"What do you think it's like to let other men go, to hang back?" he asks. There is a tightening in the small muscles around his eyes; pain mixed with a coalescing of intent—or simply bull-headedness, something she has missed seeing in him before.

Later, that night, after they climb into bed, Ena lies on her back, her body a hard, unfeeling thing, not her own. A part of her has braced for this. A part of her is unsurprised.

"Ena," he whispers, his lips on her shoulder, "I am not leaving you."

She doesn't dare touch him, her fingernails curling into her palms, her eyes boring into the darkened room. As his breathing slows and he drifts off to sleep, a fury pounds inside and then creeps up into her chest, ready to pounce, but before it can, it becomes something else—a torrent of water, silent and storming down her cheeks.

Through the hours she lies like that, afraid to close her eyes, afraid that if she does, by morning, he will vanish.

HUGH STANDS WITH JAMIE in the slushy barnyard. Jamie is sitting on a stool, his arms around a calf, a pail of grey water by his side. Another thaw has blown in from the south and the sky is cantankerous with cloud.

"Some more weather comin'."

Jamie nods and smiles but doesn't look up from the calf.

From where she is in the barn, Ena can see Hugh in profile. His arms are lashed across his chest as if to prevent something inside from escaping. His inscrutable gaze is on the wobbling calves, their black and white coats spoiled with mud.

"You sure you want to sign up?"

Jamie puts his hands deep into the bucket, pulls up the

streaming cloth and twists out the excess water. He encircles the next calf in the crook of his elbow and runs the cloth over its frail legs and belly. When he's done, he takes a small blanket and lightly buffs the little creature until its coat is a mass of silky curls.

Scuffing the ground with his toe Hugh glances narrowly at his brother. "Guess that's a yes." He's restless with watching. Going to the gate, he ruthlessly shakes the post, testing its strength. "Rotting. Thought it was. Could use a support 'til spring, when we can reset it," he calls over his shoulder.

Jamie ignores the comment and studies the calf, making sure each part of it is dry. "It's different for you, Hugh," he says suddenly, his tone measured. "You're the oldest and you got the productive farm. This one's not doing much yet. No one expects you to go over."

Ena has heard Jamie say that Hugh would be turned away from service because of his travelling eye. For several moments, the two brothers don't speak and then Hugh shifts his shoulders. "You always was the pigheaded brother."

Jamie laughs, releasing the calf that skips and shimmies away from him. "All this time, I thought that was you."

Hugh grunts. "Anyway, I brought Blain over, case you need anything done in the barn." He nods toward Blain who stands back from the men, unusually quiet, his hands dangling, his shirt askew. His eyes are planted on Jamie.

Jamie's gaze falls on another calf that stands, tottering by the gate, away from the others. He rises and traipses over to it across the muddy yard.

INSIDE THE HOUSE, Sarah is waiting for Ena. "He won't pass the exam," she says sharply.

Sarah has brought eggs and Ena carefully takes them from the basket, and then turns toward Sarah, the emptied basket in her hand. "You'll want to take this home."

"He's thin," Sarah insists. "I'm sure I'm stronger than he

is." Her face is fiery, her huge eyes roiling.

Ena puts the basket down on the worktop. "That's ridiculous. Jamie's as strong as an ox. He might not look it—"

"None of these men should be going. *Jamie* shouldn't—"

Ena says nothing. She slips on her apron. She had been baking a caramel layer cake before Hugh and Sarah came and now she scrapes the stubborn batter from the spoon.

"You have to tell him not to go. It's *foolish*, Ena. He'll listen to you."

Ena stares, unblinking into the bowl. The familiar sensation of shuttering herself descends. After all, words are useless—they won't prevent him from leaving. Hadn't she sat with Michael for hours at his bedside, listening to him chatter, his words like birds swooping, lifting, circling. Happy sounds. Still he died. She stands, walks slowly to the sideboard, and takes another spoon from the drawer.

EACH MORNING AFTER THE MILKING, Jamie leaves for his elementary training in Owen Sound. There are endless drills and exercises and route marches. He travels with the other recruits to rifle ranges that have been set-up all over the county. On both farms, Hugh does the ploughing without him that spring.

In the evenings Jamie disappears into the barn, keeping-up with his chores, taking care of the livestock; she looks for him from the kitchen window. To beat back the dread she feels, she fixes his location as if securing him to her—*he's in the third stall with the young cow, he's walking the far field with Billie.*

Sometimes, she thinks she sees in the softness of his mouth or the way his eyes glance briefly downward, a suggestion that he regrets enlisting, and for an instant she is secretly triumphant, but the feeling brings no lasting relief. The playfulness between them has stopped although he steadfastly tries to talk to her. Her responses are terse, and at night, when they lie next to one another, she flinches if his hand strays to the curve of her hip or ventures to her thigh. She knows herself to be unforgiving and she is quietly appalled, but the flow of bitterness inside won't be staunched. What would her life have been had she not met him, had she not come to live with him here, on this farm? She would be at the McLaren's still, unattached, free to work in rooms belonging to others, her feelings tamped down, too deep to be a bother.

And then, one cool spring afternoon, he takes his jacket from the back of the mudroom door. The fabric catches on the hook and he has to reach again to free it; as he does, Ena sees the naked tapering of his back, the white clear skin above his waistband, the delicate progression of his spine. She remembers with breathtaking certainty how much she loves him.

Standing in her kitchen, staring at the empty hook that just moments before held his coat, what strikes her is how starved she is. She can't remember the reason for the distance between them. She can't remember why they don't touch. She slips out and follows him over the yard and then through the barn door that he has left open. She sees the shy curl of his back as he milks.

If he hears her approach, he shows no sign, only turning his head slightly when he feels her arms reach for him under his coat. Her hands pass over his ribs and find the flat sure centre of his breast bone.

They find an empty stall and a blanket, the straw piled deep beneath them, and when they are done he takes her face between his palms.

"You won't be alone, Ena. You don't ever have to be. Hugh says he's gonna look after the place while I'm away. It's all McFarland land anyway. Blain will be around to help. But you don't have to stay here by yourself. You can stay over at the home farm."

A hay bale shifts in the loft, probably a barn cat making a nest, and Ena feels herself sink deeper into the straw bed, her arms drawing Jamie down with her.

"Or you could move back with your mother," he goes on.

Ena imagines herself in the small dark house on 7th street with Ellen and is quietly frantic.

"I won't leave the farm," she says, looking at the rough boards over their heads.

Rolling on his side, he kisses her neck. "I'm sorry, Ena."

She brings his hands to her lips. His fingers are lightly chaffed, like cinnamon bark. She lifts them to her nose and breathes.

BLAIN SPLITS HIS TIME between the two McFarland farms. In the evenings, he shadows Jamie and helps with the barn chores, all the while peppering Jamie with questions about bayoneting practice and rifle drills.

"Not much in it, Blain. Dull, most of the time. A lot of marching around, learning how to say 'yes, Sir, right away, Sir.' I'd rather be here working than standing in a muddy field waiting to stab a sack of flour."

Blain wants more from him, she can tell by the keenness in his face. Instead, Jamie shows Blain how to encourage the bull into the paddock. "It's best if you have help to move him," he says, giving Blain the animal's lead. "But you might have to handle him yourself if Clem or Hugh aren't here." Jamie nods at the bull. "Don't pull on him if his tail is arched or his eyes roll. And don't try and move him unless the cows are pastured and out of his sight."

Blain is more assured around the animal now, guiding it into the paddock with only a staff and the lead. Swinging his leg over the rail and jumping in with the bull, he grins at Ena and Jamie who watch from the other side of the fence. When he's done, he ambles over and tells them a story about a bull that charged a motor truck up Wiarton way, how the truck ran the bull down, killing it. "Bugger didn't know it met its match," Blain says with satisfaction. "Didn't know what hit him."

IN EARLY MAY, a letter from the newly designated regimental office arrives for Jamie at the post office in Owen Sound. Jamie and Ena sit together on the wagon, the back of the wagon half-filled with supplies, Ted still secured to the hitching post as people on the street stroll past.

"The regimental train will depart Owen Sound later this month for Camp Niagara," Jamie reads out loud. He turns over the page, his eyes narrowing. "Says in the fall, before going overseas, we'll have a week's home-leave."

"What else does it say?"

He shrugs. "Just confirms what supplies the army will issue, what personal things I can take with me. Confirms the rate of pay. They've already told me all of this."

When they get back to the farm, they unload the wagon and Jamie absently drops the letter onto the table. Ena busies herself with sorting what they bought in town—two sacks of flour, a tin of cinnamon, a glass bottle of lemon juice, gelatin, fresh yeast. Earlier, she harvested some rhubarb, and it now sits limp and wilting on the worktop. She had gone out early, and sliced the fleshy stalks, anticipating the conserve she would make, the rhubarb cake; she had thought about the fragile colour of the veins, how the rhubarb will turn the water to a blushing pink when she simmers it. But the letter consumes her now.

Jamie has gone to the field to put fresh water in the troughs for the cows. She sees him through the window carrying pails, his back straight, his stride easy. He wears his straw hat low on his forehead and his shirtsleeves are rolled to his elbows. They seldom talk about the war but since Jamie enlisted, she reads the paper front to back. She wants the war to be over, won or lost, before he is supposed to leave, but nothing in the paper gives her a bit of hope.

She turns her back on the rhubarb, her hand resting on the letter, lifting it, unfolding it. Just as Jamie said, it gives the date and time that his train will leave Owen Sound for advanced training, and it provides a specific list of what he should take. But there is also, near the bottom, a suggestion that all volunteers use the weeks ahead to make certain that their affairs are in order. *Recruits,* the letter urges, *are to make the practical and financial arrangements necessary to care for their dependents throughout the duration of their absence, and they are strongly encouraged to draw up a last will and testament before embarking for overseas.*

JAMIE WRITES TO HER REGULARLY from Camp Niagara where he goes for higher formation training, and then from Pine Plains, the new training grounds that the 147th are helping to build. He writes that building makes for dull work. "We had digging practice in Owen Sound," he observes, "and now we are digging here, even when it rains. We'll be good diggers at least, once we go over." There are football matches and card games, pranks played on one another.

Twice over the summer he comes home for a week's furlough to help Hugh and his crew with the farm work. Each time he goes away again, she sets her mind on the next leave, the next time he will be home, her bones lighter with anticipation. And then his final leave in October comes and no matter how she tries, she cannot see past it.

The week before their final departure, the 147th puts on exhibitions, and marching bands play on the parade route from the armoury to the Market Square. The unit's championship bayonet fighting team stages a display that disgusts Sarah who turns away, striding off alone toward the river. "Just a lot of nonsense to entice more boys to join up," she tells Ena later. "It's criminal to even witness it."

Ena doesn't say so but she wishes she hadn't seen the bayoneting. The shouts of the men, their head-long run, the thrusting knives—the spectators cheering as though they were watching a lacrosse match or a game of football.

HUGH AND SARAH HOLD A FAMILY REUNION on the Saturday before Jamie and two of his cousins will leave with the regiment, and relatives come from as far as Chesley and Hanover.

Long tables are set on the grass and the arriving women set out cold ham and beef tongue, large wedges of cheese, carrot salads, potato salads, relishes and pickles and hard-boiled eggs. There are plum cakes and buns, and Ena's brown bread, and three of her deep, double-crust peach pies.

A golden day, light clouds and blue sky. All afternoon, Jamie's uncles pump his hand in encouragement. His aunts present him with thick knitted socks and scarves. Little cousins—boys and girls—wave toy flags and no one talks about the recent losses at the Somme.

Hugh has laid out a long hemp rope on the grass for a game of tug-of-war and men, their jackets peeled away, take their places on either side of the centre knot. Hugh is the anchor man for his team, his thighs set, his heels dug-in. Jamie is in front of him, his back angled into his brother, his feet shifting slightly to find the best advantage. There are many matches over the afternoon but no team can beat them.

Late in the day, when the sun is low and everyone is stunned with food and sun, Hugh announces that the arm wrestling will start. A table is cleared and men sit two to a side, each man facing his opponent with elbows planted, eyes locked, jaws screwed tight. After each match, the victors wrestle.

At last, with the light vanishing from the sky, Jamie sits across from Hugh. Hugh wears a gleaming grin, his hand held out to Jamie, and in that moment, it is like Hugh is making an offering—a handshake or a promise. The brothers' hands connect, their knuckles hard and white beneath their skin.

Family members keep a respectful distance from the men, and Ena, standing among them, is held rapt. For a long time Jamie and Hugh are perfectly counter-posed, their arms solid with no quiver and no give. She is inside the effort, her own muscles straining, her fingers digging into her palms. And then Jamie gracefully relinquishes, his arm inching back and over, Hugh's strength finally prevailing. Jamie's knuckles stop just short of the table.

The change is so sudden it is difficult to credit. In a rush and with startling swiftness, there is an arc of movement, arms sweeping in the opposite direction, the back of Hugh's hand thudding painfully down. No one moves or speaks. Hugh stares, incredulous at his own defeat. He frowns at his pinned arm. "God Damn!" Jamie loosens his grip and Hugh is up and around the table, guffawing, affectionately cuffing Jamie's ears. Other men tug Jamie's shoulders and clap him on the back. Jamie laughs and laughs and Hugh shakes his head, grinning. "You done all right, Jamie." The brothers clasp hands once again, Hugh pulling Jamie hard into him, and in that moment Ena is both exuberant and sad.

From inside the house, the piano starts and is soon joined by a fiddle, and suddenly the evening is filled with jaunty chords and whirling rhythms. Ena is carried in a throng of McFarlands up toward the sound.

ON THE DAY BEFORE JAMIE'S TRAIN will leave, they sit with Sarah and Hugh at the McFarland's dining table. Hugh is at the head of the table, his elbows encircling his empty plate. His pale hair is combed back and creamed into place, the ends neatly trimmed around his ears. Without the fall of hair, the long smooth ridge of bone across his eyes is visible. He forces a grin and instantly his cheeks swell with the effort.

Sarah makes a show of collecting the plates, stacking them onto a platter of half-consumed roast, her irritation palpable. Her hatred for the war has peaked with the losses at the Somme. She declares herself a pacifist, furious that there are no other pacifists in Owen Sound.

"A nation of children," she spits out.

Pushing back his chair, Hugh ignores her. He grunts and rises to a stand, his eyes on Jamie. "We've things to talk about. Let's take a walk." Jamie nods and slides from the table. For a moment, the two brothers don't move, their eyes on the swirl of carpet at their feet, the threads bare from decades of use.

Little has changed at the McFarland farm since Mr. and Mrs. McFarland died. The farmhouse is full of their furniture. Their wedding china is in the walnut sideboard; Mrs. McFarland's canning jars are dusty and stored in the cellar (no use to Sarah who doesn't care about canning). Sheets and tablecloths—things put to use at the McFarland farm for decades, all still in drawers and wardrobes. Ena's parents brought almost nothing with them from Ireland. No linens, no plates. And then Michael had lost the store. As she watches the brothers, their pale heads angled and close, Ena sees the untested faith they share in this place.

Jamie gestures with his eyes in the direction of the barn and Hugh gives an answering shrug of his chin. When Ena rises to help Sarah, Hugh puts his outsized hand on her arm.

"We got by over the summer just fine with me working both farms, Ena. It's all gonna work out. I'll take care of it. You'll see."

11. AUTUMN 1916

OCTOBER 5TH, THE DAY SLIGHTLY COOL, a wind blowing off the bay. The flags outside of the courthouse snap smartly, and the brightly-coloured banners and bunting thrash and threaten to tear away. Ena and Jamie stand in a sea of people—handshakes, giddy chatter; a man quavers resolutely into song and other voices, out of sync, break in. The crowd is taken over with silly anticipation, a heady rush toward departure.

The troop train is scheduled to leave from the station at three-forty-five p.m. Hours to go, thinks Ena, steadying herself. On a decorated riser stands the Mayor, his face shiny above a starched white collar, his round spectacles glinting in the sun. He squints into the crowd and places his ringed fingers flat on the polished surface of an oak lectern that has been set before him. Clearing his throat, he readies himself to speak to the crowd.

Time stretches but not enough. Everything in Ena inclines toward a refusal of movement and her body, next to Jamie's has gone rigid. Jamie slides his ungloved hand into hers and gently prods her fingers with his thumb.

The Mayor is recovering from a recent illness and his voice, once he begins his congratulatory address, is rough and difficult to hear. Wind gusts snatch away words and entire phrases. Not certain that his speech is done, the crowd breaks into "God Save the King" too early and after there is an eruption of cheers. He stops and waves—more cheers—and then he hurries from the podium.

The band plays on, people's faces flushed with pride, chatting, sharing sandwiches, shaking the hands of the volunteers. Regimental pictures are taken: the 147th Bugle Band, the 147th Machine Gun Platoon, the 147th Medical Section and Stretcher-Bearers, and on and on it goes. Done up and trim in their khaki, the men blink into the glare of the day.

After Jamie's photograph is taken, he picks up his duffle bag and he and Ena slip away from the huddle of people. They walk along tree-lined streets, past stolid redbrick houses where entire families sit on porches, chatting, playing checkers. Seeing Jamie's khaki, children shout and parents wave.

Flags have been tied to trees with red and white ribbon. A small black and white dog perches on an old man's knee, one ear cocked to the sounds of ragged singing—hymns and anthems. The signs of departure are undeniable.

Jamie tilts his head, adjusts his bag on his shoulder, his pace slowing. He studies the ground. "Ena, you'll have to order the crop seeds early. Remember how it was last spring? They were late delivering. Put our order together with Hugh's if you want. He'll handle it."

"I'll go to town and put it in myself. Early February. Is that enough time?"

"Yes, should be." They are quiet for a few moments. "Best if Hugh does the costing for the dairy. The man there will try and talk you down. I've seen that happen."

"They won't talk me down," she says quietly, taking his arm. "I had to deal with him all summer. It will be all right."

He is nodding, his head lost in his worries. "I wrote down all the names of people you might need. But of course, there's Hugh."

She has heard all of this before but she lets him go on, focusing on the up and down of his voice, the timbre of it. She would bottle the sound if she could, sleep with it under her pillow.

"I remember everything you have told me. I won't forget," she says simply.

"Of course, Ena. I know."

The courthouse is open, the foyer set with long tables, the YMCA women serving apple cider, sandwiches, chocolate-walnut squares, and maple-sugar cookies. Ena fills a plate for them to share, Jamie holding the two steaming mugs, and they find a place to sit down, away from the milling crowd of people. Neither of them eat. Six men start to sing, a comical tune that Ena has never heard. A round-eyed boy in suspenders goes from group to group and does magic tricks with a deck of cards. Jamie, transfixed, watches him then turns to Ena and smiles.

When the clock on the wall shows three, some of the crowd begins to drift toward the door. Jamie rubs his palms down his long thighs and then looks apologetically at Ena. "Well…" he says. Outside, the air feels fresh and Ena breathes, momentarily lulled into relief.

When at three-fifteen, the troop train pulls in beside the packed platform it already seems over-full, boys and men leaning out every window, and taking chocolate bars from the women of the auxiliary. Some of the men clown, some grin, others look frankly sad and frightened. *There is no room for him*, thinks Ena. *With so many, they can't possibly need anyone else to go.* Her arms feel heavy, her fingers tensed. Now, so close to departure, she finds she can no longer look into Jamie's face.

From behind them, Hugh steps out of the press of people, his huge hand on Jamie's shoulder and then pulling him into a hug. "Goodbye, brother," he says, clapping Jamie on the back. Sarah is there too, perplexed and anxious-looking. She presses Jamie's arm and then scowls at the train as though she'll do battle with it. Hugh takes her hand and together they disappear into the swarm of people.

Ena will not permit tears. Jamie holds her to him with firmness, his head bent low. "It will be fine, Ena. I'll be home in no time."

Ena straightens his collar, frowning into her clumsy-seeming hands. After a long moment of fiddling, she stands on her toes and presses him close.

She steps brusquely away, takes a wrapped package of ham, bread, and a small tin filled with her lemon biscuits from her bag. "For the journey," she says evenly, placing the food in his hands.

All the men are boarded. The train bellows and steam curls up from its wheels, obscuring the figures at the windows. As it begins to move, Ena looks for Jamie among the passing stream of male faces but can't find him. She blinks, her faced turned in the direction of the departing train, not moving until long after it has utterly vanished from her view.

12. NOVEMBER 1916

B LAIN, STILL GROGGY WITH SLEEP, thinks vaguely about the weight his father has lost over the last two years. It's early on a cold November morning and the old man is making his breakfast, his face grey and stubbled, dark pulpy rings around his eyes. His suspenders dangle from his belt and he pushes off the table and then staggers to the icebox. He hikes up his trousers and painfully coughs.

When Mum was here, there were regular meals and she always served the old man first—a portion of meat, lashings of potatoes, sometimes a slice of pie. He only ate a few mouthfuls then, but now he barely eats anything at all.

Blain has memories of the old man and Mum—Clem and Auntie Annie sitting across the table from them, a deck of cards in between. Blain was five or six. His father was sleekly muscled then with a youthful strength, a glow about him, Blain sitting secure in his lap. Euchre, Blain imagines, although he has never learned to play it. Mum laughing excitedly, her eyes bright and quick as she dealt the cards.

They played cards every Saturday night back then, and there was talk about right bowers, left bowers, tricks and kitties. Blain had liked the strangeness of the words, the mystery of them.

Those were the years before the still. But even if he chooses to blame the still for everything that's happened, Blain only has scraps of memory to go on, a mere scattering, and not enough to know what took Jack Carter down into the black morass he now lives in.

Auntie Annie sends home food—roasted chickens, pots of stew with buttermilk biscuits, a whole braised beef-tongue. And Ena McFarland keeps them in baked goods— loaves of bread, rolls, tins of cookies, and tarts. Blain has learned to cook a few basics but he could stand to learn more.

Rubbing his nose with his thumb, the old man peers into the icebox and pulls out a jar. Owen has abandoned a mason jar near the back, the glass now frosted and hoary. Next to it is a jar of apple butter, Mum's last, the label turned and out of view.

Jack Carter sets down the jar on the table and then pours himself out some muddy-looking coffee. There is a loaf on the table—one of Ena's, the crust an unbroken gold. The old man saws himself off a slice and tears it in two.

He sets down the knife and opens the lid of the jar.

Christ, he bellows. *Little bugger.* Inside is a shrivelled spider, big, the body bulbous, slightly hairy. Blain remembers when Owen caught it in the house last fall, cleverly using two empty cans to trap it, then dropping it into the jar. Owen had tried to feed it flies at first but the spider was morose and turgid. Before long, it stopped moving altogether and Owen put it in the icebox, near the back, where no one ever thought to look.

Blain is spooning porridge from a saucepan into Owen's bowl when the old man discovers the spider corpse. Usually Blain predicts an eruption by the slight tightening of muscles at his father's mouth, the pinch above his eyes, the pull of skin across his sharpened cheekbones making his ears rise against his narrow skull. But Blain is tired this morning, bleary-eyed, his brain turned inward, still dreaming. He doesn't see his father's backhand coming at him from across the table and there isn't enough time to get out of the way. The force of it spins him back and his head bounces dully off the cast iron stove. For a few seconds he sprawls on the floor.

His first thought is that he shouldn't let himself be caught off-guard like this. His second thought is that the old man still has plenty of strength, despite looking like he's half-starved.

"You're supposed to be keeping an eye on him, Blain," Carter says, his head jerking violently toward Owen. His voice is thin and reedy even when he is enraged. He jabs his finger at Blain's chest as if he intends to make a point, the gesture almost comic because he's already laid Blain flat out on the floor—nothing's to be gained now by upbraiding. Blain remembers how the old man used to wag his head, a serious look on his face: *If you want, I'll give you somethin' to really cry about.* That was when Blain was just a kid, when he would sometimes cry after a beating. He doesn't cry anymore but Owen does, and although Blain tries to cover for him, shushing and guffawing—distracting their father with long-winded stories Owen has become a thorn in the old man's hide.

Blain drags himself up from the floor not bothering to brush off the weeks-old crumbs from his clothes. He doesn't meet the old man's eye. Instead, he takes the jar with the spider to the kitchen door and sets it carefully out on the stoop. His legs are a little shaky and he breathes in the cold air, willing himself toward a more level head. Back in the kitchen, he casually goes to the icebox and pulls out his mother's apple butter. Unceremoniously, he puts it on the table, in front of the old man. It isn't a careful gesture, though not exactly bold. Blain lacks patience; patience is more Owen's strength, sitting by the hour, waiting for tiny creatures to venture out and reveal themselves. *Lucky* is how Blain thinks of himself. He picks his way around Carter like he's walking barefoot through thistle, and he doesn't protest when Carter is acting crazy. Blain dodges, retreats into a good humour, his mind on sunny skies.

But his old skill is proving less reliable. A fury gathers, a blind, hot hatred for Carter, for the still, for the cramped and smothering house, the glowering trees and swamp, for his mother because she's gone. And for Owen—for the simple fact that he is a child and has no one else to rely on but Blain.

"Shut up," Blain has yelled on occasion when Owen couldn't be comforted. Owen stared at him, his dark eyes liquid and brimming. Later, the love for Owen swelled in his chest so much that Blain could hardly breathe. He lay beside him and spun tales about the wild west, the stories snaking and uncoiling from Blain's head. Owen touched Blain's shoulder and peered into his face. "I know you can't be her, Blain. You don't gotta try."

Now, Blain shakes off the buzzing between his ears and then sets himself into his chair.

"You hear me, Blain? A goddamn spider!"

"Yup. I must'a missed that."

Blain smiles over at Owen and manages to wink. Owen is staring at him like he's seen a ghost.

IT WAS MUM WHO INTRODUCED them to storytelling. She and Owen and Blain lay beside one another on her bed, and Mum, snug in the middle, would start off. The story was about far away places, which she made up because she hadn't been anywhere but Owen Sound. There were strange animals and trees that could talk, and bugs with faces like people. Always, there were two boys at the story's heart and they joined travelling circuses, took long boat rides. Breathless, she paused when something momentous was about to happen, her eyes sliding conspiratorially over to Blain. Blain would take over then, adding all sorts of colourful details—funny things that would have Mum giggling, her hand held over her mouth, her eyes on Blain's lips, bright as stars. And then it was Owen's turn, but Owen wasn't good at taking up the story. He was too young, or maybe he was too serious.

Blain and Mum would coax him, and then Mum would finish up—the grand finale—the two boys in the story always happier in the end, and better for the adventure.

Once, Blain asked Mum why she thought Owen couldn't come up with magical stories. He wondered if there was something wrong with Owen, something missing. Mum said Owen's mind was already too full with seeing what was in front of him—at understanding what she called "the mysteries right under our noses." He didn't have to look further than the leaves and moss and beetles and stones that were everywhere. All of that, his mum said—if a person could *really* see it—was likely more than enough.

Blain, on the other hand, feels an unstoppable drift at his centre, a draw toward something—a place, a life, he cannot name. His mum had that whimsy, but she also had true direction, like there was a compass inside of her that always led straight to him and Owen. When he thinks of Mum now, he smiles—a giddy joy bubbling up. And strangely, with that lightness also comes a wringing-out of his insides, a swirling and furious sorrow.

THE DAY THE SPIDER CORPSE is found happens to be Friday. Pay day. Blain is paid by Hugh McFarland every two weeks in cash. Hugh drives the Model T into Owen Sound every other Friday, wearing his good coat and his low boots, dressed that way because he's going to the bank. It doesn't take him long and when he comes back, he walks straight to the barn, the money in a brown envelope that he has tucked securely into his coat. Clem and Blain meet him by the door and when Hugh hands each of them their wages, he seems pleased to do it. "Thanks, boys," he says.

When Clem takes his pay, he usually makes a joke about the money being like a hot potato that he has to hand off to Annie lest he get burned.

Blain grins, taking his. "Sure enough thanks, Mr. McFarland." He folds the bills in half and thrusts them into his pocket where they riotously unfurl. (He wishes he had a silver money clip for them, like Hugh McFarland's.)

"Spend it smart, boy," Hugh barks but they all know that Blain's pay goes straight to Jack Carter.

When Blain gets home, it is late afternoon, the old man waiting for him outside of the house, the truck already loaded and set for the trip up to the Queens. Blain puts the money directly into Carter's hands and Carter churlishly turns his back and counts it. "McFarland ought to give you more since you're working at the brother's place now, too." Since Jamie left, Blain goes over to Ena's place for part of each day, helps her with the chores, keeps her company. He sees her burrowing down into solitude, clinging fast to work. He worries sometimes that she might go too far.

The old man grunts and shoves the money down the front of his pants, saunters over to his truck, starts it, and clamours down the rutted lane.

When he's out of sight, Blain stands thoughtfully, shrewdly beside the shed; he's seen the old man collect payment a hundred times over. He knows the old man's habits (Blain's eyes are keen in the darkness, something he supposes, that comes from growing up in the bush and watching the old man's nocturnal comings and goings). Carter's approach to the gathering of men who stand in the lane, their wagons and trucks newly loaded, is always the same. He struts—the old rooster—his hand out, his thin neck craned over their wallets and money clips—he's a laughable enough figure from afar, but not so laughable up close. After they drive off, Carter heads straight to the shed.

Blain knows that the old man will drink himself into oblivion at the Queens tonight. He puts his hand on the shed's rusted doorknob and slips inside. With the sun down the shed is even colder inside than it is out. Blain and Owen are forbidden by Carter to be in here, but Carter never knows when Blain has crept around the place, it being in complete disarray with empty jars, tools, upturned boxes of nails, saws too rusted for use, half-finished tins of oil, sharpening stones, an enormous broken winch for hauling logs that for years has waited for repair.

Blain stamps his feet and shrugs his shoulders up to his ears and takes a couple of steps toward the littered work bench.

The window above the bench is grimy and veiled with ragged and abandoned spider webs—broken whorls of grey—but there is no sign of the spider and he thinks of Owen.

He glances outside, making sure the old man hasn't come back, but he sees only the glum and naked trees, the house, the spindly cedars that conceal the creek and still.

Blain thinks of the tidy drive shed at the McFarland farm, Hugh and Clem both sticklers—sterilizing pails, cleaning the muck from shovels before they are hung, polishing barn lamps. Blain hadn't known much about looking after equipment until he went to work at the farm. Hugh had shaken his head when he first watched Blain work and he commented darkly to Clem, "Looks like that boy's been raised by a pack of wild dogs." Clem had assured him he'd show Blain what was what, but Blain still makes a mess of things at times, the old man showing himself in him like blood that rises to a blister. "Boy's got a temper," Hugh complained to Clem. "Good natured enough 'til he gets frustrated. And he'd forget his head if it weren't screwed on."

Blain drops to his knees and pulls up the filthy oilcloth that the old man has thrown over the bench and finds the boot box. Carter has put a heavy padlock on the box and he keeps the key on a chain around his neck. The box's sides and top are a faded marine blue and the metal boot-hold is black with old polish, probably from the time of Blain's grandfather who was a sailor in Owen Sound. A man who travelled.

He slides his hands over the roughened sides of the box and imagines the ports on the shores of Lake Michigan and Lake Superior. From those places, a man could go overland and get to the other side of the continent.

The padlock hangs sullenly from the latch and there is no sound in the shed except for the rush of blood in his ears. His mouth tastes of metal, as if he has taken a bite from the lock, as if it is inside of him, rusting and flaking, no impediment at all.

EACH MORNING, AFTER GOING EARLY to the barn to tend to the animals, Ena washes, eats a small breakfast and then begins her baking. It is six weeks since Jamie's left, and now she has no home leave to look forward to. His absence is as close as her shadow, and she often thinks she hears him, whistling to Billie, latching the door to the barn, treading softly up the stairs to her at night. The idea of Jamie—the slight angling of his long back, the descending V of his torso, his ambling walk—has become her silent companion.

In the first days, Billie paced the barnyard, pausing only to sniff at the barn door, one ear cocked as if to listen for the sound of Jamie's voice, her eyes scanning the fields. But she attaches herself to Ena now, waiting patiently for her in the woodshed each morning, trotting behind her to the barn.

In the late afternoon, Blain walks up the long laneway, his boots scuffing the December snow, his head bent into the wind. A foundry worker gives him a lift part-way, otherwise it would take him close to an hour to walk. She wonders why he doesn't wear gloves.

"Have you eaten?" she asks him the first time.

"I ate," he says, grinning. "But I'll eat some more." While he devours a plate of her biscuits and blackberry jam, he talks to her about working at the McFarland's, what he is learning from Clem. He is cheerful, overflowing with talk, but she sees agitation in the way his shoulders jump in his lean frame, and while he chatters, he casts long looks at the road behind him. He works hard enough although he forgets to tidy after himself some days. Ena has to remind him, pointing out a forgotten pail or an abandoned cart. She worries that her tone is too severe, but he nods agreeably. An ease has grown up between them and she's glad of his company, always feeling lighter for it after he has gone.

HER EVENINGS, AFTER BLAIN LEAVES, stretch painfully and to fill the empty hours, and for extra income, she takes orders for baking. Most of the work comes from the Presbyterian, Anglican, and Methodist churches in Owen Sound, whose auxiliaries are taken up with the first waves of returning veterans.

Brusque and forthright, Flora Stewart of the Imperial Order Daughters of the Empire had arranged for Ena to provide her baking services for a fee. "When they get back, some of them can't run a saw in the mill or work a lathe in the boatyard. There are farm boys who can't lift a bag of potatoes. I've known men who can't see their own shadows without being frightened. Those are the difficult cases, the ones who are able-bodied but won't come out from under the covers. Sometimes, they'll drink themselves half to death, wander away from their families." She sniffed in distaste. "They suffer a kind of weakness that the bootleggers in Grey County prey on." (Flora is tireless in her efforts to eradicate bootleggers and liquor from Owen Sound. Hugh jokes that she should join the 147th and ship overseas—that the mere sight of her leading the troops would send the Germans calling for their mothers.)

Flora had speared Ena with a hard admiring look. "You've done your part, letting your man go over and serve. I'm sure you can use the extra income now."

"Yes," said Ena simply. "I can."

The income from the IODE leaves a bitter taste; it isn't lost on Ena that the organization is part of the war effort, perpetuating enlistment, drumming up patriotic sentiments, shaming those who turn their backs on service. But it is money she earns, money she will use to carry the farm without having to ask for extra from Hugh.

Besides, the work itself is relieving. The drawing up of lists and the careful selection of ingredients absorbs her—molasses and honey, mace, cream-of-tartar, flour and yeast and berries. Nuts and raisins, cinnamon, allspice, and nutmeg. The cream and butter she can take from her own farm (Ena never tires of that particular pleasure). The eggs she continues to get from Sarah. What she loves best is the baking itself, the hold it has on her, the way in which each small task—the whisking of egg whites, the turning of dough—is essential.

She has a growing sympathy for the people for whom she bakes, her feelings pushing beyond her usual restraint. When she can, she makes the deliveries herself. The state of the farms she visits is a shock. Standing on forlorn laneways, she takes in shabby gardens, filthy yards. What she sees is a surrender to hopelessness. Slipping a box through a half-opened door, she glimpses a black dress and veil, a long string of mourning beads. An exhausted face looks back, and more often than not, it holds resignation. The woman might whisper *God Bless,* as though Ena is part of a divine plan for comfort, for charity. Ena nods, steps back from the closing door, and although in her quiet reserve she might appear to be pious, there is no trace of the believer in her.

THEY HADN'T REGULARLY ATTENDED church when Ena was a child. "We're not Catholics," Michael said. "We don't have to be popping in and out of a church every day of the week. We don't need clergy poking long noses in our business." Ellen had apparently agreed. Even so, growing up in Owen Sound, Ena was subjected to bible stories at school; there had been an earnest and relentless prodding to trust in God's goodness, His care—the Shepherd who keeps an unwavering eye on His sheep. She had no sense of Him, no feeling of His presence.

When Michael died, she hadn't felt the protective arms of God around her, only a certain prod toward self-reliance.

Ena thinks back to that last morning with Michael, a sly brightness that promised more warmth than the day delivered. April, but there was still ice in the bay.

"To help the poultices work best, Darling, you must open the window. Open it wide."

When she slid up the sash, the rush of cold took her breath away. She wanted to close it. The room was growing too chill, the wind sweeping away the comforting funk. Michael had been feverish for days and Ellen was forever piling more blankets on top of him.

Ena resolved that she would close the window and lock out the sharp wind. She had to stand on her toes to reach the top of the sash, but she would manage.

"Don't close it, Ena. I'm feeling much better today with the poultices. Let them do their work, with the air coming in. I can promise you I'll be on my feet by tomorrow."

She took a step back from the window and looked at him. His words were breezy and light, his tone almost playful. Trusting him, she'd done as he asked.

Seeing her standing frozen at the end of his bed, he'd opened his arms to her and she went to him, drawing up the quilt. His face was hollow and dark with shadows, his stubble peppered with grey. She put her two hands on his cheeks.

For Ena, it was the cold wind that came in from the open window that took him, bearing him on eddies of air, sweeping him over the still frigid water of the bay, ushering him through blushing woods, over black and thawing fields and forever out of the world.

SARAH, WHO STILL RELIES ON ENA for her baking, puts in a regular order for Ena's brown bread and buttermilk biscuits. Ena harnesses Ted to the wagon and loads Sarah's order along with two other deliveries she will make along the way. It's a grey, flat day, a January thaw and warm enough for the snow to be slushy, the wheels of the cart often plunging into small craters of mud.

When she arrives at the McFarland farm, Sarah is behind the house, bundled up in a marten coat, tall thick-leathered boots on her feet—men's work boots which are too small to be Hugh's—a fur hat pulled low on her forehead. She sits on a red-painted chair, her back to the laneway, her eyes on the barn and fields. It isn't until Ena comes quite close that she sees the easel.

Turning, Sarah's face leaps into a smile. "Oh good! It's you."

Standing now, Sarah stretches out her arms and then swings them back and forth. "I get cramps sometimes, sitting so long," she explains. She studies the painting from under her hat, pressing her shoulder into Ena's, Ena anticipating rather than feeling the warmth radiating through the layers of fur and serge between them.

Ena peers at the canvas. "I'm not sure what it is." She puts her hands behind her back as if the gesture will prompt understanding. The painting is made of tiny points of paint, all converging to give the impression of mass and weight and texture. There is strength in it, even fearlessness.

"When did you learn that?"

"When I was still in school. It wasn't a new technique, even then. It's cubes now, and other geometric shapes that artists are playing with. I read about it in the art journals when I can get them. But everything comes very late here." Ena thinks of the bundles of art journals sitting next to the wood stove in the McFarland kitchen, some of them printed in French. Hugh seems to take pleasure using them to stoke the fire, his eyes squinting into the flames.

Taking a few steps away from the easel, Sarah leaves a slushy trail, the melting snow making her footprints appear oversized, like a giant's. She puts her hands on her hips and looks across the fields that appear subdued and patient in the weak light. Sarah has painted them in colour, the landscape holding its breath, its heart beating wildly, heat rising in the midst of cold.

"Craig Murray showed us this technique—mostly landscapes, lots of them done with slashes of paint so you had to stand back to really see—"

"Slashes..." says Ena, taken aback, trying to work it out.

Sarah laughs and turns to the easel and to Ena. "He said painting was changing. Colours were different—not so drab as before, and painters were finding new ways to *show* things. Not just how they looked, like in a photograph, but what was underneath."

"Craig Murray taught you a lot then," Ena says, her eyes still on the painting.

Sarah doesn't answer at first. "By then, I was sketching whenever I could, and it worried my mother. I had to sneak away to draw, sometimes down to the park or behind the school. I showed Craig Murray my sketchbook. He said I was quite good. He thought I might go far." She is speaking loudly, as though there is an audience waiting to hear her, a hint of bitterness in her tone. "He taught four of us that spring, until June, when school was out. But he kept me on. All through that summer, I met with him. It was a secret. I had to tell my mother I was volunteering at the school, tutoring younger children," she smiled and sniffed with the cold. "My mother would have been shocked if she knew."

She turns, her eyes finding Ena. Her voice drops and warms. "I shouldn't be telling you all of this, Ena. It's boring and you must be freezing sitting there."

"Go on," says Ena. She wants to hear Sarah talk about Craig Murray. It helps her to understand the paintings, how she feels about them. "I'm used to the cold," she says. Since living at the farm, she finds she can stand all kinds of weather.

They are quiet together, Sarah back at the easel again, looking at the canvas from different angles, shaking her head. "At the time, I had a girl's crush on him. That isn't a surprise, I guess—he was older, he'd travelled, and he loved to paint." She daubs some diffuse blue onto the sky in the canvas, the strokes quick, assured. "He had free ideas about a lot of things. For a man who had spent so much of his time in Europe, he could cope in the rough country, taking long trips by himself, canoeing, living in tents, always painting. He wasn't like anyone else I knew."

A cutter and a team of horses emerge from the bush. They drag an enormous log and Sarah follows the motion with her eyes. "Do you miss Jamie, Ena? It must be very hard."

Ena thinks about the shadow spot at her centre where Jamie is, how it pains her sometimes, how she wraps Billie in her arms and closes her eyes and tries to bring Jamie close.

"I do," she says simply.

Sarah puts her brush in the can with the others and then blows on her fingers. "Lots of times I think I should give up."

Ena wonders if Sarah means the painting. She looks back at the canvas, so sweeping, consuming in its energy. "You can't just stop because it's easier."

Sarah shrugs and pulls the dense coat tighter around herself. "I don't know what I'm doing." She tips her face up and squeezes her eyes shut, something a child might do. Ena watches the colossal force of her, stopped like a clock that needs winding.

"What do you want?" Ena asks her plainly.

Sarah's eyebrows shoot up and Ena blinks back. It doesn't seem like such a strange question, and her mind goes to Ellen, now living alone in the narrow, dark house in Owen Sound, how when Ena visits her, Ellen seems cross that Ena has stayed so long away. *I'm here now,* is what Ena wants to say, but she doesn't. It's no use talking to Ellen. Her unhappiness is like a fortress. Now, Ena looks at Sarah who seems strangely blind to her horizons, caught like Ellen in her way.

"You said you wanted this life with Hugh." Ena squeezes her hands together to force the blood to flow. "And you said you wanted to paint."

Water is running down Sarah's cheeks, her nose streaming. She stamps her feet a couple of times as if to signal a change. "Not as simple as it seems, to be a painter, an artist, a *woman,* living here."

Ena's mind tries to untangle what Sarah is saying. "It is what you *are* doing now. A woman, *painting*—"

"There is more to it."

Ena is nonplussed. "*What* more? We have what we have."

Sarah smiles suddenly and shakes out her hands, the way a dog will shake itself after rain.

"I'm beginning to freeze out here," Sarah says. "I think I need some tea."

~

February brings the heavy snow, the drifts bullying the barn and creeping over the lane. Some days, Blain and Ted plough a track first thing in the morning and then have to do it again before nightfall.

The cows will be calving soon. When Hugh had dropped Blain in Ena's laneway, he'd sternly instructed the boy to stay for the night should he be needed.

"Staying to calf overnight isn't what you're hired for," she'd said as they walked to the barn. "I'll pay you for your time, Blain. On top of what Hugh gives you."

Blain grinned and then tossed his hat in the air. He swung his arm behind his back, his fingers stretching to catch the hat but missing it. More and more, he looked like a scarecrow, his wrists bony, his coat too short. In the cold, the tips of his uncovered ears flamed red.

"Mr. McFarland already took care of that." He picked up the hat, slapping it over his thighs. "Don't mind staying, long as I get home early enough that I can get my brother off to school. He likes school, not like me. He *asks* to go." Blain shook his head in disbelief. "Clem will swing me back home after milking."

She pinned her eyes on him. "You can use it Blain, I'm sure. For something. You'll know what for." She walked purposively to the house, found the tin where she kept her cash and took out two dollars. He didn't refuse it when she gave it to him. He stared at it, there in his palm, a shadowy look passing quickly over his features, and then he pocketed it.

THEY SIT TOGETHER IN A STALL, Ena on a low stool, a green plaid blanket across her legs, Blain squatting, his back rounded against the rough barn boards. A cow is labouring with two calves. Blain will keep the tension on the birthing chains while Ena has her hands deep inside the cow, guiding and easing each calf as it births.

They eat thick slices of bread and butter, gulp cocoa from mugs, while Blain chatters, his stories meandering, sometimes crashing one into the other: there is a bear, he says, wiping his mouth on his sleeve, living in the McFarland bush. Clem says there haven't been bears for years. But Blain's seen signs of one. When he walks home along the side road, there are long ragged scratches in the trunks of trees, and twice he's heard growling.

"A dog," says Ena flatly. He ignores what she says and tells her about a man stabbed in a bar fight up in Wiarton. "The man who did it took off, likely got away in a car, then a train somewhere. Who knows where." He has a lit-up sort of look that makes Ena smile.

"He'll get caught," she says. "They'll be after him."

Excitement blazes in Blain's eyes. "Maybe not. Maybe he'll just disappear."

The hours wear on and the cow seems calm enough. Ena smooths the blanket over the straw beside her. "Sleep, if you want," she says to Blain. "I'll wake you."

He laughs and shakes his head no.

He begins to tell her about a man from the west who taught his horse to do tricks. "Horse could count," he says, "same as you or me." Although Ena likes his voice, the brightness in it, she is only half-listening. Her mind drifts to the other sounds. The barn is a restless place, the cows shifting their heavy bodies, trying to find ease in their stalls, and Billie alert, rising with each new grunt or moan.

THE YEAR BEFORE, JAMIE HAD LED the calving, teaching her as they worked. She thought of him positioning a wide set of hips, his hand steady and reassuring on the cow's broad flank. Just yesterday, she had received a letter from him, the first from the front, and holding it, reading it, she had become very still. The letter bore the usual YMCA and Canadian War Contingent Association mark in the top left-hand corner.

January 17, 1917

Dear Ena,

Just writing to let you know we have come from England to France now. We are near a place called (There is a square cut out here where he named the place). Yesterday, I got the box you sent. The fruitcake is so good, Ena. I divided it with Mathew Rolly and Pat Marshall who both said it was the best they ever had. The cap you sent is very warm and I sleep in it at night. If you could send tea, that would be good. The common kind, black Tabloid if you have it. We are on a rest now from the line and it is a chance for a bath. We didn't have a bath or shave for the whole time we were up the line! We are back from the fighting, but can still hear the roar of the artillery. I see Bruce Cammeron every day (from Chatsworth way. We were at school together) and he seems very cheerful. He says his mother is ill this winter. I am sorry for that. I hope the bull isn't giving you any trouble. If he is, you should get Hugh to come. I think the animal might be too much for Blain. It is raining something awful now and the mud is no good when we are at the line. We walk on boardwalks across it so we don't sink or drown. My boots and puttees are covered in mud. My feet give me some trouble but I am not the only one. Yesterday, some of our men trapped rats and set them on fire. It was horrible. The squealing and the smell. Farm life did not prepare me for what happens here.

I think about the farm, and about you every day. I am quite well here so you don't have to worry.

Your loving husband, Jamie.

His first letter, the one before this, had come from England, a place called Storeham-by-the Sea, sections about his voyage from Halifax cut from the page. The excision of his words had sent her into a silent fury. How dare they *hide* him from her; she wants to think of him precisely where he *is*—to see the place, to know it. Now, she has grown used to the blank spots and she thinks instead of how he misses the farm. For Jamie, the farm is like an appendage—one of his arms or a foot.

She thinks of the day he had driven them to the back of Ross's land, to the far end of the bush. Winter time and some months before they married. "I came here all the time when

I was a boy. Ross never minded." They left Ted at the road and followed the line of the old stone fence, up and around a rocky spring and then west toward an outer boundary of hawthorn and scrub, the taller, cleaner outlines of maple and beech a fortress behind. At first she had to push hard to keep up to him, but when he saw her effort he slowed his pace. He wasn't used to walking there with anyone else but Billie. Now Billie was just ahead, weaving through a solemn line of spruce, her tracks making figure eights in the snow.

The slanted sunlight that dropped onto the forest floor was criss-crossed with dense shadows. The land was hollowed in places, and elsewhere broken with rock. Fallen trees lay across their path, Ena hopping over them and feeling an unusual impulse toward gaiety in her feet, almost a skip.

"You're part goat," Jamie said, looking back at her, grinning.

Billie had bounded off over a crest and left them. Everywhere was the upward thrust of leafless trees. Light and shadow, no colour except the shock of blue above them. Jamie stopped ahead of her, a concentrated certainty in the length of him, in the dark wool of his coat. Suddenly, he cocked his head to one side, his gaze riveted. He was listening to something, a sharp eruption of cries, alarming, urgent.

Jamie put his hands in his pockets and planted his feet. "Billie's frightened a fox. She's likely sniffing around a den." He knew the language of the place. His face was bright, his cheeks scarlet from the brisk air. From below his cap, his blue eyes peered out at her, translucent and bottomless.

"There's deer too, and a lot of birds," he went on, "all sorts of animals. I'll show you."

Above them was nothing but clean sky. "This is the best place," he'd said, laughing. "Even better now because we're here together."

SHE HAS BEEN LOST IN HER THOUGHTS about Jamie, about the afternoon they spent together in Ross's bush, the first time she had allowed herself to really love him. Blain has grown quiet although she hasn't noticed until now. Looking over at him, she sees that he is curled on the blanket, his back to her, his hands in fists at his chin. A hint of the child he must have been. He would have made Margaret happy, this boy, pouring out his stories. Hugh has put a telephone in at their farm and Ena imagines Blain speaking into it, his voice travelling down a line, his words delivered directly into Margaret's ear. That's what he might have been for her—a conduit and she thinks perhaps that is what he has become for her in her solitude.

His shirt has ridden up and her eyes travel to a square of exposed white skin, goose fleshed and stretched between his lower rib and his hip. He *is* thin. She isn't mistaken about the neglect she's seen. She thinks about Douglas McLaren, Dr. McLaren's son, how broad he was in the shoulders, how his shirt strained across his back. Had Douglas been the same age that Blain is now? She is looking at Blain, thinking she's glad that Hugh has sent him. Not grateful exactly, because Ena feels a wariness about Hugh's generosity. She worries that Hugh will become too much a part of this place and this farm. That Jamie won't matter in the running of it.

Her eyes still rest on Blain's trunk when he shifts and sighs and a new patch of skin comes into view—a peninsula of red which runs toward Blain's ribs, one part of it encrusted with blood. He is breathing deeply, evenly. She rolls off her blanket and covers him with it but he doesn't move. They have been up for hours. It must be almost three in the morning. She thinks about the welt on his back, uneasy questions forming in her mind. Blain can be clumsy, distracted. He might have fallen on the ice. Her mind turns to a more plausible explanation and she immediately knows it to be true. What she sees on him are undeniable marks of violence.

A sickness rises in her, thoughts that are red and tearing. She wills recognition away. She lets herself rest for a few moments, closing her eyes. She tries to entreat Jamie to appear, and for the briefest time, she feels him converge with the small movements, the inhalations and exhalations of Blain and the creatures around her. She can't hold on to him. She opens her eyes, startled. He could be dead, she thinks, and would she know? How long would it take for word to reach her?

She straightens herself, gets to her feet as lightly as a child, and then takes her attention to the heifers, particularly those whose time is close, scouring her mind, as she does every night, for everything that Jamie taught her about birthing calves. She remembers the signs of readiness—the pacing, the fretting and snorting, the frequent ups and downs, and then finally the characteristic water sac hanging from her rear end like a giant balloon. "Look for both front feet to appear," he said. "If the base of the feet point to the ground, an easy birth is likely not a problem, but there will always be cows who struggle." Jamie seldom needed restraints, he was so deft with the animal, but he had showed Ena how to use a head gate to hold the heifer steady while the calf was pulled.

The cow with the multiple calves is very close. Ena is careful to wash her hands and arms. She knows how to probe the heifer, to determine the position of the first calf. She remembers how Jamie had guided her hands with his and showed her how to reposition a head, a foreleg.

She imagines Blain dead to the world in the stall. For a little while longer she will let him sleep.

15. MAY 1917

HUGH ARRIVES WITH CLEM and his team of horses for ploughing.

"We can use Ted," she says, turning toward the barn. "I can lead him."

"Nope." There is a hint of a chuckle in his voice. "Don't take it hard but we're faster on our own."

Ena watches their progress from the fence, taking pleasure in the sight of the horses, their heads swaying in tandem, their great hooves gouging the field. Clem steers the plough and Hugh drives the team, Blain walking behind to clear the clots of earth from the plough's blades. Against a spare April horizon, the horses and men appear newly hatched from the heaving ground, every bit a match for it.

The ploughing takes four full days and on the last afternoon, when the work is done, Hugh comes into the woodshed and kicks off his boots. He strides into her kitchen, ruddy-faced, glowing, and Ena sets out butter, a plate of warmed cream biscuits, and a bowl of rhubarb conserve. While she pours out strong black tea, he talks about his neighbours, the war, how hard it is to find good help. She is quiet with him, keenly aware of his presence, which is too large for this house.

"If I had a nickel for every word you *don't* speak Ena, I'd be rich. You could make a job out of it—travel around with a troupe, charge people to try and get a rise out of you."

She laughs. "I say enough." It's a puzzle to Ena what people want from her, as though they are stumbling through fog, trying to locate themselves, straining to hear an answering call. She has never sought reassurance in words, except as a child, when her father's voice would hold her spellbound.

Hugh surveys her kitchen, taking in the organized clutter of pie shells, mixing bowls, two racks of cooling bread loaves. Canning jars boil in the large kettle on the stove. "It's kind'a ridiculous, you doing all this baking." Leaning back in his chair, he regards her, crumbs from the last biscuit still on the edges of his lips. His eye swims to the left and then travels, wavering more because he's tired, although there is no other discernible sign of wear in him. "The farm's gonna be enough, as long as we can keep the yields up. You won't need extra income." He doesn't wait for her to speak. "Ross wasn't much of a farmer—he never did raise this place above a hand-to-mouth operation." Sipping his tea he closes his eyes contentedly. "Dad was the better farmer. That's where I learned."

Hugh doesn't mention Jamie. He talks about himself, offering himself up as a distraction from Jamie's absence. It hurts her, this deliberate exclusion, as if Jamie isn't coming back.

"You can read Jamie's last letter to me if you want," she says now, her eyes steady on him.

Hugh vigorously rubs the back of his neck and slides down a little in his chair, his legs outstretched. "I read quite a bit in the paper about things over there."

For Ena, there is little of Jamie in the newspapers. Nothing of what he eats for breakfast, how he sleeps with the hammering of the guns and the shelling, how he keeps himself clean.

"You'll want to know how he is," she says. "What he has to cope with. Of course, he doesn't write about everything."

Hugh plays with his spoon and squints in the direction of the barn.

"He says you don't write to him, Hugh. I'm to tell you to send him a letter."

"I'm not much for writin'."

"You can read his letter, then."

"All right."

She hands the letter to him. "He doesn't name where he is. They aren't supposed to. But a few weeks back the papers said Vimy Ridge."

April 16, 1917

Dear Ena,

I am on a rest and haven't been able to write before now because I was up the line. It is hard to write in the trenches but some men can do it.

Maybe there is still snow in the fields? Hugh will get to ploughing as soon as he can. On Easter Monday it snowed here. That was the first day of the big battle. Think of a thunderstorm Ena, the loudest you have ever heard and that still isn't what the guns sounded like when they started that day. I ended up with a piece of shrapnel in my arm and had to go to the Casualty Station but things could have been much worse. The wound was not so deep and I was patched up in no time. The Casualty Station is very good to us. Fritz uses gas now and that has been very bad. I hope my lungs will be okay when I come home. Mathew Rolly was sent back to England with welts on his face and neck from the gas, terrible as kerosene burns.

I got your box, Ena. I can use as many socks as you can knit. Aunt Rose has sent a box of knit things too and I gave some of those away. The cakes and tea are good. Some lads don't have anyone sending them parcels. We get one loaf of bread to three men now. The bread isn't good like yours and it isn't filling. I think of your rhubarb pies because soon you will be making them fresh.

Soon you will be at your garden and things will

be coming up green all over. Did Hugh get his binding machine fixed over the winter?

I know Hugh is helping so I won't ask. I hope Blain is helping enough. He needs to keep the stalls very clean in spring, with all the wet and muck. The cows shouldn't get hoof rot. That would be bad for you!

I think of home and you every minute but I am quite well and fine.

Your loving husband, Jamie

Hugh reads carefully, the wavering eye working to keep up, his face absorbed and clouded. When he's finished, he reads the letter again. It's a long while before he speaks.

"Jamie's too soft for all this." Defiance creeps over his features. "Probably should be me over there, but I *had* to stay back to look after things. That's how it is on farms. Course, if conscription comes in, maybe I'll go anyway. Clem will stay back—he's too old. He'll look after all this."

The room feels too close. Ena moves and opens the mudroom door a crack and cooler air wafts in. She plants her gaze on him, his moving eye struggling to stay pinned to her before finally breaking away.

16. SUMMER 1917

S TANDING ON ELLEN'S FRONT PORCH, Ena glances needless-
ly at Ted to reassure herself he hasn't bolted. The house,
which is a tall and narrow duplex, has never been a home, at
least not since Michael lived there. Although the small rooms
are tidy, exhaustion has settled over the worn armchairs, the
peeling wallpaper, the swollen window frames. As Ena is poised
to knock, there is the usual silent turmoil—the urge to turn
away. Ellen opens the door, her face sharpened, her eyes bright.
"Well," she says, "you've found you're way here. What has
it been—a month? Six weeks? You have your hands full over
there, I know. Anyway, glad to see you."

The air is thick and heavy with summer heat. After she drags
two wooden kitchen chairs onto the back stoop, Ellen hands
Ena a cup of tea, tepid and milky and bitter. (Ellen always serves
tea, regardless of the weather.) She cuts them each a slice of
soda bread and drops a dollop of raspberry jam on their plates.

With the back of her chair pressed to the brick, Ellen takes
her palm to her neck, her eyes drilling into the hazy afternoon
light. "There must be rain in it," she says. "There has to be
some relief."

"No sign of that," says Ena. "It's fine out."

Ellen's features, in profile, are delicate, precise, as if cut out
with scissors. She seems to have shrunk, a boniness in her
shoulders, a softening at her centre. She won't be able to work
indefinitely at the Maclaren's. She has already suggested that

Ena might like to take over the work. "You know they lost Douglas over there, just a few weeks back in that big fight. The McLarens have changed since," she says. "Mary, the daughter is still there. A serious girl. She takes care of her mother."

Mary, Ena thinks, has managed to secure her mother's attention only after Douglas is gone. "The McLarens didn't like me, and I didn't like them much."

Turning her gaze on Ena, Ellen's eyes are an unlikely china blue, like those of a doll. "What do you mean? Mrs. McLaren raves about your baking still. You could take over some of my hours at the house. Let the McFarland's look after their farm—it isn't smart to think you can manage it on your own. Come live here, with me, until Jamie comes back. You can help out a little with the rent."

Ena's face settles reflexively into a mask. "I have help. And I don't want to leave the farm."

"Wanting has nothing to do with it."

RELIEVED TO BE OUT FROM UNDERNEATH the shadows in Ellen's house, Ena drives Ted toward St. Andrew's Church, the wagon filled with crates of peach pies and brown loaves, buttermilk tea biscuits, jars of strawberry and blackberry jams. A warm push of air comes off of the bay, batting her collar, moving a loose strand of hair at the nape of her neck. She takes a breath and can smell the horse, the peaches in the pies, grass that has been newly cut.

She drives past the harbour and catches a glimpse of striking blue between the stacks of the foundry. Owen Sound sits on the crossroads of rivers, on the shores of Georgian Bay. A town in the crook of a valley with an expanse of fresh water at its feet, and at its back, a spiny escarpment. Growing up here, she spent little time by the water, and now, since living at the farm, it is the sullen streams and rivers, the tumbledown stone fences that hold her. She is suddenly quite sure that she has no wish to live in the town again.

She turns the corner, past the squat, stone Presbyterian church. Salvation Corner where four churches face one another. Across the street, Sarah is stepping from a car Ena hasn't seen before. Her shoes are mucky, her long skirt mud-spattered. She wears an emerald-green scarf, too warm for the weather, which she has wrapped twice around her throat. The wind is gusting and Sarah seems distracted by it, her head turning right and left, her gloved hands busy with securing her hat, smoothing her skirt.

Ena brings Ted to a stop, sensing that she is seeing something she shouldn't, some part of Sarah's life that Sarah hasn't yet shared. Sarah doesn't see Ena; her eyes are on the stocky man who strides toward her, his coat open, his face set in a wide and unrestrained grin. He carries a large leather satchel and he wears no hat or gloves. Just as he reaches Sarah, a gust picks up and the two bodies are pushed closer, Sarah's hand on his shoulder for balance. After a long moment, Sarah stumbles back, laughing, taking the satchel from his arms and sliding it into the car.

Driving back to the farm, the air, which had been blustery a short time before, is now eerily still. The sun is swallowed by a building cloud. Ted doesn't trot, preferring to plod under the flattening heat. Ena thinks of Ellen complaining about the oppressive air, prophesizing incoming rain. She had been right about the day, and as Ena turns up the lane, sullen drops begin to fall.

The yellow brick of the house looks grey in the dull light. Blain is on her front step, Billie next to him, her nose planted on his lap. Standing now, Ena welcomes the cooling touch of rain on her neck. The seat of the buggy is loaded with the food and supplies from the market and she gathers what she can in her hands. She expects that he will amble over to her, take hold of the bags, but he is raggedy-looking and limp, his hand heavy on the dog.

"Blain?"

When he does meet her eye, she feels an instant jolt. His face is a mass of bruises. One of his eyes is a purple mound; his cheek is split and gaping, his lower lip bulging. Most shocking is the missing patch of hair, his exposed scalp a red mash.

Suddenly, the rain is torrential, dousing the dusty lane and instantly forming puddles. Ena abandons the bags on the porch and crouches next to Blain, something in the way he sits, the tilt of his torso, his shallow breathing, making her wonder if he's hurt in places she can't see. A fork of lightning strikes the field nearby and brings Billie off the step, her nose insistently butting the back of Ena's thigh. Ted must be taken into the barn and out of his harness.

"Can you move?" she asks Blain, her hand on his arm. He nods and then dully turns away, levering himself up to a stand. Limping, his arm held protectively around his belly, he makes his way into the house with Ena following. "Lie down, there," she says, pointing firmly at the chesterfield.

When she returns to the sodden yard, her mind is on the mess that is Blain's scalp. A slight queasiness vanishes almost before it is felt, and what is left is a vibration, distant and rumbling—a disturbance, both angry and appalled. The horse is quiet, his head down despite the storm. With the buggy still attached, she pulls him into the barn, unhitches him and lifts the harness from his back.

There is fresh toweling and disinfectant soap in the wood-shed. Bringing it to the kitchen, she takes the kettle and pours lukewarm water into a basin, soaks the toweling, and drops in the soap. The water becomes milky, the towel softening. She washes her own hands at the sink and then slushes the towel with her fingers.

Blain is staring at her as she comes into the parlour, his eyes vague, the pupils huge. Slipping onto the edge of the chesterfield, she takes his chin firmly between her fingers and studies his broken face. "*Who* did this?" The fiery feeling has completely taken hold. She shouldn't be angry with Blain, but she is. She bites her lip before speaking—teeth hard against her lip.

"Blain. *Who?*"

He looks away from her and shifts painfully onto his back. "It's not that bad. I just needed someplace to go, is all."

"Where were you before?" She is swooshing the cloth in the warm water, wringing it out. Now she carefully begins to wipe away the blood from his face that later will bruise terribly, she sees, the tissue mottled and swollen.

"Home."

She pauses and takes a breath in, measuring what to say next. "So this was done to you at home—"

He has her by the wrist, her hand stranded above him. "Sometimes the old man gets things in his mind. Like I hold money back. Or I'm not really workin' and I just say I am."

She gently unclasps his fingers and curls them into her palm. "Let me do this now," she says.

He's silent, his eyes closed, and she thinks that the only time Blain is quiet with her is when he is asleep. But he isn't sleeping now. He's keeping her out, closing a door. When she puts down the cloth and looks at him, it is frank outrage that she feels. An anger that is unlike any feeling she has ever known.

"You won't go home today, Blain. Not like this." Her voice is stern, like a school teacher's voice.

He opens his eyes. "Well, I'll have to go sooner or later. For Owen."

"Fine," she says. "But not now. Let's see if there's anything broken. And then we'll think about what to do."

17. MAY 1917

BLAIN LIES IN A BEDROOM next to Jamie's and Ena's room. There is a scuffed black steamer trunk at the foot of the bed, a pine writing table by the window and beside it, a wicker basket full of clothes for mending. Hanging on a hook on the back of the door is a blue knit sweater, slightly askew as if Jamie had just hung it there, one sleeve tucked up, the collar partly folded back on itself. He thinks of Ena seeing it there and choosing not to straighten it.

The jabbing pain in his ribs is manageable if he keeps his breaths shallow. He floats overtop of the day's events, and sees himself on the run, stumbling, falling, leaving Jack Carter and the glowering house behind. He followed the creek, angry branches clawing at his clothes, his breathing ragged, until he found the place where the creek sidled up sweetly next to the road. From there, he knew if he cut across the Timneys' field and then headed south on the county road, he would emerge at the back of Ena McFarland's farm. He could follow the old fence up through the ramshackle orchard, to the crest of bush, and then make his way down to the house.

When he got as far as the field, Billie made a beeline for him. She danced and jumped, but recognizing he was hurt, she didn't press herself. Blain touched her silky skull. Reassured by her softness, he made his way down to the barn.

SINCE JAMIE LEFT FOR THE WAR, Hugh McFarland gives him

extra money because of the help Blain gives to Ena. Hugh can be a hard man but he's fair and he's been generous.

After receiving his wages, standing alone at the bottom of the McFarland lane, Blain slides a bill between his sock and his ankle. (A creeping habit has taken hold in Blain—a craving to *take* from Carter and it goes a long way in dulling the hammering anger he feels. Periodic filching had been enough at first, but it isn't any longer. He wants to see his father on his knees, to howl with loss. To cry.)

Later, when he amiably surrenders the balance of his wages to Carter, Blain doesn't blink or look away. He jams his hand down deep in his pocket and fishes for the wad, absently smiling while he places the mess into his father's hand. Back in the dark house, he takes the small sum he has secreted away and slides it under his mattress. He tells himself there should be some money in the house for Owen in case something happens. He hasn't accumulated much; the skimming is hardly worth the risk.

On top of what Hugh pays, there is what Ena provides, kept safe in a tin on Ena's farm. A few dollars here and there (sometimes more), Ena solemnly slipping the bills into his hand with no explanation and nothing asked.

They don't speak about this arrangement—not ever. Hugh wouldn't take kindly to Ena interfering with matters concerning pay (Blain's wages, and Clem's, are strictly Hugh McFarland's business). What's more, Blain would be fired on the spot for taking her money.

Each time Blain leaves her, Ena loads his rucksack with raisin buns, biscuits, loaves of fresh bread, a brick of butter, a handful of eggs. It's what women do on farms. But the money she gives him is different. It means more than common generosity; in giving it, Ena permits a secret to grow. She goes that far for him—a bold gesture for someone who holds herself close, her edges wrapped tight.

What Ena doesn't know is that Blain has often stolen the

old man's moonshine from the shed, taken at night and right from under Jack Carter's nose. At first it was a jug or two, sold to men like old Mr. Savage, but now Blain is so brazen.

He had waited for the opportunity to approach Freddie DeWitt, a log man who occasionally transported loads of the old man's timber. For a fee, DeWitt agreed to barter a secret deal with Ben Fourtier, the owner of the Queens Hotel. For a discount that was frankly shameful, Fourtier would buy Jack Carter's stolen moonshine, his payment passed from DeWitt to Blain, less a good-sized cut for DeWitt.

Blain is stealthy and careful when he packs the jars, lining the crates with rags to stop the glass from clattering. Using the log-hauling sled, he drags the loaded crates through the cedar bush and leaves them covered beneath a blanket in a ditch by the road where DeWitt picks them up in the morning.

"That McFarland woman's on her own, eh?" DeWitt had just brought Blain his first payment from Fourtier, the bills jammed inside a smudged envelop. He was staying out of Carter's site, skulking moose-like in the brush behind the log splitter. A big-boned, rangy man, DeWitt's face was broad and flat, his small pale eyes deeply recessed. There was a cunning smirk about his mouth. Blain didn't like doing business with him.

DeWitt had leered, talking about Ena. "No man around the place except *you*, Blain. No one there with her at night."

Blain's insides churned and heat leapt into his face; he wished Ena had taken Hugh McFarland up on his offer, stayed at the home farm, let Hugh keep a watchful eye on her. Staunch and determined as she was, Ena could be hurt. Men like DeWitt and Jack Carter — selfish men—took what they wanted and trampled what got in their way. Ena's strength was the sort that could be crushed, ground like glass under the heel. He'd thought of his mum, her strength like a boisterous stream but stoppable.

"Oh, the McFarland's look well-enough after their own." The lie tripped out brightly, effortlessly: "McFarland has his hired hands staying with her, Ena getting their meals and doin' their washing. Not me of course." He'd grinned stupidly. "Got my *own* work to do right here."

There have been two hefty deliveries over the last two months; Blain added Fourtier's payments to the money Ena gave him, the money growing like a fat worm inside the tin kept high in the rafters of her barn. Because Carter drank many of his own jars, he was in a constant state of being stewed and didn't have a firm grasp on variances in his stock. A week after DeWitt's last shipment to the Queens, the old man started whining that someone was undercutting his business; "Fourtier's not takin' anywhere's near what he was from me, yet he seems well greased."

"Maybe someone else got himself a still and is selling to him," Blain said, scratching behind his ear. The old man stared at him and then jumped in his truck and tore through the county, looking for signs of new operations. If there were any, he didn't find them.

SWEAT SOAKED THROUGH BLAIN'S SHIRT and blood was caking and drying across his nose and eyes. Cloud had buried the sun and the air was awful and still, making it a chore to breathe. He dragged himself across the yard and then heaved open the barn door, but there was no sign of Ena, and Ted and the buggy were gone.

He'd felt a crashing hollowness at not finding her. And then hopelessness, and with it a terrible wish to cry. He'd settled himself on the step, determined that she would come up the lane and find him. He wouldn't leave until she did.

When Ena finally came, her back straight as a broomstick, the horse faithfully lumbering toward him, it was like his heart had been wrung out. He'd let out a small groan, like an animal might.

She'd been shocked at first, and for a small moment, her face showed horror before it closed over again. She hadn't wasted time getting him inside. The storm was on top of them and there was the horse to shelter. It wouldn't have been right to leave Ted out, bound up in his harness, the hard rain stony on his flanks. Blain thinks of Jamie, how his first thought was for the animals—for their care—and how Ena now does the same for them. He thinks quite suddenly that his own parents had never cared about the same things.

Ena had given him a good going over, an unsettling glint of anger in the deep brown of her eyes. After all, he was causing her to worry. Working beside her these last months he has seen her bear down on what was in front of her, her attention closely funnelled. Ena's way of taking care, of holding on.

Inspecting his head, her fingers tugging this way and that, Ena bit down on her lip, and he took her wrist and held on to it, a small flat rod, the bone dense as iron. Ena McFarland was hurting him but there was no other way. After she'd cleaned him up, she put the kettle on to boil.

She spooned some tea between his lips and then helped him upstairs to the spare cot in the room where he now listens to the rain as it hammers the roof. She has taken off his boots and covered him with a light cotton quilt because, despite the heat, he is shivering.

Blain closes his eyes, a throb in his head, blood rushing in his ears.

Jack Carter, his mind pitching and roiling with moonshine, must have gathered up his suspicions over the last weeks. This morning, while Blain slept, Carter had slipped into the room and with Blain still in the bed, he'd flipped the mattress over. The pilfered wages were there, paltry compared to what he'd made from the Queens, that moonshine money along with Ena's safely laid up in the rafters of Ena's barn. But what Carter found was enough to send him into a rage.

Blain found himself on the ground, his father's boots buried in his ribs, and then the pummeling of knuckles, the scrape of his head against the bedstead.

"Get your sorry arse out of here, Blain. Don't never come back."

After a few moments, everything was black. He heard the sounds of the old man's grunts, quiet like an animal's. He hadn't *felt* anything at all.

18.

THE TRUCK JOGS AND BOUNCES over a road that is still awash from yesterday's hard rain. Hugh has one wrist on the wheel and his elbow pokes out of the open window of the truck with Ena, uncomfortable, sitting next to him.

"Does Blain's father make any money or does his child do it for him, working on McFarland farms?" It's evening, the day after Blain showed up, torn and bloodied on Ena's doorstep.

Hugh squints, a smile pulling at the sides of his face. "To hear him tell it, Carter doesn't make much money. Small-time logging, a woodlot in behind their place. Mostly sells the lumber for firewood. Course, there's the still and he does just fine with *that*. More money in moonshine these days than second-rate lumber, but he wouldn't dare brag, not with the by-laws what they are."

"Why doesn't someone shut him down?"

Hugh chuckles and then looks over at her with an indulgent expression. "Plenty of people, some of them muckety-mucks like bankers and mill owners, count on getting their hands on his stuff. Convenient, being that Carter is so close, and there's a steady supply. As long as Jack Carter stays out of Owen Sound, the police won't bother with him."

Ena isn't from a family of teetotallers. Michael was known to pull a plain glass decanter from the cabinet in the parlour and pour out a finger or two of whisky. She'd even seen Ellen join him on occasion. And on Sundays, over lunch, they would sometimes split a bottle of beer, the foam breezily high in the glass, Michael inviting Ena to write her name in it with her little finger. But Owen Sound, a port town, had a history of sporting houses and liquor and loose women, and so the town had decided to launch an assault on all vice. After 1905, Michael's orders of whisky arrived nestled in between skeins of Irish wool, packed in crates sent from County Donegal.

She'd never seen anyone in Jamie's family drink a single drop although Sarah sometimes griped that the McFarland's were puritans. "I'd kill for a taste of brandy, or a glass of Claret," she'd say. Hugh would bellow out a laugh, his great arms around her waist, his chin burrowing into her hair. "You shouldn't have married a Scot. We're too pure for the English." Sarah would playfully throw off his arm, her face glowing, her eyes bright. "In my view, purity is overrated."

"Carter's too keen on his own stuff," Hugh is saying now. "Wonder there's anything left to sell to those sad sacks at the Queens Hotel or any place else for that matter."

Ena thinks of Blain and wonders about what part he has played in Jack Carter's operation, what else has happened to him besides the beating he took. A shadow passes over her, a darkening apprehension.

"Sad about Margaret Carter. When she started working at our place, Jamie was just a little kid. He had a soft spot for her, I remember—used to follow her around like a puppy." Hugh is smiling, his teeth a flash in the truck's light-dappled interior. He is remembering Jamie—a boy, a brother. Ena looks out of her window and sees restless land, rocky and dense with scrub. Greyish foliage reaches into them from the road. She feels uneasy, aware that she is travelling through countryside that is new to her, a place she has never been.

Suddenly serious, Hugh glances at her and then looks away. "Not sure this is the right thing to be doing, Ena. Not sure it's our business, going in and telling a man how to deal with his boy." Hugh shrugs. "And if Carter thinks the boy was stealing from him...."

She is frankly glaring at him now, Hugh avoiding her gaze, adjusting his window, first down and then up.

"I just mean to say that boys get up to things," he goes on vaguely. "Jamie and me got the switch more than once. We likely had it comin'. And *Blain*. Blain needs a firm hand. Boy's as bothersome as a deerfly."

"So the harm done to him was of the usual kind. It was earned." Her tone is deadened, the words muffled by the relentless motor. She presses her hands between her knees and feels a surprising surge of sadness come over her.

He turns his head and scowls into the dim and ragged bush. "I wouldn't say that."

They fall into silence, Hugh's fingers drumming the wheel. "It isn't far," he says, his tone lightening. "Just the next lane up. See there? Where a road goes off?"

Ahead, a dirt track angles away from the road and quickly disappears into a press of trees. Hugh slows and takes the turn. "How about you stay in the truck to start," he says. "I'll see if I can talk some sense into him. Put things right."

Ena nods but she is thinking of Blain, the pulpy scalp, the dulled expression on his face when she found him. Her knowledge of what Jack Carter did cannot be undone now. There won't be any putting things to right.

The house in front of them is a sunken wood frame structure that is pitifully peeling, the windows half-rotted in their frames. One side of the porch has completely collapsed. Trees close in on the house from all sides, and the grass has been left so long, they only see the tail of the large yellow dog which now bounds toward the lane, snapping, its muzzle wrinkled into a snarl.

"These people..." mutters Hugh, pulling a staff from the backseat and slowly pushing open the door. Ena watches as he raises his arms high and shouts at the dog, who cowers, growling, before retreating under the porch. She rolls down the window of the truck, intent on hearing.

"Mr. Carter?" Hugh's voice is strong but not threatening. "Like a word, if you don't mind. Won't take a minute." After a moment, Hugh lumbers up the tilted steps and glances left and right. From a half-hidden shack a few yards into the surrounding trees, a figure emerges, slight, his head a greying mass of black curls. He looks too small, too fragile to do the kind of damage she'd seen on Blain. He walks stiffly, as if his joints are hampered by rust. His eyes are set doggedly on Hugh.

"Well, there you are," says Hugh smiling and amiable. "Mind if I have a word? About your boy, Blain?"

Carter turns his face to the truck and eyes Ena. "What's he done now?" His tone is sad, almost gentle. He doesn't take Hugh's outstretched hand. "If he lied or stole, that ain't no problem of mine."

Hugh laughs. "No, no. He's pretty good. A good boy. Just needs a little training. You know, he'd forget his head if it weren't screwed on. Clem's been overseeing him. I just wondered about some trouble with his earnings. Seems he might'a come-up short the last time." Hugh reaches in his pocket and pulls out his clip. He peels off a bill and hands it to Carter. "Sure it must'a been a mistake—maybe mine." Hugh fixes his quaking gaze on Carter, his mouth still wearing a smile, but a tension now coming into his jaw. "This ought'a right things," he nods. "No need for more action. No need for you to *correct* the boy. How about I pay you direct from now on? That way, Blain can stay out of it. Sure you have use for the money."

Carter looks blankly at Hugh, his expression unreadable. "Think there should be extra pay, since he's lookin' after your brother's place too."

Hugh plants the staff firmly into the rotting floorboards, a frown forming, and he pulls himself up to his full height. "My brother's place and my place is the same thing."

Carter shakes his head morosely. "*I* ain't seen extra money."

"Like I said, this should cover it."

Just then, a voice comes from inside of the house, cutting and bleak, although Carter doesn't turn.

Blain?

With a small, neat hand, Carter slides the bills Hugh has given into the front of his pants and puts his back more definitely to the front door. Hugh doesn't look at the house but Ena knows that he hears the voice too.

Blain? That you?

She doesn't know why she feels the pull of it the way she does but she is out of the truck, her heels grinding into the stony lane.

"That ain't Mrs. McFarland," says Carter watching her, his gaze flat and heavy.

Shaking his head, Hugh shoos Ena with his hand. "That's my brother's wife, Mr. Carter. That's Ena. Ena McFarland."

Carter's dark eyes sink into Ena, eyes that are drawn down at the corners as if they are on a string, stagnant ponds, no evidence of life. Ena faces him, the child still calling from inside the house, the dog growling at the bottom of the stairs. Ena feels herself contract.

"You won't hurt Blain again. Or that boy inside." Her voice is quiet. She looks at the house and then back at Carter who stares sullenly. She has never been this forceful with anyone in her life before. She has never cared to.

"I look after them. I do what I can." His voice is hoarse, more of a whisper. "Lost my wife a couple of years ago—I'm on my own here."

The still air, the weight of it, has made Ena unbearably hot and she pushes at her buttoned sleeves. The exploitation of his loss revolts her. The Carter place hems her in—the swampy smells, the spindly trees, light that is half-choked—so different from the openness of the farm. She understands why Blain wants to be away.

Carter watches her like a spider. "Send Blain back," he drawls, "or I'll come get him."

The next moment, Hugh has Carter's arm, and then he spins him, pinning him to the side of the house, the staff clattering to the porch floor, both hands at the man's collar. He towers over Carter. "You won't go on our land without asking or being invited. You don't come near us—not Ena, not me and Sarah, not nobody. And you keep your hands off those boys. You understand me?"

Carter goes limp and looks blankly at Hugh. "Don't recall inviting *you* here, on my land."

It's a long while before Hugh speaks. "Next time won't be a social call, Mr. Carter." He lets go of him, snatches up the staff, and takes Ena by the elbow, half-dragging her to the truck. He steers her into the seat, and then jumps behind the wheel and starts the engine. With the engine roaring, he backs down the rutted lane. Carter stands on the porch, staring at them, his shoulders bent as though he's been hit.

Hugh curses under his breath. "That man's a menace. We got no business getting caught up with people like that. I want nothing more to do with him."

She looks out the windshield, woods and swamps on both sides of the road. Dead cedars poking up and pointing at the sky. A terrible question comes into her mind. It expands and presses on her until she has to ask. "What happened to Margaret Carter, Hugh? How'd she die?"

Hugh rolls his shoulders back and then eases himself further down into his seat.

He clears his throat. "Wandered out and drowned." He looks away from Ena, toward the scattering of half-dead trees and mossy water. "Out there, in Carter's swamp."

19

July 11, 1917

Dearest Ena,

    I got your last box all right and the cakes were not crushed even though you worried they would be. The lads wait for your boxes because they know they will have something good! Sarah sent a wonderful packet of cards inside a box with chocolate bars and maple sugar. She wrote that Hugh picked up more acres and that he is keeping very busy. I don't know how he will work it all, but he is a good worker and so he'll do fine. How is the hay crop this year? I'm glad the binder machine got fixed. I wish I was there to help. The cows will be fattening up with grazing. Are the new calves doing all right? It was too bad about Maeve and Harry's place being burned down. Lightening is a terrible thing. They will rebuild but it won't feel like the old place for them.

    I have a new job up the line. A few weeks ago, the fighting was very bad, and shrapnel hit our trench. After the dust and smoke cleared, one of our boys, Alec Miller, lay missing a leg and with a wound to his shoulder. He was in a bad way and I went to help him. I put a tourniquet on the leg and put pressure on the shoulder. The medics took a long while to get through all the debris and by the time they got to us, Alec was gone. There are too many injured for the medical corps to keep up now. Someone must have told my C.O. that I am all right with the wounded, and so I have taken up the job of stretcher-bearer. We try to help the injured men, if we can, and then transfer them to the Casualty Station. This is better for me than fighting. I feel like I can maybe do some good. It is terrible to see some of the injuries though.

Don't work too hard, Ena. Ask for help! You don't ask for it enough.

I am quite well and you don't have to worry. I am thinking of you every minute.

Your Loving Jamie

Ena keeps Jamie's letters in an old flour tin on the top shelf of her pantry, behind a jar of currants. Not that she is hiding the letters. When she slides the tin into place, a temporary assurance moves through her, as though for the moment, she keeps him safe.

The letters she writes back to him are stripped of any hint of worry. She writes earnestly of the weaning of calves, of a wild dog shot in the neighbour's field, the progress of crops—she ends the letters with the same line: *I am keeping you in my heart always.* Each time she writes it, although she knows the impulse is foolish, she wants to strike the words out, as if there is some curse in them, a jinx, the power to do him harm.

WHEN THE GRAIN IS READY for harvest, Hugh arrives with a threshing crew. One of the crew unhitches Hugh's horses from the steam engine while another quickly puts the wheel chocks in place. Two more unroll a long fat belt and attach it to the thresher, their movements light, quick, and strangely antic. Watching them, it becomes clear to Ena that not one of the crew is over the age of fourteen.

Although Blain and Ena hadn't talked about Blain staying, he is still here and she's secretly relieved. The purple bruising on his face has turned to a yellow wash, and the gash on his cheek is disappearing. The broken ribs will take a long time to heal but his mood is bright. He tends to the animals but he isn't able to do much else.

To help with the food during threshing, Ena has hired two sisters from a neighbouring farm. They are close in age, around sixteen, grinning, their skin nut brown from the sun. The sisters wash utensils and watch over the oven. Whispering to one another, they flit about her kitchen, their lips as busy as the wings of bees.

With the baking in hand, Ena is free to go to the field and into the windrows. Taking Ted with her, she loads the stooks onto the cart, takes them to the barn, and then, with one of the boys, she transfers them via a ramp to the press in the loft.

She is strong, levering the bundles with a fork, using strength in her thighs to make up for what she lacks in her arms. Her hands crack and swell around the fork's handle and the sun lies hot as iron on her back. She lifts and loads, returns to the windrows, lifts and loads again. Hugh stays with his team, transporting bundles of grain to the belt; she catches glimpses of him heaving the bundles from the wagon, his fork piercing the load, shifting it with a lift of one arm while exerting a convincing downward thrust with the other. And then, for a moment the bundles are airborne, pale discs sailing upward into the blue.

Near lunchtime, Ena walks to the outdoor washtub where two of the boys from the crew are wrestling—elbows needling fragile ribs, knuckles grating bristled hair—their tumbling sending up dust. "They're not much younger than you," she says to Blain who has wandered over.

He nods, his eyes narrowing. "They're some older than my brother Owen." A rare tension comes into his eyes. "Course, Owen's small for his age. My mum was small. Like you, Ena."

Hugh finds them. The sun has bleached his hair to a paler blond and his eyebrows look like the tassels of wheat. His face is a deep honey-brown. Glaring at Blain, he says, "You look half- mended. Some, anyway. Why don't you go take care of them horses? They could use a drink of water and a rubdown with a rag. Then you can eat."

"His ribs are still bad," says Ena, frowning, studying Blain.

Blain smiles. "I'm all right." He shuffles off to where the standing horses shift their feet, their coats slick with sweat, flies finding them. Hugh is quiet for a moment.

"Carter's been over, demanding the boy's wages. Told him since Blain was stayin' with us, getting his meals free, he wasn't costing Carter a nickel. Said it was up to the boy to do what he wanted with his wages."

Ena looks at him but Hugh keeps his eyes on Blain.

"I told Clem I don't like the man. Don't think I have a place for Blain anymore. Too much trouble. But we'll get someone else, Ena, someone better. You won't be without help for the winter."

Ena repositions herself, blocking his view of Blain. "Keep him, Hugh. Keep him on until spring and then we'll see."

They take their midday meal at a long table on the grass behind the house and under the shade of a towering elm. The boys devour everything Ena places in front of them—four or five thick slices of bread each, slabs of cheese and meat, two, or even three wedges of pie. As the heat thickens and the day wears on, the girls set out fresh glasses and jugs of cold water, and late in the afternoon, lemonade and trays of buttermilk biscuits, peach tarts, a cherry cake.

After they have taken out the last of the food to the crew, Ena stacks the plates in the kitchen while the girls sit for a few minutes on the back stoop of the woodshed, their blouses open at their throats, their stockings rolled down to their ankles. Still they look overheated.

Blain is with them, his shoulder against the door frame, his hands shoved deep in his pockets. As he talks, the girls giggle but they stop when they fall under Ena's gaze, a flush spreading across their throats and into their cheeks.

"Is he your brother?" The younger of the two asks Ena as she brings them lemonade.

Ena pauses.

"Yes," she says evenly. Her eyes meet Blain's. He's looking surprised, a smile playing on his lips. Ena has never told a lie before, not even as a child and now the idea that Blain is her brother fills her as if with bright water; there is a frank recognition that she was thirsty and now she isn't. Her imagination has never gone this far. In an instant, it changes what she sees, what she knows. It changes what she believes.

On the second day, with the rain falling hard on the fields, the work stops and Hugh sends the hired hands away. All but Blain who waits in the kitchen while Hugh checks the new binds in the barn.

"Ena, read to me," says Blain sitting at the kitchen table.

"*Can't* you read?"

When he grins, his lean cheeks surrender to dimples and something shines in him. "Yes, but you read better."

There are not many books in their house—a cookbook Ellen had given Ena when she got married, readers from her days at school, and Jamie's copy of *The Virginian* by Owen Wister. The frayed front cover is amber-coloured, with the image of a squiggle of rope and a red pistol in a decorated holster.

"This one," she says bringing it in from the parlour. She'd first seen a copy of the Wister book at school, and for a time, all the boys in the school were reading it. And then later, she'd seen a copy at the McLaren's, jammed into a small bookcase in Douglas McLaren's room. She imagines it is a book that a boy like Blain would like although she's never read it.

She reads to him while a streak of pink light steals into the heavy sky. Blain sits with his chin in his hands, a dreamy look on his face. Ena is in her chair, a pot of tea in front of her. She doesn't know the story of *The Virginian* and it seems silly, with shootouts and hangings, and a landscape that is too big for real people. But as she reads about the sprawling vistas and lives driven by adventure, she sees that Blain likes it.

"You read good, Ena."

She gives him a hard look, but is secretly pleased. "And how would you know? I could be making things up."

A short series of delighted whoops. He closes his eyes and listens. "Don't matter if you do."

20.

NOT YET NINE IN THE MORNING and Ena has harvested all the beets, pulling enough to fill four baskets. She vigorously hoes the length of garden where the beets had been. The earth easily turns over, plain and brown and clotted. No hint of the bounty it has pushed up over the last several weeks. Ena holds the garden in awe. She is taken over with thoughts of the beet relishes she'll make (she'll add lemon juice, baby onion, mustard seed to the usual recipe). And the pickled beets—jars and jars will line the shelves in the root cellar below the house.

A motorcar rumbles up the lane, raising a cloud of dust, and Billie streaks from the barn to meet it. Ena recognizes the car at once as the one she'd seen Sarah with in town.

"The car beats all, Ena," Sarah says, stepping out, breathless, her eyes gleaming. She'd been in a hurry to leave the farm Ena guesses, and hasn't bothered to change out of her painting smock, which is splashed with reds and yellows. Her hair is haphazardly bound up in a colourful headscarf. She looks both exultant and untamed.

"It took no time to learn," she goes on, peeling off her leather gloves. "Hugh taught me. We took it over to South Hampton and back, and then into town." She glances at the car and frowns. "Parking it is still a problem. You have to line it up properly, and then reverse." She grimaces. "But I'll get better at it. Hugh likes the idea of me driving around Owen Sound in a car of my own."

Ena lets her eyes run over the boxy car. "It sure is something."
Sarah frowns. "You mean, *not* beautiful, not like a horse.
It's all right, Ena. I don't care about the car. Just what it can
do for me." She looks over Ena's shoulder at the house and
then holds Ena's eyes with her own. There is a fierceness about
Sarah's friendship, an affection that can bully itself into Ena's
most determined reserve.

"I haven't seen you in weeks, and I *could* have come to see
you, and I'm sorry I didn't. Anyway, you had your hands full
and I've been painting a lot. The time just gets away...."

High, dark-bellied clouds race across the sky, the sun disappearing and then bursting through again. It isn't clear to Ena
why Sarah thinks she should have come; Ena doesn't expect
other people to fill the gap that Jamie leaves. She shutters herself,
pushing away the thought of company, a feeling of irritation
climbing over her when Hugh arrives, or Clem. Anyone really,
except for Blain.

"I can never tell if you are glad to see me or not," Sarah goes
on, her tone both affectionate and chiding.

Ena laughs and props up the hoe on the side of the house.
"Well, I *am* glad to see you. I don't have time to think of much
else but the farm."

Sarah examines the garden plot as though the answer to the
puzzle of Ena is in the work she does. "You're always up to
your wrists in something. The livestock, the milking, the gar-
dening. And then the baking, all that work you do for those
church people—the IODE women. You don't like them, Ena.
You can't. All their preaching about *doing one's duty* and
fighting on the side of God. If they were really Christians,
they'd be pacifists."

"I don't care about what they say. I don't *belong* to them, I
just *work* for them. And the baking is something I like to do."

Sarah tightens, her lips pressed together. Ena knows she is
offended by the IODE work. In truth, Ena too is appalled by
the war. She hates living in a state of constant apprehension

about Jamie. What she knows is that men come back or they don't; either way, women and families who care for them—or grieve for them—are deeply affected, burdened, changed. It isn't solidarity with them that Ena feels but something far more wrenching.

"Hugh says you don't need the money. He'll take care of any extra expenses."

Bending, her face tilted away from Sarah's, she picks up the baskets of beets. She will wash the beets first, scrub the earth from their scored skins, and then boil them. She is anxious to get at the job, not wanting to wait until the kitchen gets too warm, the sun still strong, even in September. She could use the summer kitchen but she prefers the larger stove, never surrendering her oven, even on the hottest days. "I put money aside, for when Jamie gets back. He's talking about buying a truck." It's true that she manages to save a good deal of the money she makes, but she's also given quite a lot of it to Blain. She sets her gaze on Sarah, keeping her growing bond with Blain to herself, feeling strangely proprietary about it.

Sarah sighs, worry storming over her features. "You'll need more help—another hired man and someone more experienced than Blain." Sarah presses. "Besides, there's the trouble with Jack Carter coming around our place, his hand out for more money. Hugh won't put up with it for long." She strides along the borders of Ena's garden, studying it, the squash coming along, the turnips, still some late green beans. "Hugh told me to tell you he's going to send over extra hands. And don't feel too grateful. He does it for all of the McFarland farms."

Something in Sarah's words needle: *All the McFarland farms*—as though this place isn't Jamie and hers. Sarah isn't looking at her now; her head tilts up toward the sky, her face filled with intense curiosity.

"You miss Jamie terribly, Ena," she says. "I *know* you worry." It's always difficult to hide from Sarah. For a moment Ena is exposed—there are tears in her eyes but she doesn't let Sarah see. She straightens her back and looks at the house. "Having Blain around has been a help," she says evenly. "And he's good company. He makes me laugh. As long as Jamie is away, I want Blain here."

Sarah stands like a giant at the edge of the garden. "Well, I have some place to be." She walks toward the car and then, as if thinking better of it, she turns, takes Ena by the shoulders, and looks intently into her face. Sarah at her full height, her hair swept up and under the scarf, the sleeves of her blouse rolled so that Ena can see the firmness in her arms, looks nothing but determined. "Come for a drive with me — it will be good for you to get away from here. I want to show you something." Her hand opens toward the motorcar, both entreating and insistent.

Ena glares at the gleaming car, boastful, pompous in the bright summer sun. "I don't like cars, Sarah," she says truthfully.

Sarah laughs.

"There's milking," Ena adds.

"Isn't that why you have Blain here? You say he's so much help...."

Ena looks doubtfully at the barn and brushes her hands on her skirt. "All right, but not too far. I don't like to be away for long."

IN ENA'S OPINION, Sarah is driving too fast. She keeps the car close to the shoulder, her fingers gripping the steering wheel. There is a change in Sarah—a focus to her energy, a bright and almost dangerous shine.

"The work I'm doing this summer, the painting, it's different." She tilts her head, her eyes narrowing. "Craig Murray is here," she says almost tersely, "and he's helping me." Reaching, she briefly squeezes Ena's hand. "No one else knows but you, Ena. You understand, about the painting, how much it matters...."

Sarah's work, her secret life, sits between them, whipped up by the thrum of the car's engine. Ena thinks about seeing Sarah and her car in Owen Sound, the man she met on the street, the two bodies inevitably colliding.

"I tell Hugh I'm going into town to give drawing lessons to school children—I *do* give lessons but nowhere near as much as he thinks. I don't like telling lies. But it's the painting. Hugh doesn't understand...." Her voice trails off but Ena waits, knowing that Sarah will say more. A frank, unapologetic light falls across the fields and bush. Sarah looks to be drinking it in, her eyes gleaming. "The car has made things easier. You'd be surprised how much I've been able to do."

They take the shore road, north of Owen Sound, and beside them, Georgian Bay comes and goes, a trumpeting blue. "We're going a long way from town." Ena's voice is raised, sharpened over the motor's roar.

Sarah looks over at her, unyielding.. "It's still early. I'll have you back before dark."

Farms roll past, tiny outposts in a sea of golds and greens. So many tiny worlds, thinks Ena. "Are we going up the west side of the sound?"

Sarah doesn't seem to have heard her. "Sometimes, when I drive down the lane, away from the farm, I feel like I'm not going to go back. But I always do, of course. It's like having different parts of yourself scattered here and there." She pushes roughly at her headscarf. "I want to show you where I've been painting."

Ena stares straight ahead, her mind travelling over what Sarah is saying. Sarah's life is cracked, like a mirror, brilliant shards strewn over the countryside. It is painful to imagine it. Ena has never known that sort of pulling-apart. How will Sarah ever put the pieces together? She looks out of the window again. At once, there are no farms, only trees and passing glimpses of water.

"I'm going to introduce you to Craig. He's helped me so much."

"Why can't you paint at the farm? Like you always have?"

"Because it's not enough." A spray of stones suddenly pelts the undercarriage of the car and Sarah's grip on the wheel grows even tighter. She glances at Ena, a rueful look. "Don't be upset with me, Ena. I don't want to hurt Hugh. It isn't like that."

The effort of talking over the motor is too much of a strain. There is a fork in the road, one track broad and straight, the other winding to the right, a narrow stony tract that leads toward the bay. Sarah takes the right one and they are quickly in a hardwood forest, the trees a crowded mix of greens. Their branches batter the sides of Sarah's car and Ena wonders what Hugh will think when he sees its condition. It occurs to her that Sarah's explanations will have to be endlessly inventive.

Before long, the water comes into full view, and then a dark-timbered cabin, a scattering of thick-legged chairs and tables set in front. Sarah pulls the car into the yard and climbs out. From the far side of the cabin, a figure emerges, short, broad, wearing a red shirt and cap, his shirtsleeves rolled up. The man Ena saw in Owen Sound. He grins widely when he sees Sarah. He comes to Ena directly and extends his hand, which is strong and sure in her own.

Up close, his face is both boyish and not, his skin firm, slightly pocked like the peel of an orange. His gaze is direct, open, and when he speaks, the vowels swim a little lazily in his mouth.

"Sarah has told me a lot about you," he says. "We were awfully sure you wouldn't come." An American accent and when she hears it, Ena thinks of summer visitors, wealthy people from Michigan.

It's strange seeing Sarah next to Craig. She's an inch or two taller, and the difference makes her seem off-balance. "Come and see Craig's workshop while the light's still so good," Sarah says, taking Ena firmly by the hand.

Although the windows that face the road are small, inside the cabin light pours in. Craig has enlarged the two windows on the east side, installing the glass himself, he tells Ena. The effect is of trees and water, as if there are no walls. At one end of the room is a wood stove and a small table with two blue paint-chipped chairs. Someone has put a jug of dried purple and white flowers on the table. Perhaps it was Sarah, Ena thinks. To the right is a narrow bed and some hooks on the wall. The rest of the cabin is given over to canvases, palettes, hardboards, stretchers. Two easels stand outside, set up on a narrow wood platform overlooking the bay.

"When the weather is fine, we work outside," says Craig simply. "But the light is good enough to work in here if we have to."

Ena takes in each object, recognizing at once the utility, the careful organization. Canvases are everywhere, some leaning against a wall, while others have been stacked on narrow shelves that appear to have been especially installed for that purpose. A few of the finished pieces have been done on hardboard and they are set apart from the rest. Gesso and paints are grouped by colour or type, and brushes stand clean and ready in milk pails, sorted by size and bristle. Clean rags are folded in a wicker basket, used rags set apart in a pail by the back door. A large basin sits filled with water. The floor is swept clean, the rough walls whitewashed, Ena assumes, to increase the vaulting light. She wraps her arms around herself, liking the feel of the place.

Craig appears satisfied and easy. "The place belonged to an uncle who came up here for the fishing and hunting." He keeps his hands in his pockets. "No one in the family cares about it now but me. Of course, I won't live here in the winter. If I stay, I'll take a couple of rooms in Owen Sound when the weather turns."

Sarah, who is impatient with interiors, preferring a front porch, a field, a bit of lawn even on the worst day, appears rangy and restless in the small cabin. She looks longingly out at the bay. "How about you show Ena a piece you've finished, Craig?"

When he nods there is something hard and determined around his eyes although his mouth wears a generous grin. He goes over to one of the stacks. After leafing through the canvases he pulls out two large pieces.

"Let's take them out into the light," Sarah says, her hand already on the back door knob. On the wooden platform, the light is sparkling, effervescent. Craig places the first piece up on the easel—a large square canvas, angular, all triangles and squares—the colours mostly blues and greys.

"That one is from a sketch I did in Paris—a modern street-scape."

Now, Ena can make out the outline of large buildings, cars like insects moving along broad streets. She has never been to a big city but she has seen photographs in newspapers and magazines. "Yes, I see," she says.

"Of course, Paris doesn't look like that," Sarah leans in closer to the canvas. "This is what it is, underneath. You see the life there, behind all the machines. Machines are taking over. Even here."

Ena thinks about Owen Sound and the appearance of auto-mobiles, trucks, mechanized farm equipment, the improvements to appliances.

Resting his hand on Sarah's shoulder and standing back from the canvas, Craig regards the painting as though he is regarding someone else's work. "Cities are changing," he says, his voice warm and broad. "All over Europe and America. Painting is harder to understand than it was. The modern stuff like this isn't to everyone's liking, but that would be too much to expect."

Ena looks at Craig, and then back to the canvas. She thinks about Hugh ploughing the field behind his team of horses, the strength of him as relentless as a machine. The same force and thrust is there in Craig too, and in his pictures.

"Well, let's have a look at another," Craig says, wheeling around, graceful, almost acrobatic in his movement, snatching up another painting and putting it on the easel. It is all white, grey, a horizontal line across the midsection, the image of an infinite cold, a world of snow and ice.

"No need to explain this one," he says, a pipe now between his teeth. It's a plain pipe, the step curved and without a silver band. "I did this from a sketch taken up the peninsula, several winters ago." He looks warmly at Sarah. "I truly love the landscape here. So many faces, but the bones are strong and unchanging."

Looking at Craig Murray's paintings is bewildering. Ena feels no spark or jolt and she wonders if she doesn't know enough of the world to understand them. "And what about Sarah's work?" she asks too quickly.

With no sign of offense, Craig nods. "Of course you'll want to see. What you think of her work matters so much to Sarah. You're somewhat of an inspiration to her—your husband away, fighting, you very much taken up with your farm, the work you do."

"It's true," Sarah says, touching Ena's sleeve.

"It's hard to describe what she's doing now," Craig goes on, something of the teacher in his tone, "but I'll try. I'm glad you'll see it for yourself. Sarah's lack of training gives her work passion. It seems completely natural. Very humane. She's coming into her own, mastering something—a style that I can't begin to tackle myself."

While he is in the cabin, retrieving a piece for them to look at, Sarah walks the short distance to where the small patch of grass falls away to a ravine and a rocky beach below. "He gets worked up when it comes to painting," she says, laughing. Poised there, the water radiating out behind her, Sarah looks as though she might spread wings and burst into flight. The bright tension surrounding her leaves Ena with uncertainty, anticipation mixed with caution. She realizes she has never been this far up the peninsula. She has never been this far from Owen Sound.

Craig returns carrying one small canvas. "This one is finished, and ready to be viewed I think. Is that all right, Sarah? Do you approve of my choice of this one?"

Sarah walks back, frowning and looks at the one in his arms. "Well, yes—that could be one...."

Craig puts the small canvas on the easel and Ena is immediately overtaken with recognition. The colour is what hits her first, vivid, colliding shades: darks that hold deep veins of red and lashings of grey. There are brown and barren trees, twisted wire. Although there are no people in it, there is panic in the picture. A feeling of being held in a storm. Ena thinks of Jamie's letters, his brief and measured descriptions of the war, the horrible things he sees and does.

"It's too much, Ena. I know. It's overblown. It's how I think of it—what's going on over there."

Craig is nodding his head appreciatively. "I know a few war artists. This wouldn't be far off how they describe it, although they don't paint it this way. They are paid to be patriotic, not interpretive."

Ena looks at Sarah. "Can I see another?" She is greedy for more—the burst of feeling that comes as she is taken to the heart of things without words or explanations.

Sarah hesitates. "Not yet, but there will be more, once I've had time with them."

Pulling the pipe from his mouth Craig holds the bowl and stretches his arms about their shoulders. "What about some lunch? I know you can't stay forever—and I want you to eat before you go."

He leads them to the front of the cabin, to a small square table under a low-limbed tree. Sarah spreads a canvas cloth over the table and Craig brings chairs, two at a time, and then a third that he holds over his head like a lion tamer. He brings out a tray loaded with ham, a bowl of pickles, butter and thick slices of bread. At first, they talk about the war, but soon the talk turns to art, the exhibit that Craig is preparing for.

The late afternoon has settled in and the sun is now well behind the cabin. Ena is thinking of Blain, of the livestock, Billie waiting for her at the gate.

"We must go," she says to Sarah,

After she clears the table, Sarah walks toward the cabin, Craig following, his eyes searching the line of sky above the trees. Ena stays behind and shakes the crumbs from the cloth. It seems like a long time before they emerge. Craig is smoking his pipe, Sarah giving the cabin a wistful backward glance.

"Well, goodbye then, Craig," says Sarah, lingering for a moment before settling herself in the driver's seat.

From the passenger's window, Ena puts out her hand to him. "It was good to meet you. I hope we meet again."

Craig instantly breaks into a grin. "I count on it. Goodbye, Sarah. Until next time." As they drive away, he sticks his pipe forcefully between his teeth. When Ena looks back, she can see him still standing there, his back to the dark cabin, a slash of hard light behind him from the bay.

21

THERE ARE JOBS ON THE FARM that neither Blain nor Ena are experienced enough to do—repairs to be made, and the new birthing stalls that must be ready in advance of spring calving. Hugh comes by, his truck rattling with tools. The day is dark with incoming rain and Ena lights the barn lanterns.

Inexplicably, Ted has gone partially lame. "I'll have a look," says Hugh, sliding a stool in close to the horse. He leans heavily into the horse's flank, small grunts escaping from him as he bends Ted's knee and lifts the foreleg. Holding the massive hoof between his thighs, he frowns. "You know anything about Sarah's teaching in town?"

Ena looks at him blankly. "I know she goes to town a lot."

Hugh peers at the hoof, probing it in a desultory way with the hoof pick. Heaving a great sigh, he drops Ted's hoof and stands stiffly from the stool. "It's what she *says* she does, but I know different." He shakes out his legs and gives the horse a sharp slap on the rump. "I know she's doing her pictures somewhere."

Ena puts her hand on Ted's neck, willing Hugh to stop talking about Sarah. He expects her to offer some relief but nothing she can say, nothing truthful, will help him. She combs out Ted's mane with her fingers and then slides her hand down the length of the horse's nose. "It's hard for her to paint at the farm."

Hugh's eyes ramble up to the loft and beams as if to find

something on which to pin his thoughts. "I don't understand her."

"The painting is important to her."

"The pictures are for children."

"I don't think a child could make what Sarah makes."

He looks down at his own hands, squeezing the fingers closed, clenching his hands into fists. A bristling tension pulls between them. He gestures at Ted with his chin. "*I* don't know what to do for the damn horse. It's Jamie's horse. Write and ask him." His gaze catches on Ena, his face combative. "I'll go outside and work some on that gate that's givin' you trouble before the rain starts up."

"I can take over with Ted if you want."

Hugh stares at something in the corner of Ted's stall and sets his jaw. "You're gonna have to give up that boy." His head jerks toward the back of the barn where Blain is milking. "Carter's been back 'round, asking for more money."

She lowers herself onto the vacated stool and gently lifts Ted's hoof, beginning to clean it with the pick. Buried deep, she finds a hard fragment of wood. She pries it out and then massages the horse's foreleg with her hands.

"I don't want to be bothered by Carter or his boy anymore, Ena. They're a thorn in my side, both of 'em. I got enough to do, runnin' two damn farms all on my own."

His back is turned to Ena now, his face toward the door and the yard where the broken gate is waiting for him, his loneliness there in the hang of his shoulders.

"I have it," she whispers, carefully holding up the splinter to the light. "He'll be all right now."

Hugh looks back at her, his expression pained. "Ena, I mean it about Blain. I'm gonna let him go."

She stands up from the stool, her spine unfurling.

"Not yet. Not until Jamie comes home."

22

September 24, 1917

Dearest Ena,

I got your last letter yesterday and the sugar and cakes and tea. We are on a rest now. The fighting has been very bad here and we have been up the line a lot. I was sorry to hear about Tommy Creston being killed. He was a good lad. His mum and dad and sister will be awful torn up about it. Ralph Brown was transferred to C company and so I don't see him anymore. We are very spread around now and few of us are together from the 147th.

You are taking wonderful care of everything, especially poor Ted who had trouble with his hooves many times before. I would have soaked the bad hoof in saltwater, just as you did, and then massage his legs. He is a good horse and I am glad he is there with you and not in with the horses here.

It is very wet. We stay in a small village a few miles back. We walked away from the line of fighting, dead on our feet. Now we are away from it, we can still hear the guns. It gets so you don't notice it so much. I still carry stretchers helping the wounded up on the line. I never knew I could move so fast. Running while carrying half the weight of a man is not easy. Some of the other men call me Daddy for Daddy Long Legs. It's *funny being called Daddy. I don't know that anyone else outside of this war will ever call me that but we can hope!*

I don't have very much to say. So much of it is too bad to write down. But please don't stop writing to me, about the farm, about you, about everything.

I am fine so don't worry.

Your loving husband, Jamie.

LATE SEPTEMBER AND HARVEST TIME and Ena has been out in the field with Blain, pulling up potatoes. A thin rain has begun to fall, at first neither of them noticing, but now they are soaked through and chilled. They lead Ted and the loaded wagon into the barn, unhitch him, rub him down, Blain pouring out the horse's feed. He is good with Ted, thorough, patient, able to put aside his own discomfort for a time.

"We'll get some tea to warm us up," she tells Blain wearily as they head toward the house. He wears one of Jamie's old coats, his hands drawn up into the sleeves. She has continued to give him extra cash—she should encourage him to buy a coat of his own, one that fits him.

Stepping out of her boots, she leaves Blain waiting in the woodshed. In the kitchen she takes the warm kettle from the stove and brings it back to him. Blain has the coat off and his sleeves rolled up, his hands hovering over a basin.

Her mind is numb, her back throbbing dully from bending in the field. When it is her turn to wash, the carbolic soap stings her skin and briefly her senses sharpen; she dries her hands and then gives Blain the roll of linen. The stove needs to be lit. She pulls back the grate and adds some more kindling, then lights it with a match. A second filled kettle sits ready and waiting on the worktop and she puts it on the stove to boil.

They should eat something. She should butter some bread. When the water boils, she pours it into the brown pot, pulls two cups from the shelf, and takes the pitcher of milk from the icebox.

Some part of her registers that Blain is no longer in the kitchen. He must be in the parlour although she can't hear him. Perhaps he has fallen asleep. She imagines him on the chesterfield, his bony knees drawn up to his chin, no blanket, no pillow. The woodstove hasn't been lit in the parlour for hours and the room must be cold. She swallows down exhaustion and thinks about lighting it, imagining the warmth invading the room, drawing out the damp from their clothes and hair. She told Blain to take off his wet things, to put on a sweater, but she hasn't heard him climb the stairs.

After the first blistering sip, the tea revives her. As she sighs and straightens herself, she thinks *move now or sleep on your feet*. She hasn't yet turned when she feels someone behind her, an undeniable presence.

A ragged sound of breathing; "Where's Blain?"

Recognition swoops down, sudden, unequivocal. *Jack Carter*. She sets down her tea on the worktop and turns to face him. He looks dishevelled, his eyes swollen and hooded, and he wears the same sad and deadened look he had when she last saw him. She blinks back shock. He has walked into her house, into her kitchen. She goes rigid, a sickening mix of fear and outrage pushing up.

Taking a loose step toward her, his face shows no malice but rather a vacancy of expression. Sweat glistens on his forehead despite the chill in the room. When he moves in closer she smells the alcohol, and something acrid yet sweet beneath it.

"Word at the Queens is that him and DeWitt had quite a scheme goin' for a bit. Boy thinks he's too smart for me, eh? Thinks he can beat me at my own game. Well, DeWitt's taken off, gone north, so that leaves Blain to answer for what they done.

His voice is lazy, the words slurred.

"Your making no sense," she says.

"And then there's the wages," he goes on. "Either Blain's holding back on me or you haven't paid up. Either way, I'm not partial to being taken advantage of." His face is hang-dog and sullen. His eyes look weepy.

"*Leave—*"

He leans in, one hand steadying himself on the worktop. "Just. Get. Blain."

He doesn't expect her to resist. He sees no threat in her at all. From a deep vein of stubbornness, an orphaned word rises: "No."

He blinks, staggers a little and then he resets his balance before he grabs her by the wrist, his grip surprisingly strong. He twists her arm, watching her face impassively. "I just want what's mine."

Over his shoulder, she sees movement, an elongated shadow on the wall. When it gets closer, Blain comes into her view, his face creased from recent sleep. He seems transfixed, and for a moment, she wonders if he is really awake. Mindlessly, he slides his belt from his trousers.

His movement is like a swift moving cloud. In one fluid motion he throws the belt around his father's neck just as he might halter an animal, and then he crosses his arms and tugs. Carter flails, his arms clawing at his throat, his body twisting, his legs kicking. Blain doesn't yield and soon Carter has slumped to his knees.

Ena is on Blain now, her hands prying open his fingers. "Stop, Blain!" Blain is long past words. Seeing that he won't let go, she wraps herself across his back, hooking her arms around his, forcing them back, wrenching his shoulders until he drops the belt. He staggers into her and they both tumble.

On the floor beside them, Carter gasps for air. "You little bastard," he says, spitting onto the floorboards. He grasps the edge of the worktop and pulls himself to stand.

Blain's face is bright, his chest is heaving, and there is a concentration in him that she has never seen before. For a moment, the boy inside Blain has completely vanished. Staggering to the door, Jack Carter hesitates before turning. "I told you before—don't you come back, Blain, not to see your brother. I know you been to see him when I'm not around, that you go see him at the school. Keep doin' that and Owen's gonna have to pay for the visit." They hear the bang of the woodshed door.

Blain is on his knees and staring, his face blanched, his hands shaking, the wrists bony and exposed. Neither of them move, unsure that Carter has really gone. Blain has the leather belt still held between his hands and he regards it with a look that is close to wonder. "He was gonna hurt you, Ena."

She takes his face in her hands, something inside of her breaking open, tears streaming freely down her face. "You took care of that."

"He might come back."

Standing, Ena takes him by the hand to the bottom of the stairs. "Now, go and sleep. Try. I'll watch until it's light. I'll call out if he does come. I promise."

She watches him go.

"Ena? What's gonna happen to Owen now?" He turns to her from the landing.

She doesn't answer and he staggers off to bed. For most of the night, she sits on a hard kitchen chair, her hands tight in her lap, wondering at the violence she has just witnessed, the suddenness of it. How it changes everything.

23. OCTOBER 1917

ENA RECEIVES A TELEGRAM: Jamie is recovering in a field hospital, the result of having been gassed, and he will return to Owen Sound in November. At first it's as if she is lifted from the ground. After reading the telegram twice, she catches hold of Billie, wrapping the dog in her arms, her face buried in the silky ruff. Minutes pass. She plants her gaze on the woods and fields. The land rolls away beyond the structures of barn and house, past Billie and reaches for Jamie. The vision is whole, complete, and when she is overcome with its generosity, she closes her eyes, her fingers still wrapped up in the warmth of the dog and dares to believe that Jamie is finally coming home.

Later, in the quiet of her room, a worry settles over her. He has been gone for a year; half as long as they have lived together, and lately, he writes less and less. His most recent letter, written September 29th, seemed remote, a spidery angle to the handwriting, the sentences thinning, trailing, thoughts vanishing.

Filled with apprehension, over the next days she sets about preparing the house and garden, ruthlessly cleaning the floors and windows, starching sheets, making tomato relish, canning plums, drying apples. There are moments where she is almost dizzy with anticipation and a shy but certain joy steals in.

Blain and Billie pasture the cows each morning after milking, and while the weather remains fine, the bull stays apart from the cows and in the paddock. Blain feeds it, fills its water trough after safely studying the animal from the other side of the fence. His foolishness vanishes in those moments, a new assuredness in his ropey forearms, his gaze steady on the bull.

Blain has continued to sleep in the room next to hers. Even if he could go back to his father, Ena would do anything to prevent it. Her care for Blain has stretched and lengthened since Carter's intrusion, fuelled by something she struggles to name; indignation, fury, love. She tells Blain to scrub and whitewash the stalls in the barn, polish the glass in the barn lanterns, sort the tools and equipment. He scratches his short-cropped head with ragged fingernails, the missing patch of hair grown back like moss over stone. "Will he give a hoot 'bout all that, first thing when he's home?"

Ena gives Blain a hard look and tells him to get on with the work. The truth is that she doesn't know what Jamie will care about. She has no idea.

WHEN THE DAY OF HIS RETURN finally comes, she goes to the station alone, having turned down Sarah and Hugh's offer to wait with her. It would be too much, for both of them, to be watched and fussed over.

It is afternoon, strangely warm for late autumn and a dusty dry wind blows through the town, catching up brown leaves and old newspapers. Blain has brushed and combed out Ted, and his long mane and tail move like strands of silk. Ena strokes the horse's neck, her stomach in knots, her eyes pinned to the train track.

With a sullen hiss of steam, the train pulls in and then shudders to a stop. There is a terrible wait before the men spill out, just a handful at first, clad in grey and khaki, and then more step down, their eyes scanning the platform. The men show no sign of interest in one another, no camaraderie; having disembarked, they instantly separate and then disperse.

Ena sees Jamie as soon as he emerges. He is taller than the others, slightly stooped, and he's thinner than he was before the war, his features angled. The sun seems to bother his eyes and he puts a hand up to shield them.

She feels a stab of dismay, seeing how changed he is. Straightening her back, she hesitates and then walks toward him, putting her arms around his neck, her cheek against his rough wool lapel. At first the words don't come. When he holds his hand out to her, she takes it, relishing the living certainty of it.

"E-n-n-n-a, I..."

It is there, immediately in his voice, the trouble with words, the stammer. He takes off his heavy great coat and slings it over his arm; it hangs from him, brown and extinguished.

"No, you won't need that today," she says, taking it from him. "The weather isn't cold enough."

He nods, his blue eyes watering in the brightness.

"We'll go and find Ted," she says. "They've made the station bigger over the last year. So many people coming and going." He is listening to her intently, but the effort it takes for Ena to be chatty is immense. For a moment, she panics, wondering if they will ever know what to say to one another again.

"Here. Here's Ted," she says taking his hand and placing it on Ted's broad and shining flank. She goes to the horse's neck and strokes him herself. Ted's coat has warmed in the sun and for a few moments, all three stand quietly as departing coaches and motorcars rattle past.

"You must be so tired, Jamie. Such a long trip."

"Yes," he says vacantly. "It was a j-j-j-ourney."

She doesn't ask if he wants to drive and takes the reins herself. Around them are empty fields, farmhouses naked of any greenery or bloom, which makes the unseasonable warmth seem like illusion. Ena wills herself toward conversation, filling the gap between them with stories about the farms they pass, the families they know. Finally, they pull up the lane and Billie comes tearing around the corner of the barn, barking and jumping at the wagon. She leaps up before Jamie has a chance to stand. He smiles and strokes the silky ears.

"She had to put up with me for a long time. You must look pretty good to her."

Jamie shows a hint of real amusement. "You've t- t- taken good care of her. And T-t-t-ted."

His eyes shift to the barn and catch on Blain, awkwardly standing in the half-open door, his eyes intent and curious.

"Blain's staying here now," says Ena quickly. "It makes things easier for chores."

Jamie nods as though this new arrangement is no surprise. She motions to Blain who steps out of the shadowed doorway, his face screwed up against the sun and the blowing dust. When he reaches them, he is strangely tongue-tied, nodding his hello, turning to put his hands on Ted's reins.

"I'll take care of Ted if you want, Ena."

He turns and looks up at Jamie, his head tilted his eyes widening. "Course, you might want to do that, Mr. McFarland?"

Sliding his gaunt frame from the buggy, Jamie says, "I'd l-l-l-ike that."

Blain grins and unhitches the buggy, and then helps Jamie slip off the heavy harness. Jamie arranges it over his shoulder and walks toward the barn, Ted doggedly following, Billie dancing circles at his feet.

The smile disappears from Blain's face and bemused, he turns to Ena, his eyes searching hers. She says nothing and reaches into the buggy for Jamie's things but Blain gets to them first, folding the coat across his arm, just as Jamie had done, slinging the duffle bag over his shoulder, and together they walk to the house. Blain heaves the bag and coat onto the woodshed floor.

"You want me back tomorrow?" He looks out the window toward the barn. They had decided that Blain would go to Clem and Annie's for the night. Now, there is quiet between them, Ena wanting him to stay after all, to bridge the gap, but she's thought of Jamie coming home so often; she's longed for it. "Be back in time for evening chores tomorrow," she says to Blain. "That's enough of a holiday for you."

Blain grins and nods his head. "See you, Ena."

After he's gone, she takes Jamie's duffle bag and coat into the parlour, the bag surprisingly light, only half-filled. How had he managed with so few things? She kneels and touches the bag, the canvas coarse, salty beneath her fingers. She buries her nose in it, trying to place the scent, a mixture of earth, smoke, something ancient. A smell of mildew and decay. Not for the first time, she tries to imagine where he has been.

Going into the kitchen, she begins to lay out food. When he steps inside the woodshed, streams of late afternoon sunlight follow him, eclipsing his face. "Close the door after," she gently reminds him. The day is cooling now. He is exhausted, his breathing hard and raspy. But despite that, being in the barn has relaxed him.

"The place is looking g-g-g-good."

She smiles, glad that he's noticed the care she's taken. "We've done all right," she says, meaning she and Blain. He looks at her and nods.

In the woodshed, he stands in front of the basin and rolls up his shirt sleeves, his hands trembling. When he turns he catches her looking at them and he glances down as though he were noticing the tremor for the first time. "They told me it might g-g-g-go away." He shrugs. "I don't think it will g-g-get in my way."

She had thought a long while about what to serve him that first evening. In the end, she decided on a simple roast of beef, with pickled beets, potatoes, fresh milk, and a French Apple pie made that morning and served with whipped cream and cinnamon. They don't look at one another as they sit down at the crisply laid table. Jamie's fork shakes when he holds it to his mouth but he eats steadily, apparently enjoying each bite.

When they are finished eating, she makes tea and talks to him about the farm. Every so often, he asks her a question and in this way, their conversation takes on a unique rhythm, a gentle to and fro, with Ena speaking more and Jamie speaking less. There were repairs made to the barn, which Hugh helped with, she says. The milk production has been growing, the dairy buys as much as she can provide, and Blain delivers the milk to town for her.

"G-g-glad that Hugh's l-l-let the boy c-c-come over to help." In her letters to Jamie, she hasn't mentioned the storm that surrounds Blain; the violence that clings to him alongside his sweetness.

"Blain's been a help," she says now, a hole in the conversation opening. She should tell Jamie about the extra money she gives to Blain. She should explain the dead-centre tug she feels to protect him, her worry silently tucked inside the modest fold of bills. That she wants to tether Blain to safety with the money. Instead, she says, "He could be a help still."

Jamie nods and a new familiarity descends on them, lasting only until Ena rises to clear away the dishes. When they climb the stairs, their steps are tentative, their heads down. Once they reach the landing, she pauses outside the open door to their room.

"You won't stay here with me t-t-t-tonight?" He is shy about asking.

She searches his face. "I wasn't sure what you would want…"

"Just lie n-n-n-next to me, Ena."

They undress without the lamp. A three-quarter moon hangs in the window, a watery, cool light falling over the bed. His skin feels chalky beneath her hands, and the spare outline of his bones has altered the landscape of his body. His scent is different—sharp and acidic.

A white scar snakes across his shoulder from the shrapnel wound, healed long ago, and she traces it with her finger.

When she places her lips to the flat plane of his chest, she feels the firmness of him beneath the surface, dense like a second skin.

24.

THE SPELLS OF SILENCE THAT FALL are not entirely compan-
ionable like they were before the war, but frayed like rope,
singed and hardened and knotted. Jamie's sleep is broken.
He wakes with startling energy, shouting words, fragments
of conversations without the stammer that is now strangely
characteristic of him. There are names: *Over here, Brady.*
Or *Get Walsh. Oh God. We can't carry him like that.* In the
mornings, the bedding is drenched with his sweat.

Watching him Ena feels she is uselessly peering down a black
road—the road he has just come from—and there is nothing
familiar about it, no reassuring landmarks, no way to know
where he's been.

On the third night, going to the kitchen to get a cloth and a
basin of water for him, Ena finds Blain crouched in the hall-
way, knees splayed, his hands holding his head as if to keep
it from cracking. She kneels down and tries to look into his
face. "What happened to him, Ena?" he whispers. "He's all
right in the barn. He don't holler and shout."

"I don't know. He doesn't talk about it."

Blain looks at her, his face haunted. "Does he hurt you when
he's like that?"

Ena takes his chin in her hands and tilts his face. His cheekbones make purple shadows against his skin. "No. Jamie
wouldn't do that."

The nightshirt Blain wears is too big. It puddles around him on the floorboards. Wiping an arm across his nose, he slides himself to a stand.

"Morning comes early, Blain. Go back to bed."

ON SUNDAY, THEY GO TO the McFarland farm for supper. Hugh meets them in the lane, his face taken up in a wide smile. In an instant, he has Jamie in an iron-clad bear hug, his open hand thumping Jamie's back.

Resting his forehead against Hugh's chin, Jamie looks as if he has surrendered all of his energy now. His hand comes up to his brother's neck and lingers there, and then he steps away.

When they wander to the house, Sarah takes Ena alone into the kitchen and pulls out a chair for her to sit. "What's wrong with Jamie?"

Ena doesn't know exactly. The time he spends in the barn sends him into violent coughing spells, contorting his features, making his eyes stream, turning them blood-red. He's left exhausted. "He's like this because of the gas, I think."

Sarah has her arms crossed and she looks at Ena. "It's more than that. He's different. I think he has shell shock."

Ena has heard the term. Some of the shut-ins she's made deliveries to for the IODE are shell shocked, but unlike them, Jamie manages to go out to the barn, to work. Just yesterday, he and Blain spent the day together splitting wood.

"Craig tells me there are hospitals especially for it in Britain. But not here."

Ena looks at her. Sarah speaks about Craig Murray so casually now and it strikes Ena as reckless. "You still see him a lot," Ena says.

Sarah prods the gravy on the stove with a wooden spoon. "I paint more now than I ever did."

Over the meal, Hugh talks, his tone breezy and assured. He speaks about the new farms he's acquired: the Donaldson's, the Wiley's, the McRae's. All of them had men in service. The families had to sell their land when operating the farm became too much. "We picked-up several hundred acres, all told." He winks conspiratorially at Jamie.

Jamie doesn't appear to be listening. He lifts his glass and drinks deeply, water splashing down his chin.

"It's gonna take time for you to get on your feet. You don't have to go it alone."

No one speaks. Sarah passes a basket of Ena's walnut bread and Hugh takes a slice.

"They don't give you fella's much when you come back."

Ena thought of the small lump sum pay-out Jamie received, some of it considered as recompense for the "minor" damage to his lungs. There had been an additional pittance for civilian clothes.

"It's about time you got yourself a truck," Hugh presses on. "Goin' around with that horse is foolish. I'm going to give you some cash to buy one." He takes a bite of the bread and then nods to Ena in appreciation. Ena is about to say that she has money saved, that in a few months they will have enough without Hugh's help.

"I d-d-d-on't need it." The words erupt from Jamie with a terrible effort. "We manage j-j-j-j-just f-f-f-f-fine."

Hugh carefully sets his fork down. "Things have changed over the last while. *Everyone* who farms needs a truck."

Jamie stares down at his plate, half-eaten mounds of food pushed to the rim, a hole in the centre. "You won't t-t-t-t-tell me w-w-w-w-hat to do."

Hugh is stunned and for a moment his jaw hinges loose. "You're takin' good advice hard. You won't make a go of farming, clinging to the past. You won't be able to hold on to the farm." He rubs his broad hand over his face and then vexed, he fixes his gaze on Jamie. "Men coming back *have* to take their place. They *have* to or lose everything. I've seen it happen."

Across the table, Sarah shakes her head in disbelief. "Stop badgering, Hugh. Jamie is just back."

Hugh's palm rises in way of defense. "Jamie, you *know* I'm right. I mean to help until you've got yourself sorted."

Jamie is staring absently out of the window. "You helped m-m-m-me and En-n-na a lot, Hugh. I appreciate it. We'll b-b-b-be all right now." Ena can see that he has retreated to another place, far from the McFarland's' oak table and his mother's china, the linen cloth embroidered in pale blue with *Mc*. She feels him falling away and his distance from her isn't tolerable.

Some newly found part of Ena pushes forward as if to stake his place for him. She folds her hands together and puts them on the table between herself and Hugh. "We have Blain. He's learned a lot about livestock and keeping up the barn. He can drive Ted in and out of Owen Sound. When it comes time for calving, Blain's not afraid to stay up half the night if we need him to." She nods solemnly toward Jamie. "And Jamie will keep showing him things. Blain's a pretty fast learner—more than what he seems. We'll pay him ourselves—room and board and a little extra." Her eyes are steady on Hugh. "With Blain, and with me working for the IODE, we'll manage—"

Hugh's eyebrows raise and he glares openly at Ena. "You got a lot to say all of a sudden, Ena. Guess you have strong feelings on the subject of Blain Carter. I can give you hired hands who *know* what they're doing. Hell, take Clem for a time if you want. But not that boy. He's trouble enough, let alone Carter. You know it."

Jamie's features look fixed and distant. "Blain s-s-s-stays," he says.

On the way back, a fine sleet begins to fall. Ena is chilled through. She puts her arm through Jamie's for warmth but he does nothing to encourage her. His coat is done up high over his chin and he keeps his eyes straight ahead.

THE NEXT MORNING, BEFORE DAWN, Jamie and Blain milk the cows in the barn, and alone in her kitchen, Ena stokes the stove. When the kitchen is warm enough, she starts the yeast for the brown bread, scalding the milk, pouring out molasses, adding Graham Crumbs and flour that have been measured in equal parts. Finally, with gentle precision, she pours in the frothing, living yeast. With a broad wooden spoon she turns the heavy molasses dough, and she can tell from the consistency that the brown bread will be just right, the texture perfect. For a brief moment, her world is balanced between what is and what will be.

When Jamie and Blain return, she ladles out steaming porridge into their bowls and then spoons out the brown sugar. There is fresh cream on the table, and an octagonal plate with a mound of high, sweet biscuits. A jar of apple butter sits open with a spoon.

Jamie barely manages half a bowl of the porridge while Blain scrapes his bowl clean. When they are done, she puts on her barn coat and her boots, and wraps up four of the biscuits into a clean bread cloth.

"That's a dandy idea, Ena," Blain says, looking happily at the biscuits. "A little something more for later."

"That hollow leg of yours, Blain. I was thinking of Jamie." She smiles and does up her buttons. "There might be one or two for you."

Blain guffaws and then all three trudge across the dreary yard. There are stalls to be cleaned, pails to be filled; Ena and Blain do the work quickly and easily, as they have done together for months, but Jamie is slower, his breathing raspy. After a while, he sits on a stool, his long fingers playing across the face of a heifer. He isn't speaking so much as showing Blain how to examine the eyes, the ears. Blain leans over Jamie's shoulder, watching intently, every so often his hand going to his cap, removing it to rub his head, putting it back on, tugging it into place. It's as if so much focus hurts him. He's quieter with Jamie than he is with her, his usual chatter slowed, a restrained eagerness in his movements, although from time to time, torrents of stories do burst in. Instead of *Mr. McFarland*, lately he's taken to calling Jamie, *Captain*.

Blain's eagerness, his light-heartedness, loosens something in Jamie. A smile creeps into the corners of his mouth. "N-n-n-ot a Captain," Jamie corrects, but Blain just grins. Jamie sends him to clean the other stalls and then ambles over to Ena.

"A g-g-g-good boy," he says quietly and as if to himself.

Ena smiles. "Perhaps not *good*. Perhaps sweet."

Jamie laughs, his head shaking as if he is remembering something forgotten. Something delightful. "G-g-g-good enough, anyway."

In one of the stalls, a spotted calf lies in the straw, its eyes languid, the lids heavy and slow. No matter what Ena has tried, it drops weight. The bones stick out from its hips like antlers and it doesn't get up to nurse.

Jamie rests his arms across the gate, his body very close to Ena's. His features are less guarded here in the barn, his eyes softer. "I g-g-g-gave it s-s-some milk earlier," he says, looking thoughtfully at the calf. "From a b-b-b-ottle."

Ena shakes her head. "I think it will die anyway."

Instantly, she feels him stiffen. "D-d-d-d-don't say that."

He is hidden from her again, a brittleness coming into the skin around his eyes. The divide between them strikes her as unfair, too sharp a blow, and unexpected in the warmth of the barn, with Blain so close. Her eyes sting and she reaches and touches his arm. "Tell me what happened to you."

She must ask. It isn't enough to stay silent and she fears she will lose him if she does. She doesn't think he will tell her. He opens the gate to the pen where the calf is resting, its long ears folded back on its neck, its eyes half-closed. He squats next to it, and then runs his hands slowly along the ridge of its spotted spine.

IT TAKES DAYS FOR HIM TO GET THROUGH the story. He can only tell it in small bursts, his speech too muddled for more, his lungs filling with dust, sending him into fits of coughing. He will only tell her when they are in the barn together, and only when he thinks they are alone. (Once or twice she catches a partial impression of Blain crouching in the shadows, the cropped head, the unmistakable shape of his ear, the bony, looping wrists that supports his narrow chin.)

Each time Jamie stops, exhausted from the effort, she thinks he won't go on and she feels the awful weight of silence return. When he starts again, relief floods her. She is surprised how attached she is to words now. How much she needs them. He is here, with her and she can feel the erratic rise and fall of his breath, but she wants more. She wants to see where he has been. To be that close.

She had known that Jamie wasn't meant to be in the medical corps. He hadn't been trained for it but in the spring, after Vimy—after so many casualties—men were shuffled around to where they were most needed.

"A t-t-t-t-terrible battle, "Jamie says, "with a lot of shells d-d-d-ropping". Dead or dying men and horses lying for hours, even days in the bottom of huge, mud-filled craters, the stretcher-bearers awake all night, listening to the screams, knowing they couldn't risk going out until morning.

The shelling started again at first light. They were supposed to be four to a stretcher, or even six, but now, their ranks were so thin they'd been ordered to go in pairs. Jamie presses his lips closed but after a few moments, he goes on.

Walsh was the other stretcher-bearer, a man from out east, short, but very strong. He'd been a stretcher-bearer for longer than Jamie. "N-n-never wounded." Jamie's eyes show an expression of near-wonder when he says this. "Lucky and g-g-g-ood at g-g-g-getting to places other people couldn't." He'd been a miner before the war.

Jamie and Walsh were told to get to the largest hole, the furthest from the trench where Brady, an infantryman, had been heard shouting. Jamie stops here, his hand on his head, his eyes searching the rough walls of the barn. It isn't until two days later, when the ailing calf has started to feed again, that he takes up his story.

THE SHELL HOLE WAS IN THE PATH of the thickest shelling and Jamie didn't see how they could get to it. But Walsh knew. There were German trenches, recently abandoned and close. If they could get to those, Walsh said, they'd get to the hole. They'd have to keep their heads down and do a little digging but it was all right, they'd manage. Jamie could see that Walsh intended to go no matter the risk.

They took the long way around, carrying the empty stretcher between them. The trench they followed wove around and around, ever narrowing and there were fewer and fewer men and then none at all. Eventually they reached a point where the trench had completely collapsed. Using a plank to dig, Walsh began to tunnel through, falling onto his stomach, crawling. They dragged the stretcher, the two of them swimming through muck. Another stop, Jamie trailing off this time, taking up a rake, going out into the yard. The sadness in his face is almost unbearable. The next day he begins again.

ON THE OTHER SIDE was the German trench. Deep and well constructed. To show her, Jamie's long fingered hands scoop out the empty air and then come together to form a hollow bowl. They scuttled along to where the trench ended, close enough to Brady now, although he wasn't making sounds anymore.

Shells were exploding all around them, mud raining down, and they kept their heads low and waited. Then a break in the shelling; Walsh signalled to Jamie and they ran. At the hole, they pushed the stretcher down and followed it, sliding on their backs.

Jamie wasn't used to it, but he understood what men wanted: the soothing, the bandaging, the handholding while they died. "I thought I'd s-s-s-seen everything." Brady's clothing had been blown off of him by the impact of the shell and he was clutching at his belly, as if he meant to keep a coat closed around himself. But all around his fingers, his intestines were escaping, "l-l-l-ike squirming, l-l-living things." Jamie's face is wet. He wipes it with his sleeve and Ena leads him to the house, to the parlour where she lights the fire. She pours him tea and then she retreats to the kitchen to stuff a chicken with apple bread and raisins for their dinner. They don't speak about Walsh or Brady again until the next day.

JAMIE AND WALSH GAVE BRADY WATER. Gut wounds take a long time to kill, and Brady had already lasted all night in that hole by himself. Walsh had looked up at the sky, then said, "We can't move him like that. There's not enough left of him to move. No sense in trying."

They were supposed to do their best with the injured and it wasn't clear to Jamie that Brady was going to die right then. He told Walsh that they should try.

When he went to Brady's feet, ready to lift, to put him on the stretcher, Walsh did an extraordinary thing. Jamie is looking into Ena's eyes, willing her to follow.

They didn't carry weapons usually. They only got in the way of the stretcher. Now Walsh had found Brady's rifle. But it was damaged from the shelling and likely wouldn't fire.

Walsh crawled around to Brady's head and for a moment, Jamie thought he would signal to Jamie to lift him onto the stretcher. And then Walsh stood, as straight and confident as he would in a field, surveying crops. He was risking himself—making himself a target. He looked down at Brady and not pausing, he brought the rife down on Brady's head.

"B-b-b-bashed in his skull."

It was murder. And Walsh seemed completely unaffected by it.

The next day, their trench was gassed and Jamie was taken to the Casualty Station, and eventually a field hospital. He didn't see Walsh again.

"I c-c-c-could have r-r-r-eported it," he says, his face straining. "He w-w-would have b-b-b-een shot. I d-d-d-didn't open my m-m-mouth."

Ena takes his face in her hands, her thumb tracing the line from his nose to the corner of his mouth. The kindest face. "He must have wanted to end the suffering," she says.

"You d-d-d-d-didn't see W-W-W-Walsh's eyes, Ena. Empty. Like k-k-k-illing was n-n-nothing."

"No, he must have had a reason."

But even as she says it, she knows Jamie had seen something else in Walsh, that it stays with him, stealing his breath, shredding his words.

IT IS A COLD DAY, and one of the last of the season for the outdoor market in Owen Sound. Ena is neatly standing at a stall, inspecting a pyramid of golden-coloured apples when she hears Sarah call her name. A square, soft portmanteau is slung across Sarah's wide shoulders, the edges tied with emerald-green ribbon. To avoid the thin rain that has begun to fall, she steps beneath the overhang of the market, almost treading on the toes of a woman carrying a large crate of eggs. Sarah is a shot of colour in the middle of the leaden day, her face open, illuminated with excitement, her hair flaming.

"I'm getting some paintings ready for an exhibition," she says. "It's a secret, Ena. Don't say anything to anyone. Even Jamie. If Hugh finds out, he'll only put me off." Quite suddenly, the rain comes down in sheets, the stall keepers behind them packing away their trays and bins of late season vegetables—Brussels sprouts and carrots.

"It's Craig's exhibition. A friend in Chicago arranged it and he's asked me to put in a few of my pieces."

There is a thrumming of sound on the market roof, water cascading down, hitting the ground with force. Birds swoop and dip in the rafters above their heads. Strange, Ena thinks, to be both outside and in; there is something exhilarating about it, although perhaps it is just the effect of standing close to Sarah. She wonders whether Sarah has considered what will happen if Hugh finds out about the pictures and Craig Murray, the afternoons spent painting at Craig's cabin.

Reading her expression, Sarah looks impatient. "I won't use my own name, Ena. I'm going to call myself Georgina Fells."

Ena is dumbfounded. "That name doesn't sound like you at all," she says flatly.

"That's the point." There is pride in Sarah's face. And well-earned, thinks Ena now. Before Jamie returned home, Sarah had brought Ena to Craig Murray's cabin again. When Ena stood in the light-filled room, surrounded by Sarah's canvases, it was as though a spark was thrown out from her centre, a leap toward the recognition of feelings she didn't know she had. The pictures were even stronger than the ones Ena had seen before, and terrible in a way. Sarah had not continued to paint familiar fields and sky, but rather sweeps of jarring colour, broken landscapes, empty trees. The paintings were at once stark and alive. Seeing them, Ena knew that what Sarah had captured on the canvases were pieces of life, the breadth and pain of it, the shock, all deeply personal and yet shared.

It was the honesty in them that stunned her—Sarah's willingness to turn herself inside out, the confidence there, in the paintings, demanding that others really see.

In the face of the paintings, Ena had felt something inside stretch and then press, her hard shell cracking, a part of her ready to push itself out.

SHE'D MADE SEVERAL DELIVERIES after meeting Sarah at the market, the last one to the Owen Sound Inn where the inn's owner, Robert Piper, had a standing order for bread, currant breakfast buns, and three varieties of scones. Robert has given Ena good business over the last few months, and she pays little attention to the gossip and speculation that surrounds him. For years, Robert lived in Chicago where he and another man managed a small hotel, living together in one of the hotel's suites, travelling together overseas. The Pipers have always had an interest in Grey County lumber and when his mother died, Robert returned to Owen Sound to settle her affairs. He sold his share of the business to his older brother and with the proceeds, he bought the inn.

The Owen Sound Inn is considered one of the best inns north of Toronto, drawing in business travellers on lumber-buying trips, American art lovers exploring the wilds of the Georgian Bay shores, entrepreneurs, and wealthy sports fisherman. Robert Piper is accused of being a dandy by the local people, many of whom won't step inside the inn's door.

He is in his forties, broad, with a slight heaviness in his features. The clothing he wears is exotic and beautifully made: velvet jackets, brocaded coats, starched white shirts. Despite the clothes, there is an ease about him, a lack of formality Leaving the inn earlier, he'd met her at the side entrance. "Ena, have you tried your hand with fancy cakes?" She has made *many* cakes; pound cakes, lemon cakes, and maple cakes, and the inn had served her cakes often for tea. She frowned up at him, not understanding his question.

"What I mean is cakes intended for high *occasions*—society weddings, ship launches, that sort of thing."

Ena shook her head no. There were no society weddings that she knew of in Owen Sound, and she certainly knew nothing of ship launches.

Robert looked thoughtful for a moment, and then he smiled into her eyes. "Next time I go to Chicago, I'll bring back magazines for you. You'll be able to see what they are doing in the city hotels, the clubs—nothing *you* couldn't handle with the right set of instructions. You have the right temperament to be a true *pâtissière*."

She hadn't known what a *pâtissière* was and she said so now to Robert Piper. He chuckled. "There will be coloured illustrations—plates—in the magazines. You'll understand better then."

BEFORE GOING HOME, ENA VISITS her mother, Ellen, who is

perching stiffly on the edge of a chair in her kitchen, a paisley shawl draped loosely around her shoulders. "Jamie's not with you, I see." Her eyes are keenly focused on Ena.

"No," Ena says, not wanting to explain. She brings Blain with her to town if she needs an extra pair of hands. The town makes Jamie wary, the stammer worsening when he's there, his trembling hands pulled high into the sleeves of his coat. He seldom wants to leave the farm, even to visit with Sarah and Hugh, although at home his comfort grows with Ena, his arms around her waist, his hand resting on the small of her back. And he can't help but warm to the company of Blain, who, unlike many other unlucky boys, is alive, talking, roaming around the place.

"Good that you've got the inn," Ellen says to Ena, "but you won't have time for much else, not with all there is to do on the farm. There won't be space in your life for other things. "

The tea is cold, the afternoon darkening, and Ena's thoughts turn to Ted waiting in the street and the trip they will take home in the rain.

Ellen is peering at her. "And what about grandchildren?" A high, cutting voice. Ena hears a challenge in it. She stares implacably back and doesn't answer.

"Some of the men who come back from over there aren't *capable.*" The bluntness in Ellen can seem ruthless.

"What do you mean?"

"I wondered about Jamie, Ena," In speaking of Jamie, something in Ellen's tone softens. She drops her eyes from Ena's and pours out more tea. Ena hasn't thought a great deal about children. Her own childhood had offered little of a child's experience. If Ena tries very hard to remember back, she finds a thin residue of the child she had been, intermittent flashes of herself playing with a rag doll on the kitchen floor, an orange in the foot of a stocking on Christmas morning. There are images, as if viewed from the outside: herself with Michael, playing in the store, although even then, she felt the shape of her adult self within her, a spiny and focused presence.

What Ellen suggests about Jamie is partly true, although Ena won't say so. There are times when they press themselves hungrily to one another and Jamie's body cannot stir, no matter how much they try. But she can still touch him; she can still feel the length of his bones beneath her hands and kiss him deeply. And sometimes he *is* able. If a baby comes now, she will be ready to give the right care but she doesn't long to be pregnant, not like Sarah who has already carried (and miscarried) two children. Ena wonders how you can really want something until you know it, *feel* it inside. She presses her palms to the sides of her head, touching her hair, stretched and pinned into a tidy knot. She keeps it that way because it is neat, although Jamie likes it when she lets it down. "I don't know what will happen. I don't think about it."

Ellen gives a tight nod, blinks, and the conversation veers away. She tells Ena that she has accepted a live-in situation with an older couple in Toronto who need a cook and light-house-keeping. The job will be easier for her than the one she has at the McLaren's.

"No reason to stay here," she says, pressing her small hands into the tablecloth. "You certainly don't need me. Besides, the pay is better in the city."

"No," says Ena vaguely. "You shouldn't stay." She hasn't meant it maliciously, but when they part shortly after, Ellen's lips are set in a thin hard line.

THE RAIN IS SO HEAVY ON THE ROAD from Owen Sound it springs back from the ground in angry bursts. She grips Ted's reins tighter, blinking away water and focusing her eyes on Ted who plods along, his hips swaying, his head tilted down against the wet. They are close to the property line, the bush a dark blur to the left. Ted seems to quicken a little, knowing that a dry barn and some oats, will be waiting for him.

From up the road, there is the spectre of splintering lights—two of them like blurry eyes—hurtling and bouncing toward her. A spray of mud comes up from the wheels, and as it gets closer, there is the sound of an engine roaring, and then the insistent blaring of a horn. A truck. Ted is nervous. She feels him shimmy to the verge. For a moment, the truck seems to veer toward them and then it zigzags back to the other side of the road. It is rusted, battered, and it slows as it passes, just missing them. The window is pulled down and Jack Carter's face pokes out, leering at her through the curtain of rain.

"Just been to your place," he hollers, "lookin' for my boy. Lookin' for the wages. And everything else he owes me. I'll find the little bugger next time."

The truck sputters and then leaps forward, careening down the road and as soon as it is gone, Ted breaks into an urgent trot, taking them to the gate and then straight up the lane. It's Jamie and not Blain who comes out to meet her. He looks exhausted, his shoulders sunk down but he smiles deeply, seeing her.

She traces his face with her eyes, hunting for evidence of harm. "I just met Jack Carter on the road," she says, stepping down. Jamie wordlessly takes the reins from her and turns Ted toward the barn. The horse, hopeful and eager, noses his pocket.

Jamie turns from her, his face hidden beneath the peak of his cap. "He-e-e's done this b-b-b-before Ena, hasn't he." Not a question. He's known the threat all along. He's seen it. Wordlessly, she follows him as he leads the horse into the barn. He lifts the heavy harness from the horse's back and Ena takes a cloth and begins to rub down the animal's neck and flanks.

"Where's Blain?" she asks, gazing across Ted's back.

He nods his head in the direction of the house. "Safe." He takes off his cap and wipes his forehead, fixing her with a level, unflinching gaze. "I g-g-g-gave Jack Carter m-m-money to m-m-m-ake him l-l-l-leave."

Turning, he studies the bull who stands obtusely in its pen. Her eyes follow, but the bull is so still, it might be asleep on its feet. She wonders what Jamie sees, looking at him.

"He-h-he w-w-w-won't get m-m-money from us again." A stubbornness is there, a bristling against losing more. She blinks at him, realizing that the same resolve is in her, grown strong in the months she spent alone, her attention and concern pinned to the animals and the farm, to her livelihood, to Blain.

They are not the same people, either of them.

JUST BEFORE CHRISTMAS, dogs invade their bush, eight or nine of them, strays and their offspring, hunting at night, frightening the cattle. Jamie keeps Billie in the barn so they can't draw her out. She's loyal beyond sense, Jamie says affectionately, ruffling her ears, tugging on them. She'll want to protect the livestock and her people, but the wild dogs will pull her limb from limb.

The dogs come by way of the derelict farms in the county, lonely places with un-worked land and the livestock gone. Not everyone has family who can take over when a man has enlisted. People move to town to stay with relatives, and the dogs are abandoned.

The strongest and smartest ones wander in search of food, and then tangle with others who are loose and already hunting. They fight their way into the pack if they can, and mate, their offspring better hunters than they are and more cunning. Each generation is more bold, their eyes narrowing to slits, hackles bristling as they push further from the bush, marauding fields and barnyards.

The cold has set in but not the snow. It is morning, the pinkish light beginning to finger out over the fields, and Blain is in the barn. Ena and Jamie sit over a pot of tea, slices of soda bread on their plates, a bowl of cinnamon-plum conserve between them.

Often, Blain gets to the cows before Jamie. Ena hears the slam of the screen door while she washes her face in the porcelain basin. Despite his growing competence, Blain hasn't changed much and she's secretly glad, not wanting his blathering to dry up or his foolish rambling stories to end. He talks and talks, pouring himself into their silences. More and more, he screws himself down to the tasks at hand—the cleaning of equipment, the repairs of the pens. *Puts his shoulder to the wheel,* as Michael might say, a turn of phrase Ena hadn't understood. But she'd always known it had to do with faith—not in God because Michael was not religious—but in true intention that prevails against poor odds.

Ena has drained her tea cup. Without warning, Blain is inside the kitchen door, practically panting, his muddied boots still on his feet, his face and hands streaked with blood. His eyes are hard with excitement. "Ena—" he says, looking into her eyes, his body straining forward. (He knows not to come across her kitchen floor with his barn boots on. He won't dare.)

"What's happened to you?"

"Three of them dogs got hold of a calf right there in the yard," he points to the yard behind the barn, only a corner of it visible from where they sit in the kitchen. Ena tries to steady him with her eyes. "I just let the cows out with the calves and was closing the gate. Buggers was up by the bush, waitin'. They come down the field like streaks of lightning. Good thing Billie was still in the barn—" He's winding up to tell the whole story, dancing a little from foot to foot. "Left Billie inside with the bull. Didn't want her tangling with that bunch—"

"Blain!" She is cutting in, sharp and accusing, when really she's scared. "*Whose* blood is on you?"

"Calf's blood. Still kickin', poor little bugger."

Jamie is up from the table. "Where's the c-c-calf now?" He is going to the woodshed, pulling his boots from the rack, his coat from the hook.

"In the yard. Threw rocks, Captain, and they took off—" Blain puffs up a little. "Scared the b'Jesus out of 'em."

Jamie nods, giving him an encouraging smile and then he's out the door, through to the woodshed, Blain just behind him. Ena watches them go across the yard, their coats billowing like two flags. When they are past the gate and in the yard, they drop, their knees open, their heads bowed like they are in church, just shadows against the flaming sky. Ena gathers up a pail of water and some rags, slides her bare feet into her boots and throws on her coat. Closer to them now, she can see that the calf's black and white spots have merged to a pinkish brown and blood still runs freely onto the dried ground around it. Above them three enormous birds silently wheel. Vultures or hawks.

Jamie gently inspects the little body—a late summer calf, just barely three months old. There are puncture wounds at the neck, and rake-marks at the shoulder and the calf's breaths push out in frantic bursts. "We'll need a blanket to carry it," Jamie says, the stammer, strangely absent. He is looking pointedly at Blain.

Blain races to the barn and Ena offers the basin and cloth to Jamie. He starts at the neck, drawing the cloth over the animal's coat in slow, certain strokes. Every so often he rests one hand on the knobbed plain of its skull and peers into its face. When Blain returns, Jamie lays the blanket flat. "We'll use it like a sling," he says to Blain. He motions Blain to help him lift the animal onto the blanket and then they each lift an end.

Ena watches them as they carry the calf back to the barn. The day is finally breaking around them, the sun finding the fields, the bush, and for a moment, everything is engulfed in a terrible brilliance. The farm is both transformed and familiar. Trees, fieldstone, the men carrying the calf, all are fiercely possessed, changed, lit up by an unstoppable fanning light.

The scene pushes Ena outward with stunning force. Everything she relies on, what she keeps contained, is there, on the *outside*. For an instant she feels weak in the knees and strangely, she wants to cry. How is it that she has rooted herself so determinedly here, utterly given herself over to the land, the farm, and not seen it truly until this single moment? A place of shocking ends and brilliant starts.

ENA HAS NEVER GIVEN THE RIFLE much thought before. She knows it has its uses, of course—to put down livestock, or to kill a fox. She's never known Jamie to use it. He takes Blain out to the field and shows him how to shoot. First he demonstrates the right way to hold the rifle, how to check it, load it, and then he teaches him how to aim. Jamie lines up a string of cans along the fence for practise, and Ena retreats to the house. Shots crack the afternoon down the centre, the reverberations moving far out and away.

"Does he need to know how to do that?" she asks Jamie as they lie next to one another that night. She would protect Blain from the knowledge of guns if she could.

Jamie weaves his fingers through her hair. "He knows a l-l-l-lot already."

Over the next days, Jamie and Blain take turns keeping watch, surveying from a broad grey stone in the field that is half-buried, its one end high like the prow of a ship. Blain takes his place before daybreak, a surprising, new patience in his limbs, his hand resting easily on the shaft of the gun. He keeps the cattle in the barn until the sun is well up in the sky.

"You don't have to go out until the cattle are there," Ena says. "The dogs won't come without the cows."

He looks away from her, a sly smile playing at his lips. "We'll see what they do."

Two days later, Jamie and Ena wake up to shots ringing out. Jamie is unnerved by the sound and he flails at first, then shouts into the darkness of their room.

"It's Blain," Ena says, pulling at his shoulder.

They are down the stairs and Jamie takes a barn lantern from the woodshed, lighting it as they stumble outside. Billie is clamouring from inside the locked barn and they can see nothing until Blain breaks into the lamp's circle of light. He is shaking, his eyes enormous. "Killed three, Captain."

Ena steps toward him. "How?"

"Put open tins of ham out there, just by the rock. Knew the buggers would come."

A shiver goes through her. None of them speaks, Blain with his hand on his head, the old familiar scratching as though he's trying to get himself to think.

THE DAY AFTER BLAIN KILLS THE DOGS Ena wakes to find that he isn't in his room. His clothes are piled in a heap at the end of his bed, his comb and *The Virginian* on the nightstand. She still has no idea whether or not Blain can read. She frowns down into the tangle of trousers, yesterday's shirt, his worn and battered belt. His imprint is in the harmless mess, hanging in the fusty air.

She wants to search the wardrobe and under the bed, to go through the dresser drawers one by one. Eyeing *The Virginian,* she picks it up, her palm resting on the fraying cover, her head tilted as if expecting the book to speak; what does Blain carry inside his skin, what ties his heart, what loyalties? Except for Owen, he hardly speaks of his family. His chatter, his stories fitfully unspool like tangled skeins of wool—he slips beneath his words and hides, thinking no one can see.

By ten in the morning, he's walking up the lane, chin to chest, arms loose, his feet out-turned. Billie sprints to meet him and together they bounce into the barn. Seeing him, grinning so easily at her, a hard wave of feeling breaks. "What did you think you were doing?" she says, following him.

He tips off his hat and tosses it onto a hook. "Seeing Owen at night, so the old man wouldn't know. You should see how much he grew, Ena! Still nowhere near as tall as me. And I told him he don't have to stay there much longer—he's as eager to go as a flea to a dog. You should of seen how he throwed himself up on my back—"

Ena is bursting with fury now. "Do you know how stupid it is, to go near that place? He could kill you. You *will* stay here, Blain. On this farm."

Blain halts mid-story and stares at her with surprise while from the back of the barn, the bull lets out a bellow, an upward declarative sweep. Blain shifts his weight fitfully from one leg to the other. "I won't get myself killed by the old bugger."

THE FIRST REAL SNOW FALLS two days before Christmas at once filling the fields, making crests and hollows, while emptying them of all colour. There is no trace of the feral dogs and it seems that Blain has forgotten about them.

Ena has made Shrewsbury cakes, Scotch shortbread, and four loaves of bread for Hugh and Sarah. When she'd pulled up in the cutter there was no sign of Hugh but now, as she unloads, she sees him sauntering up from the barn. He's dressed in high boots and a tailored woollen overcoat, a fur hat, and leather gloves.

"Are you on your way to town?" she asks.

He grins. "Land registry. Just picked up another full fifty acres."

Ena nods. She has the basket of bread in her arms, her feet planted on the lane. She can feel the press of ice packed snow through the thin soles of her boots. It is time to pull out her winter clothes—the lined boots, her heavier coat. The cold will be with them for months.

"You've the old cutter out." Hugh is examining the faded cutter that for years belonged to the elder McFarland's. His eyes dance away. "I suppose you're here to see Sarah before she goes to town. She's already got her car loaded with her paints." He touches his nose with his glove, a slight grimace at the corner of his mouth.

They walk together toward the house, Ena willing Hugh to not discuss Sarah's trips to town, her painting, her determined migration away the farm. "More snow on the way," says Hugh seeing her look at the sky. Pronouncing on the weather, he is helpful, friendly. She is suddenly grateful to him for the care he has shown. The two Belgian horses stand amiably together in the barnyard, their butterscotch coats covered in a dusting of snow, a worry of dark clouds spreading over the sky to the west.

Hugh steps in front of her before they reach the side porch. "Ena," he says, "I want to speak about the boy."

With her hand on the wooden railing, Ena stops.

"Someone took a shot at one of my cows. Hit it in the leg. Right out in the yard." Hugh is scrutinizing her, eager for her to speak, to give relief, his one eye swimming in rapid little jerks. "It's got somethin' to do with the Carters."

"Blain wouldn't do something like that."

"Ena, I *know* Carter was at your place, lookin' for his boy. Blain told Clem and Clem told me." Hugh's jaw creeps forward. "I went out to that godawful house again, took Clem with me. I told Jack Carter to stay off our land. Next thing I know, he's got a gun pointed at us. Next night, I heard the shot and found the cow. Not dead, just hurt bad."

He hasn't mentioned Jamie and it was Jamie's land that was trespassed when Jack Carter came looking for Blain. The omission releases a sudden stinging fury. "Did you *tell* Jamie you went out there with Clem?"

Hugh's face tightens. "No. Jamie's not fit to look after somethin' like this. Besides, he doesn't take help easily now. I took matters into my own hands."

She is shaking her head, her eyes stalking him. "It isn't right, you going behind Jamie's back. He won't get stronger—he won't believe he *can*, if you take everything over."

He glares at her. "None of this would'a happened if that damn boy wasn't working on McFarland land. If his corked father wasn't brought into *our* lives. That boy's been skimming from the wages I pay him and not giving them to Carter. Now he's not handing them over at all. And there maybe worse than that. Carter's got it in his mind that you and Jamie are giving the boy extra. That he's taking that money to steel the hooch and sell it again to that goddamn hotel in Wiarton. Boy's got a head for business it seems."

"That man's unreliable. You can't believe him, Hugh."

Hugh shakes his head, his mouth tight in a grimace. "Now *you* gotta do your part, Ena. You gotta step up and take care of this family and tell that boy he's goin' *back* to his. That's the end of it. You do it by the New Year."

Ena doesn't doubt the story about Blain, how he uses her money, the profit he makes from it. Blain is a storyteller, a confabulator. Hugh is right about what Blain dragged with him into their midst, but he didn't do so willingly. She thinks of Blain's scalp after Carter beat him, the skin raked up and torn, Blain broken and waiting for her on her front steps. She studies the snow-dusted horses, the generous McFarland barn, the silver-white fields.

In that moment, she knows she will not tell anyone about the money she's given Blain, not even Jamie. Sudden anguish breaks through: she can't hold on to him. He will slip from her fingers.

"You'll send him back, Ena, or I'll have to do it myself."

27. 1918

THE ARRANGEMENT WITH FREWER, the foundry man, is simple: he will pick Blain up at the bottom of Jamie McFarland's lane at eleven p.m., and drop him at the tenth concession. The next morning, at dawn on New Year's Day, he'll collect him. This particular service costs Blain exactly twelve jars of Carter's best shine.

Blain likes the feel of the truck rumbling through a frozen night, the furious snow, the dark falling away from the headlights like a parting sea. After he scrambles out of the truck, he hurries up the road, his breath quickening as he gets close to Carter's lane.

The old dog died a few months back and although Blain was sorry, mostly for Owen who loved him, he won't miss the barking. His approach must be stealthy in case the old man has a late pick-up arranged, and if he does, Blain will wait behind the shed, crouched down; the shed offers protection from stinging wind and he won't be seen there.

The smoke from the still is like a phantom against the black sky. Blain's eyes reluctantly play over it, the melancholy smoke penetrating him, causing his heart to sink. For as long as Blain can remember, the still has jutted from the banks of the creek, the glinting metal wrong amongst the soft-limbed cedars. The old man built it himself, and its cranky appetites and yields have pinned the family down to these few sour acres far more than the woodlot has, or the house, or any tie of kinship. Mum had said, if they were given the chance to move from here, to shift their puny lives to town, she'd hire herself out, labour in a laundry again.

He squints at the glinting cylinder, the light from the moon hard on its sides and the still glares back. The way Carter tends to it—doleful and fussing, fiddling with the gauge, loosening off then tightening the cap arm, tentatively rapping the metal sides as if to test for a pulse—Mum would have known that he would never abandon it. Carter wakes in the night, fretful and dazed, his long johns pulled haphazardly up to his armpits, a moth-eaten sweater tangled around his neck. Stumbling toward the seizing creek, he hacks at the ice with an axe, frees up the flow of water, feeds the boiler. He's a slave to it.

No light comes from the house, just a remnant of smoke rising from the chimney. Blain goes to the back window where he knows Owen is, and gently taps on the pane. They've done this before, and Owen isn't scared when he sees Blain's face beaming at him from the dark. Owen sits up, eyes like an old owl, and solemnly slips from his bed. He pads over to the window and lifts the sash. Blain has his fingers to his lips and Owen's eyes stay on him, steady, expectant. Opening his rucksack, Blain pulls out Ena's sweet cream biscuits, and a slice of fig cake, which he's wrapped in a scrap of linen.

There is something reverential about Owen, how he holds each biscuit in his palm before setting it carefully on the windowsill. *Don't save 'em, Owen. They won't keep.* Blain is whispering into the whorl of Owen's ear. Grinning, Blain slips off his coat and boots, and together they hop into Owen's narrow bed.

They don't speak in case their voices wake the old man. Owen watches Blain's face for a long while and then he tucks himself into Blain's centre, wrapping himself into Blain like a puppy, and before long he's asleep.

Blain stays with him, the room cold and full with terrible and bright possibility. He imagines what will happen when daylight comes, his task finished; he thinks about his return to Jamie and Ena's place, Billie bounding up the lane. Ena will come out to meet him, her eyes dark with reckoning and then she will turn away, as she always does, her arms curled around her middle, her spine bristling. He'll talk through her silent outrage until she looks him straight in the eye. Her look will pin down his heart. He'll lie to her though, just the same.

"You won't go again, Blain. You'll promise me." He *will* promise, a grin on his face, his fist behind his ear.

His hands travel over Owen's head, the cropped hair soft as a whisper on his palms. The shed and what's in it pull on him. When he rises, he drags the quilt up over Owen's little shoulder, leans down, kisses him on the nose. Something in him feels like it will break in two, like a tree split straight down the middle. What he's going to do he does as much for Owen as he does for himself; what he will take, he will take for them both, so that they can escape together. That's what he tells himself, his stomach queasy, his fingers lingering on Owen's cheek.

What confuses him, makes him freeze where he stands, is whether or not what he does is selfish. The truth is, Blain *wants* nothing more than to go and never come back, with or without his brother, and the desperation he feels stops just shy of ruthlessness. Perhaps he's not as far off the old man as he'd like to think. Blain imagines Carter then, his slight frame shuffling off to the still, the darkness pressing in, his mind utterly taken up with his own needs. Rage climbs up into his chest and throat. He turns back and takes another long look at Owen.

The window resists him and he wrestles up the sash. It's dark, but no matter; he locates the shed by feel, each footstep deliberate, careful as a cat's.

Blain enters the shed blind, his arms outreached, his fingers twitching to find the edges of things, the shapes. When he finds the horizontal of the bench, his hand goes to the waxy canvas and flips it back. Bending low, his fingers recognize the rough sides of the box, and then the lock. From inside his sack, he pulls the short iron crowbar that earlier he'd slipped from the wall of the Captain's shed.

It doesn't take long to pry away the old boards. Blain smiles, thinking of Carter making the discovery of what he's lost, his jaw sagging. Not the moonshine this time, but all of the cash. Everything. He'll come after the money, Blain knows, but by then he and Owen will be long gone. Now that he stands, the full sack seems almost weightless. A strange burden—nothing to do with what he's really after —except for Owen. He wants the money for him.

Outside a crack of eastern light finds the still, the cylinder drum winking back coldly at the breaking day. Blain has to drag out that pallet of jars to the road for the foundry man. He has a lot to do before his ride comes.

T HE NEW YEAR BRINGS ON FURIOUS SNOWS. The wind cuts down Ena and Jamie and Blain as they trudge back and forth from the barn, their footprints disappearing in a dervish of white. Smells vanish from the air, except in the barn where the rich odours of the animals weave into their clothes and hair. In the third week of the year, Jamie's damaged lungs seem to utterly collapse; he swings between sweats and chills, soaking his nightclothes. Later, Ena would think that she couldn't have gotten through without Blain, his willingness to take up the chores, to work without being told what to do.

Doctor Granton makes the trip in from Owen Sound in his cutter. He's an old man and very careful. Pushing his spectacles up to his forehead, he leans in close and listens to Jamie's chest. He asks Jamie about his service in France, where he fought, who was his C.O., and when Jamie talks, he's patient and unperturbed by Jamie's stutter.

"And nightmares," he asks almost casually. "Do you suffer with those since coming home?"

Jamie looks up at the ceiling. "M-m-m-more at f-f-f-first. S-still s-s-sometimes."

Dr. Granton guides Jamie to a sitting position and then taps at his back ribs, loosening an eruption of coughs. With Jamie settled back on the pillow, Dr. Granton perches on a chair beside the bed.

"And during the day, do some things—normal things, or even people—seem strange to you, like they don't feel or seem the way they should?"

"N-n-not so much here."

"Other places, then?"

"P-p-p-pretty m-m-much any other p-place."

Dr. Granton nods reassuringly. "Well, quite a bad time over there, wasn't it. You've done so well, coming back to your farm, running things. Hard work, running a farm. You'll be back at it soon enough. Rest up now. Looks to me like your wife is managing."

Before Dr. Granton leaves, Ena gives him tea. "You would like something to eat, before going back out in that—?"

"No, I'm fine." After a moment, he puts down his cup and studies Ena. "His lungs are quite damaged. And now there's pneumonia."

Opening his bag, he gives Ena a brown bottle. "This will ease the discomfort but it won't make him better."

"What will?"

"Time. Rest. He shouldn't be up and about, and you'll want to keep him out of that weather. But there are other problems, aren't there. The trouble with words, the shaking. We aren't very good at managing all that. More is being done in Britain, but not here, I'm sorry to say." Sliding his fingers beneath his spectacles, he rubs wearily at the corners of the eyes. He closes up his bag and stands. "I really wish I could do more."

Over the next days, Jamie worsens. Ena makes broth, and prepares poultices, carefully applying them to Jamie's drum-tight chest, but he gets little relief. Working quickly, she dries and covers him with blankets, soaks flannel in cold water that she then lays gently across his eyes.

But despite her best efforts, he slips into a rasping passivity. Sitting by him in a chair, timing his breaths, she tells Blain she thinks he might die.

Blain stands next to her, his head on an angle, his eyes on

Jamie. He rubs his head with his knuckles and grimaces. "But it's the gas that did this, you said. That *already* happened. Shouldn't he be healed up by now?"

Ena thinks about the damage on the inside of Jamie—the damage she can't see.

TEN DAYS LATER, SHE LIES QUIETLY next to him and knows that he's better. She listens for the rasps and rattles and hearing very little, a tentative relief creeps in. He has finally been able to sleep. Determined not to wake him, she rises almost silently, knocks on Blain's door anxious to hear the chirp of his reply. "I'll have tea waiting," she whispers.

Despite the care she takes to not wake him, Jamie comes down the stairs, weak but clear-eyed, and he's dressed for the barn. "You can't go out," she says, sliding porridge in front of him. "Your lungs aren't clear enough." His face is white except for deep swirls of grey beneath his eyes.

"I w-w-want to w-w-w-ork." He smiles at her, a real smile, as if he's now fully awake and only just then recognizing her.

Blain has come down, too. In the warmed kitchen, he grins sleepily and rubs at his ears before taking a cup from her, downing it, and then stuffing his feet into his boots. He pauses and waits for Jamie

Ena looks out of the window. Dawn is still a long time off. The roads have been almost impassable since the New Year, only cutters and sleighs managing to get out. The farm exists on an island in an ocean of snow, and in a way, Ena is grateful for the terrible weather, the shortened days. Blain hasn't gone on one of his night-time visits for weeks.

"There won't be d-d-d-d-deliveries again today, B-B-Blain. The roads are too b-b-b-ad."

Blain is thoughtful for a minute, as if he is remembering something, and then he shrugs. "Ready, Captain?"

Jamie nods, and with his eyes he gestures in the direction of the barn.

THE COWS HAVE BEGUN TO LABOUR, and for several nights, they all work to near exhaustion. The cold air tightens Jamie's chest, and a new round of coughing begins. The hours wear on, and Ena, her expression pinched, tells him to go inside and rest. "We'll manage on our own, Jamie," she says. "We did before." There is something of the old light in his face. "Yes. I know. But you'll m-m-manage b-b-b-better with me."

They take turns getting the pails of warm water. Together they shift and position labouring animals, set chains around unborn hooves, tug, pull, encourage. The nights are marked only by labouring animals, a birth, the poignant loss of a calf. It's as if Jamie has never been away, and Blain has always been here, and that she, Ena, has no past, no future. For a time, every part of her is held, supported by the hours she spends with them, working.

Suppertime, all three are together, bleary-eyed, at the table. Blain has his knuckles under his chin, the other hand spearing pickled beets with his fork. His eyes are bloodshot, and he moves like a sleepwalker. Still chatty, he surrenders to an endless string of yawns. Lately, he's taken to asking Jamie questions about his time in France—what it's like to bayonet a man, how does it feel when a Ross rifle jams. Jamie is patient with him, his answers scrubbed of detail.

Blain's face is dreamy and with his mouth full of food, he's finally quiet.

"I'll get up and ch-ch-ch-eck on them t-t-t-t-onight."

Ena shakes her head. "Two of them are very close to labour."

"N-n-not that c-c-close."

"You didn't sleep last night neither, Captain," Blain almost slurs his words.

Pushing himself up from the table, Jamie stretches, graceful still, the movement languid. "I d-d-don't mind. And Billie will k-k-k-keep me company."

He lifts his plate and takes it to the sink, the tremor in his hand causing the fork to slip and clatter to the floor. Looking wryly at it, he turns to Ena; "I'll s-s-s-sleep d-d-d-own h-here, then g-g-g-go out in a f-f-f-ew hours."

She's glad he wants to work, that he feels he can. Reaching her arms around his neck, her lips brush the stubble on his cheek. He clasps her firmly around her waist and draws her closer. "I'll c-c-c-come up later, once I've checked."

"If they start to labour, you will wake me if you need me, Jamie. Don't wait."

They watch Blain go upstairs, his feet dragging as he lifts them. He's so tired, he will fall into bed fully clothed. Jamie sits in the chair in the parlour, a cup of tea beside him, the newspaper on his lap. He barely ate dinner. His face is highly coloured and there is a ghostly wheeze in his lungs.

"They sound bad again, your lungs."

He shrugs. "S-s-s-same as e-v-v-v-ver."

She kisses him on the lips, her hand soft at his neck. "We'll get up early in the morning. We'll go out together."

He takes her hand loosely in his own.

Once she climbs into bed, almost immediately she's asleep, a strange hopefulness engulfing her, her dreams slipping away beneath a becalmed and bone-deep weariness.

ENA WAKES TO A SQUARE OF BLACK SKY in the window. Jamie isn't beside her. She rises, pulls on her stockings, her thick woollen skirt, her undervest, and sweater. Blain's door is open, the bed untidy. An empty room. Downstairs, everything is in darkness and no fire has been lit in the stove. There is no sign of Jamie or Blain.

"Blain?" She calls. "Jamie?" They must already be in the barn, the cows in labour. She worries; perhaps they've been out there all night.

Jamie's barn coat hangs just where he left it earlier. She brushes the wool of the coat with her fingertips, and new concern takes hold. Sliding her feet into her boots, she throws on her own coat and steps out into the frigid cold.

Before New Year's, a thaw had melted the yard into a lumpy, heaving mess, and then the temperature plummeted and the yard was frozen again. Beneath the compacted snow, the icy ruts and peaks make it treacherous and several times, as she hurries toward the barn, her feet almost go out from under her. She sees right away that the barn lanterns have not been lit. When she opens the door, Billie is frenzied, jumping wildly, whining, yipping.

"Billie, come," she commands, lighting a lantern. The dog follows her, nose to ground, eyes anxiously rolling. Lighting two more as she moves past the stalls, she calls Jamie's name again and again, but he doesn't answer.

Billie is sniffing, searching, her head low and her tail a streak, solemn as a flag. She stops at the bullpen and growls. When Ena goes to the pen, she sees the bull looking back, its hard eyes ringed with red. It stands belligerently, its breath coming out in snorts. She wonders if the bull will charge, as it does sometimes when the cows parade past on their way to the pasture, but its lead has been tied to the rail to steady it.

The wind is high. Ena can hear the large spruce trees beside the lane as they sway. And Blain. Where is Blain? She expected to find him here, with Jamie, but they must be together in the yard. The gun, usually kept in the woodshed, is set against the wall of an empty stall and she wonders if the wild dogs have come back.

Taking one of the lanterns, she steps outside. Billie is with her, circling and pawing at her skirt. When the dog breaks from her, Ena shouts, her voice harsh. The dog returns, slunk down, Ena's fingers sinking like claws into her scruff. "Stay, Billie. Stay with me."

The indentations of boots and hooves make a frozen mash. She raises the lantern and her eyes search the yard but it is empty. She looks toward the fields, which lie unbroken and dark except for a silvery path of light cast by the moon. The emptiness of them is crushing. Billie looks up at her, straining, quivering, her head keenly tilted, her eyes wide. "Find Jamie, Billie," Ena urges, pointing to the fields, gesturing madly. "Go."

In a matter of seconds, Billie is frantically barking. Climbing the fence, the lantern still in her hand, Ena sees both Billie's tracks, and footprints, not straight, but staggered, a hollow where it looks like someone stumbled before going on. Ahead of her, just outside the shaft of moonlight, Billie is a smudge in the darkness, dancing and pacing.

Closer, Ena sees the shape of him, impossibly still in the snow. She runs. Jamie is on his back. His eyes are open, frost clinging to his eyelids and around his mouth. His lips blue-grey. Ena can see right away that he is dead.

SHE IS UNABLE TO LEAVE HIM AT FIRST. To the east the sky breaks, the new light washing the fields in blue. Ena stiffly makes her way back to the yard, and into the barn where Ted whinnies in his stall, his head making giant O's in the air. She slips a halter around his neck and leads him to the barn door, but he stands, mulish and unmoving. Thwacking him on the right flank she shouts, "get." He trots a few steps and then gazes back, his head tossing, his doleful eyes on her. Looking at Ted, she thinks, *I'm sorry for being too late. I'm so very sorry,* and then she leads him to the cutter, her face streaming with tears. She goes back for the harness, carrying it over her shoulders. It's heavy, her knees close to buckling under the weight.

It takes a long time to drive to the McFarland's, the road only newly opened, boulders of snow strewn across it, patches of ice that make the cutter careen from one side to the other. When she pulls in, lights burn in the kitchen and in the barn. A figure comes from the bottom of the yard, stops; an arm waves, hesitates and then falls. It's Hugh, and he's coming toward her now, alarm in his movement, his gait strange and awkward, a giant on strings as he navigates the ice.

THEY ARE STANDING IN HER BARN, the motorized ambulance

having arrived and taken Jamie to town. Hugh is pacing, and Clem is there, quietly milking, cleaning the stalls, the slush of the milk against the sides of the pail a small comfort.

"He froze to death, Ena." Hugh's face is stretched and hard. "After living through that hell over there, he *froze.*"

She stares at him. "Yes."

"He was bruised-up bad from falling, the doctor said. He was without a coat. Jesus. What was he doing out there, without a coat?"

"He's been so ill," she says uncertainly. "We thought he was better. Happier, with the work." She searches the floor with her eyes. "I don't know why he would be there, in the field. I can't understand it."

Hugh takes his hands to his head and then he drops them, spearing Ena with a look.

"Where's the damn boy?" Except for his heaving shoulders, the frantic eye, Hugh is expressionless.

"He's gone." Her voice is hoarse, her throat unbearably dry. Her words have grown claws and they tear unmercifully at her.

"*Gone,*" he says, as if to make sense of Blain, the fact of his absence. He regards her with a kind of disbelief. "Jus' *happens* that he's not here, and my brother is dead in the field."

Ena meets his gaze. "Jamie might have wandered..."

"And the boy, Ena. Did he *wander* too?"

Her eyes widen.

"*Answer* me, Ena."

But she has no answer for him.

"Ena, that boy and Carter, they got somethin' to do with this. I *told* you to send that boy back. I *told* you weeks ago." Something brutal comes into his face, as if instead of her, Blain stands in front of him, or even Jack Carter. Without warning he hurls a shovel at a wall, nearly hitting Billie who yelps and scrambles away. He faces her, seething, taking her silence as denial, shaking his head at her in disgust.

The sound of the shovel has stirred Clem. He stands from his milking stool and slips over to where they are standing. Putting a thin hand on Ena's arm, he says softly, "All done, now. I'll take care of the cows again this evening. I'll stay with them if I think one is close to labour. If not, I'll be back in the morning, early and before you're awake. I'll feed Billie tonight. Go inside, rest. You'll need it.''

STANDING SO STILL ON THE COLD BARN FLOOR has made Ena's feet numb. She thinks about moving but doesn't. After Hugh and Clem left, she stayed in the barn, not wanting to face the emptiness of the house. As long as she remains, surrounded by the plain, broad-planked walls, she will know what to do. She imagines for a moment that she will live here surrounded by reassuring sounds and smells, and the specter of Jamie, his long back leaning against a soft, spotted flank, his hands carefully feeling the tendons in a delicate leg. The longing to stay is very strong.

Ena's hand finds Billie and the tips of her coarse hair, oily like the bristles of a pastry brush, her fingers creeping to the plane of Billie's skull where the hair is silkier. Her heart drops, thinking of Billie without Jamie.

There are the chores, the nightly vigil around the labouring animals, the cleaning of stalls, the feed. At first, there will be many offers of help.

Earlier, when the road finally opened and the ambulance came, she had gone into the house to make tea for the driver, and for Hugh and Clem. Standing at the kitchen window, she had poured herself a cup but hadn't drunk it. Over the next days, women would come, she thought wearily. They would bring oxtail soup and tea biscuits, plates of sliced ham, jellied chicken, fresh rolls, pickled eggs. Enough food for an army.

Now, the thought of the bustling women in her house, in her kitchen, makes her suddenly ill. She will have to light the stove again, change her clothes, fill the kettles. Drawing her coat more tightly around herself, she walks out into the yard. A weak sun bleeds across grey clouds while at the same time, a fine snow falls. She closes and opens her eyes to clear her sight. A surge of weariness rises up and she leans against a fencepost, at once shattered and grateful for the post's support. The temperature is frigid, and gusts of wind whip up the snow, flinging it across the yard in wild streaks. *Everything is at sixes and sevens.* Where has she heard that phrase before? Michael used to say it, when there was a jumble in the deliveries. He would peer into the crate and shake his head. *We'll put it right soon enough.* Somewhere close by, high up in the Spruce trees, a crow is calling. Its voice is hard, distant. Water streams from her eyes and Ena feels that she is turning to ice.

She's still in the yard when Sarah pulls in. Not losing a minute, Sarah takes a blanket from the back of the car, wraps Ena in it, and then rocks her in her arms. The sensation of a woman's tenderness feels foreign, unsafe. When had Ellen ever held her, she wonders? There must have been a time....

"Such sadness, Ena," Sarah says after a moment. "It's all right to let it show."

It is then that Ena feels her legs begin to fail.

"Come, let's get to the car. You'll come home with me, Ena. You probably haven't eaten anything, have you? You look like you're going to drop where you stand."

They sit in the unmoving car, silent at first and staring out at the angry snow. The sun is still fighting with the cloud.

"I thought Hugh would bring you back with him. I can't understand why he didn't."

Ena is having difficulty understanding Sarah's words. "He's furious with me—"

"Well, he can't work out what happened. None of us can. Anyway, he told me to come for you. Everything's all right here, Ena. Everything is looked after." Sarah holds Ena's hand, her strong gloved fingers insistently exerting pressure. "Clem's coming later tonight, and Clem and Hugh will be here first thing tomorrow. They don't want you anywhere near the barn. Hugh told me that quite clearly."

"I need to get things sorted here. And there will be people coming to the house. I'll have to give them something. Tea at least."

Sarah's eyebrows fly up and her head lurches forward in surprise. "We'll have them to our place, Ena. They won't expect you to be here."

Pulling her hand away Ena loses herself in the swirling snow. "Hugh believes I could have stopped this."

A storm of confusion passes over Sarah's features. "Because of Blain? I know what Hugh thinks. Look, even if he was mixed up in this, *you* didn't do anything. Hugh's upset. He's looking for someone to blame. He'll get past whatever it is."

"I'm going to stay."

"Ena! You *can't* manage all of this on your own."

"I can. And if Blain comes back, I should be here."

Sarah shakes her head, aghast, her eyes hard and staring. "He's not coming back. And if he does, Hugh will likely have him horsewhipped for what he's done."

Nothing around Ena is recognizable. The window of the car is opaque, the snow gathering and clinging to the glass. She opens the car door.

"I'll stay."

L ATER, ENA WILL REMEMBER only pieces of Jamie's funeral, single images that are vivid and lonely.

Sarah had been both alarmed and aggrieved as she eyed Ena in her dress at the church service. "You look like a child in that," she'd whispered. The dress, a dull black crepe that sagged at Ena's bust and hips, was a gift from Harold Mc-Fadden's daughter-in-law, a widow. "We would have got you something better." When Ena looked down at the spread of inky material, she saw that the dress had taken her over, that she had slipped whole, as if devoured, inside of it.

"Come back with me after this is over." Sarah's face was close, huge, eclipsing the minister, the row of somber-clothed relatives, the urns of white lilies.

To leave the farm now, even for a short time, would be to abandon Jamie, the animals, and Blain if he were to come back. "No." Ena's eyes closed against her. "Don't ask me that again."

There had been a short drive to the cemetery, the snow high beside the road. The cemetery men had made a straight clean path to the gravesite with their shovels. Ena later learned that the ground had been so frozen it took three men with pick axes to work its surface before a hole could be dug.

Jamie's casket was in a plot next to his father and mother. Hugh stood wide-footed and ponderous at the end of the rect-angular hole, his head bent, his hat in his hand, an awkward sorrow in the curl of his shoulders. Ena, a few feet away, looked down, seeing only the long oak box, a dense unyielding brown.

TO EARN MORE OF AN INCOME, each day Ena goes to work at the home of Rebecca Sword, a neighbour woman from the next concession. They were in school together and Ena still thinks of Rebecca as she was then, broad faced, with sandy colouring and thick limbs. She moves with a bovine slowness that seems both exasperating and kind.

Today, Rebecca is in her room as she is most afternoons, the blinds drawn down, the dark green curtains pulled tight. A brown glass bottle sits by her bed, a spoon resting next to it. Ena puts her head around the door, a cup and saucer in her hand. "Tea?" she asks.

Rebecca rolls her head toward her, her face white and puffy. "Thank you."

"Are you all right?"

"Just another headache."

Setting down the tea on the nightstand, Ena straightens. "I'll iron the sheets today if you like." Rebecca isn't used to having a hired woman in the house, but she has been so unwell. A friend in her congregation suggested that Ena McFarland might be a help to her, at least for a bit until Rebecca has regained some of her old strength.

"You could, Ena. I don't mind."

"I will then." Ena knows that Rebecca sees employing Ena as charity. She only endures Ena's presence.

"Is there anything more I can do?"

"Kenny will be waking soon," she says, swinging her legs heavily to the side of the bed. Last year the Swords' first child, Lucy, died from a sudden fever. Kenny remains, a boy of about three who now naps in his cot.

"I can warm some milk for him," says Ena, "and I made a checkerboard cake this morning with dates and raisins. There's coconut and almonds in the light part." Ena had bought the coconut and dates at the McFadden's Dry Goods, thinking of ingredients a child might like. "Does he know what a checkers game is? Maybe he'll like the way the cake will look on his plate?"

"I'll put it out for him. Not too much. The dates might make him sick." Rebecca prefers to care for the boy herself, leaving the meals and the cleaning to Ena. The house was buried in dust the first day Ena came, the laundry in mounds by the woodshed door. The kitchen was at once cluttered and desolate, with empty jars on the worktop, frying pans (one thick with grease), nesting on the back of the stove.

Rebecca walks wearily past Ena and goes to the child's room to wake him. No words are spoken. In a moment, she emerges with the child who rides slumped on her hip. Grave, straight-haired, Kenny regards Ena with the heavy, slow gaze of his mother. Knowing she should, Ena tries to muster a smile.

"Jo might want some tea, Ena." Rebecca puts the child down.

Joseph Sword, or "Jo," is older than Rebecca, a wiry man and bent, his hair a rough shock of grey. Besides farming, Jo sells and fixes machinery. The large shed beside the house is filled with threshers and bale presses and ploughs. He spends hours alone with the machines, only coming inside briefly for meals. Now, when Ena brings out a tray of tea and cinnamon rolls to him, he barely looks at her. "That's fine then," he mutters into his workbench. "Just leave it."

The Swords' life is a twilight world, and like them, Ena is fading, her senses dulled, a steady deliberateness engulfing her as if she is sleepwalking. Every so often, she is swept up in a surge of loneliness so vast she thinks she will be lost inside of it.

Only the piercing sound of Kenny's sobbing breaks down the quiet. He doesn't always cry, but once a week, when Rebecca persists in putting him in the tub, he shrieks uncontrollably. With her hands over her ears, Ena stays on the front porch. There is a pane of dulled glass behind her eyes that the boy's terror threatens to shatter.

EXCEPT FOR THE FUNERAL, Ena has caught a glimpse of Hugh only once; he came with Clem, very early on the day after she found Jamie's body in the frozen field. The two men had worked quietly in the barn, Hugh leaving before dawn in his truck.

The silence of her own house settles over her. Each morning, she wakes before the light, but before she can get to the cows, Clem is there, the lanterns lit, the milk already swishing into the pail. She joins him, handing him a steaming bowl of chocolate, a slice of buttered bread with jam.

While she milks, her thoughts wheel toward the livestock, the new calves, the bull that should soon be put in with the cows to breed. In the spring, she will graze the herd but perhaps not plant crops. Ploughing, planting, harvesting, and the labour it requires—she would have to give over too much of the farm's operation to Hugh. No, the livestock will be easier.

The barn is where she is herself again, if only briefly. "What happened to Blain?" She asks Clem one morning. He'd been cleaning the stalls; Clem is as patient as Jamie was in the barn, and unfailingly thorough.

He seems shy, his face drawn down, his eyes on his boots. "Don't think he'll be back. Carter's gone too. The both of 'em." He spears a fresh bale of hay with his pitchfork, shifting it closer, cutting the binding twine with his knife. He doesn't look at her but instead studies the length of severed twine. "Maybe they took off together. That moonshine contraption of his ain't been touched in weeks. Someone broke into the shed and helped themselves to whatever he had laid up. I locked the place best I could. Little one showed up at our door, just after Blain left. Makes the wife awful glad to have him there."

"Someone must have dropped Owen off, Clem. He's too little to get there on his own."

Clem's blue eyes focus on a bird's nest, high up in the rafters, the nest hollow as an empty bowl. "Didn't see. Showed up at our door with a rucksack full with bills." He shakes his head in solemn disbelief.

"What will you do?"

When Clem moves to take up the pitchfork again, his knee creaks and he slaps it, as if to coax it back toward youth. "We talked to the police about Owen. They'll look for Carter but everyone figures the boy's best with us anyway."

One of the loft windows has swung open and she glimpses the peak of her house, a pale and clouded sky surrounding it. "You think Jack Carter had something to do with what happened to Jamie, Clem?"

Clem's eyes follow hers and a tension comes into his face. "Maybe. Or maybe it's like what the doctor said. Jamie was sick and wandered. Cold got to him." He sighs. "And as for Blain. Man named Fourtier is sayin' the boy was stealing from you, Ena. That he was stealin' from Jack as well. If he shows up, there could be charges against him. Best he stays away."

"He never stole a thing from me," she says firmly.

Clem is looking at her, the blue eyes frank and pleading. "Anyway, we got to let him go."

ALONE IN THE HOUSE, Ena goes to Blain's room and sits on his bed. She gazes out of the window and from the dark landscape, rising like a moon, Blain's face shines back. She can't believe he is with Carter. The money turned up with Clem, just where Blain would have wanted it, where it could do the most good for Owen. But beyond imagining Blain delivering Owen and the money to Clem's door, ruffling Owen's hair, producing a final story, promising his little brother he'd return, Ena sees nothing. In her mind, he has stepped off the edge of the world.

30. APRIL 1918

IT'S EARLY ON A SATURDAY in spring when Ena sees Sarah again. She stands in the doorway of the kitchen wearing a lavender-coloured hat, an appliquéd violet on the rim. Despite the cool air, she wears a short summer frock and high heels, her hair cut short to her chin.

Ena breaks into a smile. A few moments before, she had been sorting Jamie's clothes; she will drop them at the Woman's Auxiliary later when she goes in to Owen Sound to do the marketing. Now, for a moment, seeing Sarah awakens a keen sense of colour. The last time they had seen one another was the funeral and Ena had been brittle. She's sorry for that, but she had been in shock then, afraid—a harassed creature burrowing deep in its hole.

"I thought I better give you time before I came," Sarah says.

Sarah hasn't given up on her and Ena now feels an unexpected surge of gratitude. "Clem says you've been getting along fine, but of course you would," Sarah goes on.

Ena nods, her eyes catching on Sarah's hands, so familiar—a carnival of paint splotches, the nails ragged. Fascinated, she reaches out to touch them. "You've been busy." Craig's exhibition. Sarah has been working, finishing her pieces. Ena has almost forgotten. She wonders if Sarah means to go to Chicago with Craig in the fall, to be there when the exhibition opens.

Sarah surrounds Ena in a hug and then steps back, puzzled.

"You look different, but maybe it's just those terrible clothes."

Although the black crepe has gone, Ena still wears dark fabric with a small print. The dress is long, almost to her ankles, and she has altered the sleeves to three-quarters so she can easily work with the pastry. Today, she wears one of her three grey aprons, pulled tight at the waist, newly laundered and pressed. And she does look older, particularly next to Sarah whose hair and skin are lustrous. Ena's features have always been angular, but since Jamie's return, her face has sharpened, storm-coloured crescents under her eyes.

"You're different too. You've cut your hair," she says to Sarah now.

Sarah takes off her hat and shakes her head. Auburn curls spring joyously, profusely to frame her face. "I got tired of it long. Hugh thinks I'm trying to look like I'm from somewhere else."

Ena thinks it might be true. Sarah could be wearing a costume. There is something child-like in Sarah, a need for notice.

"I thought maybe you were dressing for Chicago now. For Craig Murray, the paintings."

Sarah looks away. "Not really. I just need a change."

"But you're still doing the exhibition...?"

"Of course." Sarah turns and looks around the kitchen, her long tapered fingers straying to touch the flour-dusted worktop. "How long are you going to be working for those people, Ena?"

Ena presses her lips together. "The Swords?" Ena shrugs. "I need the income. And I'm still baking for the churches and the inn."

"And Jamie's pension?" Sarah throws Ena a penetrating look. "You should get something."

"Jamie came back from the war—there *isn't* a widow's pension for men who come home."

"The gas—his chest, Ena. He couldn't breathe properly after."

"He got something from the army for his lungs but not much—a gratuity, I guess. His injuries weren't thought to be bad enough for more." Ena shrugged. "Anyway, he always said other lads had much worse happen to them."

A wince seeps into the muscles around Sarah's eyes making tiny crevices. Her hands travel to her head, roughly catching hold of her curls as if to flatten them. Her face, long-boned, almost equine, looks older, the lines more vivid despite the jaunty frock. It suddenly strikes Ena that the clothes Sarah wears, the heels, the frivolity of her hair, belies the rawness in her.

"I have this place at least," Ena goes on evenly. "I can still make something of it. I'll have a lot to do over the next few months."

There is a long moment of quiet, Sarah's fingers unmoving and buried in her hair, her face fixed on Ena.

"You *can* stay here, Ena. For as long as you like. Hugh won't mind. But I don't think he means for you to farm it."

Ena had been pouring water into the teapot and she puts the kettle down, the pot half filled, her eyes boring into Sarah's. "Why would he mind if I did? Why would he care? It was Jamie's place, after all. Ours together." Even as she says it, doubt takes shape.

Sarah looks back her, startled and concerned. "Jamie worked it. And you. But it was Ross McFarland's farm, and when Ross died, the title went to Hugh, not Jamie." Her words balloon grotesquely. Ena peers at the kettle, trying to locate what she should do next, what she should say.

"It doesn't matter, Ena," Sarah goes on, "it's all McFarland land anyway." She is watching, her eyes pursuing every corner of Ena, trying to bring her toward understanding. "Hugh means to take care of you now." She sighs heavily, frustration creeping in. "I thought you knew...."

Ena frantically sorts through her memories of the first day she and Jamie had gone to see Ross's place, Jamie's eyes so translucent. *"We could make something of the place, Ena. You and me."*

"Did Hugh not give it over to Jamie? Before we married?"

Her breath is tight in her chest and her words seem to scrape the air. "Wouldn't there be papers?"

"Transferred, you mean. With a deed? No, I don't think so. Why would Hugh and Jamie bother? It was a deal. A deal between brothers. Jamie would farm Ross's place, live there, pay the expenses, and take the profits. It would make no difference who had the title because the McFarland's would never sell any of their land anyway. You *must* see it, Ena."

Ena is struck dumb. In her mind, the farm is shrinking, toy-sized, and receding to the furthest horizon. It teeters there, threatening to drop below the hard line of her imagination.

"It *doesn't* matter," Sarah persists. "Hugh said he was going to look after things if anything happened to Jamie. He *promised* Jamie that. He'll take the place over and you won't have to work so hard. You can come and live with us. Help around the place. It's how things are done in farming families, Ena—"

Sarah is restless, impatient, Ena's small kitchen closing in, her eyes now on the car that is parked in the lane. Her mind has travelled to her paintings, to Craig Murray, to the world she has beyond.

"You've told me now. You've set me straight." Ena's hand reaches for the wooden spoon.

"It's not why I came," says Sarah, openly cross with her now. "I *miss* you, Ena."

Ena has her back turned. Behind her eyelids, the world is red-black, scorched. A world of burnt offerings, she thinks.

31.

ALTHOUGH BLAIN IS FAR FROM HOME, his mind pulls him back. The nights are alive with vivid images, memories unravelling, and although some are terrible, he feels bound to them: Mum, her arms reaching as she floats on black water; Owen, standing on the green bank of the stream, his tiny hands fanned open in front of him, his head bent over something glittering and beautiful. The dull flat eye of Jamie McFarland's bull.

And the night he left. It visits him too. From a vantage point behind one of the old spruce trees, he'd watched Ena and Billie moving around the yard. He believed that Ena could see everything, like Owen, that she could sniff out every scrap of a lie. He had let Ena down, let the Captain down. His stomach lurched and he bent over, retching, staring dumbly at his boots. He would have to be well away before the morning broke.

The old man's truck was where he knew it would be—left at the road, out of sight from the house. Blain was shaking, not with cold, but with some irrepressible rattle in his bones. He didn't know how to drive but he had no other way to get to Owen.

It took some doing to make the engine turn over. Eventually after wheezing and sputtering, it started, but when he slipped it into gear, easing the clutch, the truck wouldn't move.

He got out and inspected the wheels, clearing away snow with his boot. Ice had formed a wedge in one of the wheel wells and he kicked furiously at it, a strangled sound coming from him until suddenly, surprisingly, the ice broke clean away.

He ought to have left the farm—and Grey County—weeks before, despite the snow, the impassible roads. He had enough money that if he'd made it to town, either on foot or getting a ride on a cutter, he'd have paid his way out from there. But Jamie had been sick; Ena thought he was dying, her face buttoned down against the loss, against what they both thought was coming. She wouldn't ask, but Blain could see she needed him. Besides, he thought that Carter wouldn't bother pursuing him, not in the bad weather—lazy bugger. Blain had been wrong about that.

From inside of the barn, the bull bellowed, its voice rising and breaking and then halting. The silence that came after was what made Blain hesitate, his hand on the door of the truck. He had secured the bull. Tied him to the pen, the bull's eyes rolling, his head tossing. There was nothing to go back for, nothing he could do. He slipped in behind the wheel.

When he found the headlights, it was as if they bored straight out of his own head. His feet scrabbled blindly until they found the clutch, the break, the accelerator; he'd depressed the clutch a few times and then put the truck into reverse, just managing to turn it. He'd watched Hugh McFarland drive many times, and the foundry man as well. Still, it took him several tries to not stall the truck. When he ground the gears, he was afraid someone would hear him, but the wind was so high and Billie was barking.

The headlights drilled into an empty, windswept road. So many daydreams he'd had about escape —the stories he'd told himself about the places he'd go. Now, all he saw was the next few feet of a narrow, glinting road; past that, no cowboys galloping into sunsets, no campfires under the light of a harvest moon. But somewhere, waiting for him in the dark, was Owen.

This is what he told himself: Ena would help the Captain now. And it was all right to leave Ena because Ena would

manage. Ena *always* managed. Not a lie, exactly, but a story
and inside of it a measure of truth. (Although, even then, he
had felt Ena's stoicism, the pain in it, different from Mum's,
but suffering all the same. No story was big enough or bright
enough to overshadow it.)

The truck jerked and bolted its way down the ice-covered
roads, jamming hard into ruts, the steering wheel pulling to the
left. *A junker* was what the old man called it. Good enough for
him to haul around the wood and the moonshine. Good enough
for him. The old man never thought he deserved better and he
believed that they—Blain, Owen, Mum—didn't deserve better
either. It occurred to Blain, in that moment, sitting in the old
man's truck, that something had hollowed his father, scraped
him clean like the inside of a pumpkin, nothing left, not even
evil. A life could do that to a person, but it didn't have to.

He'd thought of Mum. Smile like sun coming through a
tangle of bush, living a strangled life in that house, talking
about town, real work—streets with people, a park for walking, horses and buggies and carts and cars. It didn't have to be
Owen Sound. She would have been happy in a bigger place.
The stories she told them, Blain thought. He'd gripped the
wheel until his fingers ached.

The land was cleared. Just like the old man to keep it ploughed
out. Not good for business to have it snowed over. The headlights found the still—gleaming and yellow like an eye looking
back. Blain swallowed seeing it and then he thought about the
crates of moonshine ready for the next day's delivery. He'd
take any left in the shed and use them for barter. Something
good to come out of the damn still after all.

When he got out, he left the truck running, thinking it would
be nicer for Owen that way, warm and cheerful. He didn't
knock on Owen's window like he usually did. Instead, he went
first to the shed and loaded the crates one by one. And then,
bold as brass, he walked through the front door of the house
and lit a lamp. Owen's room, like the rest of the house, was

stone cold, the stove having gone out hours before. Owen was sitting straight up, his face on the door as if he'd been waiting for Blain. He held out his arms and when Blain lifted him, he gripped Blain around the waist with his knees and dropped his head onto his shoulder. He didn't ask where they were going.

Blain used one hand to tug the woollen blanket from Owen's bed and wrapped him, not pausing to take any of the boy's clothes. When he put Owen down on the seat in the truck, Owen settled himself onto the blanket like a cat, getting onto his knees and peering keenly through the windshield.

"Feels like we are leavin' her here," he said.

"She's *not* here." Blain's words were unusually stern but his gaze inched over the dark silhouette of cedar, suddenly reluctant to pull away. "We have to go, Owen."

Owen put a finger to his mouth as if begging for silence. His eyes were grave and huge, his face as pale as the winter moon over their heads.

"There's a beetle in the fridge, Blain. From the swamp. It's pretty—greens and blacks. Go get it for me. I want to take it."

As they drove to Clem's, the beetle between them in a jar, Blain told Owen the story of the bank robber brothers, the unending skies of the west, jagged mountains that stayed a frosty white into July.

Owen was lying down again, his body hidden in the blanket, his head in Blain's lap and just the glistening mouse-rust hair showing. Blain thought maybe he'd fallen asleep and it would be easier to leave him that way.

32.

ONE AFTERNOON, COMING HOME from the Swords, Ena sees Clem walking up the lane from the barn, his coverall muddied, his collar pulled high against the brash spring wind. She drives Ted close to the house and stops. Clem walks directly over, a slight bow to his legs, his back bent as if his hat is too heavy on his head.

As she steps down from the wagon, he rummages in his pockets, slapping at his shirt and then his trousers, finally digging out two cubes of sugar which he places, open-palmed at Ted's muzzle. "Glad you got Ted here," he says absently.

He has a kind face, with deep lines that go from his eyes, to the corners of his mouth. "Ted's a comfort," she says, smiling.

He nods and glances toward the barn, his expression unreadable. "What about the barn, Mrs. McFarland? Has Mr. McFarland said what will happen to it?"

Ena has to think about the question. The barn is in use, full of livestock, hay still piled high, equipment in the shed at the back. She has stored the cutter there. "Same as now. Why would we change things?"

A wince comes into the edges of his eyes. "Ain't no livestock left, Mrs. McFarland. I guess I thought you knew. Mr. McFarland and me come over with the large livestock wagon earlier. We loaded everything up and took it all back to the McFarland place."

Ena waits, her eyes on Clem. The animals were hers. She had

delivered them, nursed them, milked them. "Hugh told you to take the animals—all of them—to his place, Clem. That's what you're saying to me."

Clem kicks at a stone in the lane and says nothing. He has worked for Hugh and Hugh's father before him, loyalty like sap running in his veins.

"The summer is almost here," she goes on. "The cattle can stay on the land without much nuisance. Why not just leave them?"

"It's a lot of bother, him or me comin' twice a day to milk. Easier if they are over at the other place."

She hadn't asked for their help. It had been forced on her. "I could have done the milking on my own or hired someone to help me." Suddenly, she realizes that Billie isn't there. She always comes out from the barn to greet her. "Where's my dog, Clem? Where's Billie?"

Clem shrugs. "Mr. McFarland says she's a workin' dog and should be with the herd."

Ena stares, all her words dried up, her throat dust-dry.

"Anything you want me to do in the barn for you, Mrs. McFarland?" Clem asks softly. "He said I should drop by a couple of times a week, ask you what was needed. He still has the ploughing to do here. He intends to look after the place. "

She looks at the fields she and Jamie had given-over for pasture. There would be no grazing, no cattle on the top of the ridge. Everything is as Sarah said. Everything is decided.

"He has plans for the place, Clem. I see it."

Clem puts his hands in his pockets, hunches his shoulders, rocks a little on his heels. He nods toward the shell of the house. "Just to keep farmin' it. He's doing what he thinks he should. Takin' care of the place now that Jamie can't." His eyes are watery beneath his cap. "He was awful fond of Jamie. Terrible blow for him to lose him like he did."

Ena straightens and takes Ted's nose in her hand. His breath meets her palm in warm, moist puffs. She strokes the whorl of hair beneath his forelock. A star of white splashes over his eyes and there is a smattering more of white on his front hocks. The rest of Ted is the colour of brown shoe polish. She takes up his reins and leads him toward the empty barn. "And if I hadn't taken Ted with me, Clem? Would he have ended up the same as Billie? "

Clem's face colours and he grimaces at his boots.

"Tell me if Blain comes back, Clem. I want to know."

33. MAY 1918

MAY, BUT THE COLD LINGERS. Every so often, while walking to McFadden's Dry Goods, or on some other errand in town, Ena thinks she catches sight of Jamie in a stranger. It is the preoccupied expression that seems so familiar, the mindless stoop, the shambling stride, an expression of utter disconnection. Jamie, when he first came home.

The livestock would have made her losses less vicious. Without the daily tasks of milking the cows, churning the cream to make butter, Ena cannot locate herself; she retreats to what she was before she met Jamie, moving through other people's rooms at the Swords, breathing in their lives. Although she bakes and works, her heart has contracted. There is no room for joy, and she no longer tastes or feels or smells, not with any real conviction. She stands at the worktop, her hands sifting mechanically through the floury mix, going through the steps by rote.

REBECCA SWORD IS WASHING KENNY'S HAIR. He lies in the tub, his eyes squeezed shut, his mouth stretched into a howl. *No, no, no,* he cries, the soapy water streaming across his face. His small hands clutch the sides of the tub, his legs straight and rigid. His skin is raised in goosebumps. On her way to gather the sheets from the line, Ena pauses in the doorway of the kitchen, not sure whether to enter or to turn. "Should I heat the kettle for more water, Rebecca?" she asks.

Rebecca Sword's wide, soft back is to her. She is bent over the disconsolate boy, one hand holding his shoulder, the other holding a long-handled ladle. "No," she says. "It won't help." Without taking her hand from Kenny, she turns to Ena, her eyes wide and sad, a single tear inching snail-like toward her chin. "I bathed Lucy the night before her fever. Do you think Kenny remembers that? Do you think he could?" Rebecca's gaze is unwavering but there is something underneath—a spark of panic.

Ena sees the demand for reassurance. Rebecca wants to believe that no harm's been done, that she keeps Kenny protected from the sudden sweep of loss. But Ena can sense that the boy has a thorn deep inside, a memory or perhaps more the impression of pain in his mother. He won't have words for it....

"I couldn't say," says Ena.

Rebecca nods and turns to Kenny who is there, at the centre of her sorrow, his legs, his arms, his feet, his hands, not belonging to him, but to her idea of him: *my child*. The ritual of the child's bath seems suddenly morbid, awful in its compunction, its hopeless repetition.

She turns away, a rising tide of energy, a kind of sickness coming up. She puts down the basket and goes to the back of the house, vomiting into the mildewed and curling leaves of the lilac bush. When she's done, she wipes her mouth on her sleeve and goes inside.

The next afternoon, Rebecca Sword asks Ena to sit with her in the front parlour. Rebecca has prepared tea for them. Four of Ena's drop tea cakes are arranged on an etched glass serving plate.

Rebecca is unnaturally still, as if waiting for inspiration. "Your work here is fine, Ena," she says finally. Putting her cup down, Ena studies the floor, which she has recently cleaned and waxed. The parlour is dim, sepulchral, Rebecca having pulled the drapes against the afternoon sun. "I spoke to Hugh McFarland. He told me you have a place there with them, that you could cook for them and the hired hands."

"I want to stay where I am."

"At the farm?"

"Yes."

"You're a widow, Ena."

"I manage," she says.

"If you live with the McFarland's, you won't have to work."

"I'm grateful for the income."

Rebecca Sword is the picture of resignation. "The McFarland's are your husband's family. They should take care of you." She slowly shakes her head as though she sees something terrible, unstoppable in Ena. "It would be for the best."

Ena feels she can't breathe. The room is choking her. The image from the day before comes, of Rebecca Sword leaning over her child, her hand gripping him, Kenny rigid and blue. A pulse beats inside Ena, an energy clamouring at her legs, jumping and careening in her spine.

If she stays at the Swords a day longer, she will lose her ability to think, to see.

THE SAME DAY A LETTER FROM ELLEN ARRIVES, which Ena reads with her back to the kitchen window, a hard sun pushing on her neck.

May 25, 1918

Dear Ena,

I'm so very sorry about Jamie. Thank you for writing to me about his passing. For him to have come through what he did over there, and then to go in such a terrible way is beyond understanding. Life is unfair and it is foolish to close your eyes and hope for different. There is no comfort for you, I know that.

At least Jamie died in his own place, with you not far away from him. Your father, too. Your father was peaceful at the end. He knew he was going, but you didn't know it, of course. We should have prepared you. After he passed, you didn't know how to make sense of it and I was too choked with anger by then.

The first time your father took my life from me was when we left home to come here. The second was when he became ill. I have tried to get over all these things and I am ashamed I haven't. I am sorry for that. Hard for you to understand, but maybe now with Jamie gone, you will.

You wrote in your letter that you now work for the Sword family and that you stay at the farm alone. It isn't for me to ask why you are not living with the McFarland's. You and Sarah seemed quite close, I thought, and Hugh is an excellent provider. I hope there is no trouble between you. I would hate for you to make a bad time even harder than it must be. If you carry grudges like I do, let them go. You are stubborn, Ena, and you won't ask for what you need. I never asked you what you needed when you were young, so perhaps that's the reason.

You are like me in many ways, perhaps most in your toughness. But not in all ways—you have brightness, like Michael, which I never did. It shines in you. It is brilliant and marvellous and lovely. Go on with your life, Ena. I urge you to.

My position here with the Ogden's is very comfortable. It is a large home in Rosedale and I have a room of my own on the top floor. They are good people and I've told them about you, what a good hand you have with the baking. My room is big enough for two and the Ogden's will pay you on top of your room and board. Why don't you come, at least for a time?

My heart breaks for you, Ena.

All of my love, Mother

Reading Ellen's letter, a strange memory returns, astonishing in its proximity: Ellen beside Ena in the kitchen on 7th St., Ellen's forearms criss-crossed over her own, their fingers combing through a pea-textured floury mix. Ellen's body is surprisingly warm next to hers and the smell of citrus and vanilla lifts from her. She scoops some of the mixture in the palm of her hand and holds it out to Ena, flicking at a small piece with the edge of her thumbnail, her head angled sharply into Ena's. "Now, *that's* the thing—see how it separates only to be brought back together when we add the icy water?" The Irish lilt so like Michael's, but sharper, perhaps stronger. Ena pours in the ice water from a jug taken from the stoop.

Ellen stands back, her expression intent, a suggestion of pride in the curl of her mouth as Ena mixes, the dough forming a soft and gleaming ball under her hands. Putting an arm around Ena's shoulders, Ellen says; "Ahh, you know when pastry's just right, don't you Ena. You can feel it." She holds her palms out to Ena, the palms soft as new flesh, swept clean.

Ena peers down into the creamy pages of Ellen's letter. The letter is the first thing that feels truly her own since Hugh took the animals. She reads it twice more, a vivid tension filling her. Her mother's hand is neat and precise, care poured into each loop and cross and dot.

The letter is perplexing; the words carry the old weight—a ballast of disappointment, a steadying flow of caution, of pessimism, but there is a clarity in them too that dives cleanly, knowingly into Ena's centre Ellen has seen her shadows, the shuttered parts—she names them unsparingly—but she also sees what Ena has kept hidden from herself: a brightness, a perpetual awakening, a longing to hold a piece of the world in her palm, like Michael had.

Ena is growing sick in her work at the Swords, poised between an irrevocable grey descent, and an unstoppable re-emergence; like gulping air after holding one's breath for a long while, Ellen's words feel astonishingly life- giving.

She carefully slips the letter in the tin where she keeps Jamie's letters. *The way forward is in the handling of things,* she thinks suddenly. Standing in the sun-washed kitchen, she lifts her hands, confronting them as if she is reading from a book—small palms, the fingers compact, muscled, not as long as her mothers, the skin as supple but darker.

A current moves through her. What she might do with these hands. How they might save her.

FOR DAYS AFTER ELLEN'S LETTER ARRIVES, Ena can't stop thinking about baking. Her senses slowly awaken, her mind recalling the smell of fresh lemon, the silken touch of flour, the sensation of a straining muscle as she turns a heavy dough. There is a gentle nudge toward forward motion, like Ted taking his first few steps under harness, having to overcome his own weight.

Thoughts about the farm, what it could be, seep into her waking hours. When she closes her eyes, she sees the place take form, drenched in dense colour, textures that are rich and dark as earth. If she reaches out, she can touch the gold tassels in the fields with her fingertips.

If this is what you want, she asks herself, seeing her life now as she hasn't seen it in months, *why would you not put yourself there, at the centre of it?* A small possibility appears, just a speck at first, but soon it fills the horizon and takes her. She could farm again. If she saves up for long enough, she could buy the place from Hugh McFarland.

Hugh won't want to let the farm go. She thinks of the day she watched the men with the bull, Hugh's heels so dug-in that later, with the rain, puddles had filled up his footprints. She knows the force of him, stubborn, generous, unyielding.

On a Monday morning, early, before light, she harnesses Ted and drives into Owen Sound. She will need access to a larger oven, to a pantry, to a better icebox. Soon after her mother's letter arrived, the idea came to Ena that she should speak to Robert Piper, who is so admiring of her baking. Now, she imagines an agreement between them: her use of the inn's ample kitchen for her private baking business, in exchange for supplying all the inn's breakfasts as well as the afternoon teas. She would build the business slowly, adding household after household. Ena thinks of herself filling baskets with bread loaves, pallets like checkerboards loaded with pies—redcurrant and blackberry—canvas sacs with buttermilk tea biscuits, Ted taking her door-to-door and waiting patiently for her on the street.

A grey morning, the sky low, but despite the threat of rain, two or three guests take their breakfast on the inn's wide veranda. The carved double front door is slightly ajar. Inside the hall, an enormous bouquet of tiger lilies is on a side table, arranged in a brightly patterned urn. The overlay of scents strikes her right away—tobacco mixed with furniture polish, and the heady smell of the flowers.

No one is at the desk, the gas lamps set low against the rainy-day gloom. Ena sees Robert Piper in his study, apparently reviewing accounts, his heavy head bent over a disarray of papers and legers. Music is playing, the tender, warm tones of singing, a man's voice, as rich as poured chocolate. It comes from the gramophone, the first one Ena has ever seen or heard.

He looks up, smiles, gestures warmly for Ena to come in. They sit surrounded by precious objects, Ena perched on the edge of a deep brown leather armchair. The surface of his desk is an arrangement of clutter: a glass floral paperweight on top of a stack of leather-bound account books; a collection of ivory letter openers strewn over a silver tray. He has pulled his chair from behind his desk so that he can sit closer to her, their knees almost touching, Robert angling forward, his chin cupped in his palm. He wears an enormous silver and turquoise ring that seems to be embedded into his flesh—a permanent feature. She has never known a man to wear a ring before, unless it is a wedding band.

"I won't be able to work at the Swords." She knows no other way to ask but plainly and to the point: "Do you need more help here? In the kitchen? "

Robert Piper looks at her from beneath eyebrows as splendid as owl's feathers. "You are willing to reach higher, Ena? Take on the *pâtisserie* for our lecture series, and for the weddings and so on? "

"Yes," she says without hesitating. "If you get me some instruction."

"As well as the daily fare—the loaves and teacakes—what you've already been doing. We couldn't do without those."

"Of course."

He pauses, a look of open curiosity on his face. "Ena, why don't you leave Owen Sound? Work in Toronto? Train with one of the pastry chefs in a hotel? You have more than enough talent. I've told you that before."

"I don't want to leave," she says, standing, holding out her hand to him. "I have never wanted to leave."

He takes her hand in both of his and smiles. "My gain, then."

THE NEXT AFTERNOON, after spending the morning in the inn's kitchen, Ena is on a street behind the market, tall red-brick houses, pretty gardens with pansies planted at the front. She climbs onto porches and knocks on front doors. She talks to women about what she can sell to them—the types of loaves, the pies, the biscuits and tarts. When they see her in her black dress, they slide their eyes away and press their skirt fronts down anxiously with the palms of their hands.

One or two recognize her and tell her they are sorry about Jamie. Clear-eyed, Ena gives a small nod. "Thank you."

She leaves them with a basket filled with samples of her baking—a rhubarb pie, or six almond buns, always a loaf of her bread. "No obligation, of course."

Hardly a household will fail to place a standing order with her when she returns the next week for her basket.

34. AUGUST 26, 1918, ARRAS

WHEN DARKNESS FALLS OVER THE FRONT, grey vanishes—the mud, the duck boards, the dirty uniforms, the lice-ridden army blankets. Only velvet black around him, the pin-prick glow of fags, and overhead, a procession of flares. Blain squats, smoking dreamily, staring up at the sky. A few moments before, Sergeant Fossy had scuttled past, kicked at his boot, told him to look alive. "You're up for reconnaissance tonight, Carter. Don't get too comfortable, lad." The Sergeant isn't much older than Blain and formerly a private, but with the scarcity of qualified men in recent months, he has rapidly risen in rank. Blain likes him, sees how he has taken on leadership without complaint, how much care he takes with all of the men.

The 3rd Division is tucked up between a road and a shallow river, beyond which are miles of Fritz trenches and guns. Earlier today, after being squarely hammered, the Canadian 8th Brigade had managed to take Monchy. There had been much whistling and hooting and cheering among the troops. Now, the men whisper over fags and rum rations that fresh German Divisions are pouring in; tomorrow whole companies of German machine-gunners will be waiting for them.

Blain leans his head back and imagines the land around them, torn and cratered from days of furious shelling. Fritz won't have a problem finding places to hide his machine-guns.

"This is no raid, mind," Fossy had told Blain earlier when

assigning him the mission. "Leave that to others. You're just to work out location of the batteries."

It's no accident that Fossy singled-out Blain for reconnoitering. Blain's more comfortable creeping about in the dark than some of the other fellows. *Carter's got good night vision*, the men say. Blain knows how to make out the shapes of things in the absence of light. He recognizes evidence of German industry: rolls of defensive barbed wire, discarded shovels and pickaxes, the outline of a helmet poking over a ridge. Before the big battle in early August at Amiens, GHQ ordered that all movements would be at night, in secret, so as not to tip-off the enemy. The men had been taken by transport to a forest where they concealed themselves and slept in the sodden undergrowth on their ground sheets. At four in the morning, in a fog so thick it soaked them clean through, bombardment started. Blain, it was observed, walked easily through the blackness, his Ross rifle held securely in his hands, no stumbling awkwardly on rocks or feeling about for the trunks of trees. He appeared emboldened by the darkness and fog, and although he wasn't battle-hardened yet, and not the best or most experienced shot in his section, he was surprisingly accurate when shooting half-blind.

Blain prefers the sensation of movement to sitting stiff in a trench and sweating, hoping that he won't get hit, his bones rattled by the reverberation of shell fire, his guts twisting. The bombardments mostly happen during the day and Blain has at times, felt like a fish in a barrel. The dark hones cleverness, and a keenness of sight that is older in Blain than soldiering. As old as his boyhood. He thinks of nights on the Bruce Peninsula, Jack Carter coming up from the still, lurching through the gaped cedars, a jug of moonshine in his arms.

The drizzle has started. That won't help the tanks tomorrow any, he thinks. But at least there is no moon and it won't be easy for Fritz to mark him. Fossy has sent Blain out alone because the Division is now thinner in numbers. On other nights, they've gone in groups, pausing every half-hour for a well-concealed fag, Blain punctuating the long silences with jokes he's heard, or a brief saucy story. He's adjusted his storytelling since leaving home, intuiting how best to lighten and to entertain in short order. The men snort laughter into their sleeves so Fritz won't hear.

Blain grins at his own stories, entering into the spirit, embellishing here and there, changing the details. Most of what he tells is fiction. He thinks about Ena reading to him from *The Virginian*, how his mind painted pictures. It was a stupid story, but with some truth in it he supposes, the parts underneath, already laid down. The bits about courage and cruelty and what makes someone act the way he does. Sometimes, when Blain dozes, his feet clammy from rain and mud, he thinks he feels Owen's fingers on his face, willing him toward words. Owen didn't *need* the story (Blain understands that now about his brother). Owen needed the plain certainty of Blain's shoulder against his, the rise and fall of his chest, the sound of Blain's voice in the dark. When he thinks of Owen, a terrible sadness descends, a black loneliness, a wrenching guilt.

He hunches over, scuttling like a beetle past sleeping men, their collars drawn up over their exhausted faces. Scouting at night, Blain feels chance riding beneath him like a muscled animal; he feels lucky, as though he might change the course of things. Intuiting his way through the dark labyrinth, a sense of possibility begins to take hold, more shrewdly focused, more concentrated than mere excitement. He is giddy with a growing momentum, his movements invisible, his legs moving fast.

The warm August air is dense and he's slick with drizzle and sweat. He's a long way northeast now from where he started, and the shallow trenches, dug recently for daytime assaults, are mostly empty. One man he passes, a sentry, sits with his back against the trench wall, his rifle between his knees. He looks nothing but fatigued. When Blain catches his eye, the sentry places his finger to his lips almost tenderly, and jerks his head, gesturing toward someone or something over his shoulder. Blain stops, puts a hand on the man's shoulder, and the man expels air—gratitude for the brief show of camaraderie.

Not much further along, the trench runs out, its sides raggedly sloping up to the flats. There is a moment of dismay when he's confronted with the shambling wall of earth. He'd like to move further into the terrain, but he won't have cover.

He'll have to stay very still. First, he lays down the Ross. He finds a foothold and climbs, and then plants his belly on the trench's bank, sliding his head up so that his sightline clears the lip.

It takes him a few moments to penetrate the dark and he sweeps his gaze slowly over the expanse. Sullen ridges emerge, a stretch of wire, the darker impressions of shell holes in the brief light from the flares. In the far northeast corner, there is a flash, a glint that comes and goes in a rhythmic arc, and next to it, a wavering density that shifts and changes—a shoulder moving with the steady lift of a shovel, he decides. Blain rubs at his ear beneath his helmet. They're digging in, Blain thinks, and setting-up a battery.

Blain squints, pulls himself up slightly higher on the trench, his chin grinding into dirt. It isn't up to him to determine what exactly it is he sees, just to report it. To state his impression. The likelihood is if Fritz is installing a gun there, others will be found at predictable distances. Now that Blain has seen the one battery, determination to spot the others takes hold—a calm, almost sunny resolution to disarm Fritz by stealth.

Once he has a bead on where the other batteries are, he will calculate their distances from one another, and the distances of each battery from the end of the trench. He carries a pencil and a piece of paper in his upper pocket to write down the estimates, to be recorded by feel, without the benefit of a torch.

He slides away the awkward helmet and presses his ear against loose earth, hoping to catch reverberations of shovels, but there is nothing except the slightest suggestion of sound, a whirr, a gyration—flares rising and then falling to the ground. Blain never thought he was good at observation. Owen was better at really seeing. Now he thinks that those months on the farm with Ena, and later with the Captain, taught him something about looking at what is right in front of you. Or rather *feeling* what is there, not taking your attention from it, daring to really know. He thinks of the wild dogs in the bush, how he'd felt them creep over the field, knowing they were there without a bit of light.

He'll make his way back now, and rattle off his report. When he passes the sentry in the trench, the soldier straightens his back, shifting a little. A flare climbs up in the sky and the man's features are lit-up—a plain, square face, a heavy brow, eyes brown and steady. Blain is warmed by the face, assured by it, and the other man smiles good-naturedly, grateful for the sight of Blain.

Just then, a trench mortar. There is no air, just soaring clots of earth, and silence except for the terrible hum that comes from inside of his skull. He is moving, but with no way to know whether he travels up or down. He feels nothing. Darkness then, his mind strangely back in the swamp, and for a moment he peers past the tangle of half-frozen weed and into the glittering blackness. As he hits the ground, he thinks he sees her, arms stretched and reaching, and he's glad he hasn't left her behind.

35. SUMMER 1918

WHEN ENA DRIVES TED into the lane, she's surprised to find Hugh, walking tall and full of purpose from the barn, a pickaxe over one shoulder, his shirt sleeves rolled up to his elbows. A great mound of a man, wearing a broad straw hat, high boots, and a pair of coveralls, no jacket, his shirt drawn tight across the breadth of his chest. She'd seen him a few times, in the distance while ploughing, and even left a tray of currant buns and cold tea on the porch for him and Clem. But she wouldn't speak to him.

Seeing her, Hugh squares himself and swings the pickaxe down to rest its iron head on the toe of his boot. It is an aggrieved gesture, fuelled with frustration. He cups his hands around his mouth and hollers. "Ena!"

Billie too has spotted her and she tears toward the road, yipping and barking, her tail a white-tipped plume.

"Billie," she says, her eyes swimming. She levels her gaze at Hugh who whistles to Billie, the little dog slinking back to him, every few paces her head turning to Ena, her eyes abject.

Ena feels herself corked like a bottle, a storm of emotion clambering at her throat. Sitting high on the bench of the wagon, she glimpses an elongated shadow against the barn wall, a familiar line, an angled gentleness that can only be Jamie.

A cloud swallows the sun and the shadow is gone. With the abrupt absence, bitterness creeps in and with it, woven tight, a childish wish—she wants the magic of reinstatement, the miracle of resurrection. There is the surprising impulse to beg and to bargain, to ask for what's been taken. But to whom would she send such a plea? She takes in the full measure of the farm, an image gathering: what comes is Sarah's painting, the one that now hangs over her mantle, given to Ena years ago—a shock of light and dark, the thrust and pull of this place. Not a peaceful image, or a safe one either, but true. It comes to her clearly, mercilessly. He will not be returned to her, no matter how she longs for it.

Her gaze settles on Clem in the field, his hat pulled low, his face hidden, a small boy in overalls beside him. The boy is bending over and then he stands, his hands outstretched, palms together, his head bowed as if he's in prayer. *Owen.* Hugh is lumbering toward her, intent on speaking. His chest heaves, whatever is inside of him threatening to burst out. "Ena, why won't you talk to me? "

Her face is hard and stretched and she can feel the ache just below her cheekbones. "You took the livestock. You could have talked to me before you did that, but you didn't. Instead, you waited until I was in town, and then you and Clem loaded them."

Frowning up at her, Hugh's eye swims furiously toward the fields and then back again. He has planted himself solidly on her lane, doggedly. "Why *wouldn't* we move them to the other farm? I have the larger barn. Goddamn, Ena. This place *has* to be cared for. It's just practical. Jamie said if anything were to happen to him—"

She imagines Hugh and Jamie together, standing almost at this very spot, their pale heads close enough to touch, Jamie leaning ever so slightly into the stalwart mass of his brother. They had made arrangements about the farm, Jamie and Hugh.

"You intend to work the place," she says, nodding toward the ploughed fields, "while I go on living here."

Drilling the ground with his heel, he points his chin toward the fields, golden now, at the height of summer. "You don't

have to live here. You got a choice about that. And yes, I'll
work it. It's McFarland land."

"It was Jamie's—"

"I *told* him I'd look after it—and you. He'd a' done the same."

"What if I don't want to be looked after? What if I just want
a chance to farm my place, like anyone else?"

He's bewildered. She can see it. "You're *family*, Ena. You
could've stayed with me and Sarah. We'd have given you a
home. You could've helped out both places, been part of it.
You *still* could, if you weren't so stubborn."

Her eyes go back to the field, Clem squatting now, the boy
turned away from him, his face in profile. A delicate face,
ears pinned close to his skull. Hair a ruddy brown colour, the
same as Blain's.

"You blame me for keeping Blain on too long, Hugh. And
you were probably right but I wouldn't change it."

Hugh frowns, sighing. "What are you talking about, Ena?"

"You *do* blame me," she says, "for not getting rid of him. I
couldn't do it." Owen is looking at her now, his face holding
unmasked curiosity, maybe a comfort with truthfulness she
hadn't seen in Blain.

Lifting his hat, Hugh rubs furiously at his head. "Sweet Jesus,
you're not making sense. Yeah, I was mad that you kept that
boy on here. That you put him ahead of Jamie and the farm.
But I wasn't in my right mind that morning Jamie was found."
He takes in a hard breath.

"You said what you thought."

Hugh guffaws and he shakes his head. "More happened
here than you know, Ena. More than I knew then. We all got
a hand in this somewhere." He's colouring, the words costing
him something but he pushes on. "The thing is, Jamie could've
sent the boy away. All along, Jamie was makin' decisions,
too. To keep that boy on when he knew keepin' him would
be trouble."

When his eyes water, he impatiently swipes at them with his

sleeve, and seeing him do it, with Owen looking on, Ena's spine loosens. She has never thought Hugh to be a hard man. Just obstinate. It must have hurt Hugh terribly when Jamie—after coming home, tired to the bone of orders, of directives, of strong men imposing their bloody-mindedness—had turned away his help.

The barnyard is sun-drenched with no respite from the light; Ena squints, her eyes paining, and still the light streams in. Putting her hand flat on the bench of the wagon, she swings herself lightly to the ground. Billie comes straight away and rests her nose on the toe of her shoe. Bending down, Ena cups the dog's muzzle with her fingers, the dog pushing deep into her palm.

Hugh watches them, his eyes slits, emotion making slashes out of them. "I can't bring Billie here anymore. It upsets her. She goes off lookin' for him." There is a long pause, Ena close enough to see the golden hairs springing up on his arms, at his knuckles. After a moment, he straightens and gazes at her, the one eye veering. "It would have been all right if it was me that went over. I was the stronger."

There is nothing between them then but a slight stirring in the air, a turbulence of feeling. She places one hand on his chest while the other hangs loose at her side. She feels the cloth and beneath it, the warm, beating, density of him. It is the only way she knows to make him hear her.

"You couldn't have known, Hugh. None of us saw this coming."

For a long time, Ena's small hand rests on the cotton of his shirt, the fabric old, thin and fragile like an attenuated layer of skin.

A S ENA WALKS DOWN THE WEST HILL, having made her deliveries, the trees are a cascading riot of colour. Below is the town, its centre bristling with church steeples and the foundry's lean and blackened smoke stacks. Houses lie nested together, backyards neatly squared, laundry billowing on lines despite the threat of rain. Boats and ships slip easily in and out of the harbour, their decks piled high. Except for the beetling of motorcars and trucks, from here, the town seems unmarked by the last four years of war.

From the open window of her car, Sarah calls to her, "Lift?" She doesn't wait for Ena's answer. "On my way to paint."

Each afternoon, Sarah leaves the farm in her painting smock and when she returns, Hugh is in the fields, ornery and sullen. "I have nothing to say to him," she told Ena hotly when they last visited.

Now, Ena imagines Sarah, glassy-eyed, flattened by the hours spent with her work and with Craig Murray, near to extinguished, but still a twist of smoke inside of her. Hugh won't know what to make of it.

Sarah pulls the car over to an unconvincing stop. "I wish I had another month."

Gusts of wind kick up leaves that clatter across the road and a thin rain begins to fall. Ena thinks about getting in. "You have to push through," she says, looking uncertainly at the car. She doesn't trust Sarah's driving. She shifts her empty basket from one hand to the other. "If it's important to you, you have to keep going."

Putting an elbow out of the window, Sarah narrows her eyes against the sight of Owen Sound. For a long while they don't say anything, the car jittering restlessly between them, Ena thinking that Sarah will drive off, but then she speaks. "I can't keep doing this. Living two lives."

ENA IS IN THE KITCHEN at the inn. She has made more than a hundred jars of conserves—jams, jellies, preserves. She identifies each in her neat and precise hand—a hand like her mother's—and then pastes cream-coloured labels to the fluted glass.

Last year, she had done her canning at the farm. She'd had Blain to load the jars into crates and carry them to the root cellar. Waiting while she finished the labelling, he'd sat in a kitchen chair and chattered aimlessly about a two-headed foal Clem told him about down in Goderich. "Lived for *hours*," he said, his voice breathless, his expression caught-up in the fantastic occurrence of such a thing. "Wonder what would'a happened if it *had* kept living, Ena? Just think of it—one head wanting to go one way and the other wanting to go someplace else?" She'd laughed, and then he did too, his *hee, hee, heeing* making his chest seem to shiver and his over-sized ears wiggle up and down. Foolish Blain. Anger flares inside, remembering how, without a word, he simply left.

She'd asked Sarah if she'd heard anything about where he was. Did Clem ever talk about him? And Jack Carter. Had he turned up? Come back for the money? Sarah knew nothing of Blain, but the talk on the peninsula—the Queens and so on—was that Carter disappeared up to Sault Ste. Marie. "No one's very interested in finding him," Sarah said wryly. Owen was doing well. Ena had been relieved to hear it. Clem said he was bright—good at his lessons. Annie was making certain he got as many books as he could read.

Surveying the gleaming jars of coloured fruit, Ena feels a

frank satisfaction. The counting is no less satisfying: *30 peach preserve; 42 blackberry jam; 36 sour cherry jelly; 50 apple butter.* She can sell these door-to-door, the money she makes added to the growing balance of funds, and when there is enough, even if it takes her years to do it, she will go to Hugh with an offer to purchase.

She makes her entries in a wide green-jacketed ledger kept on a kitchen shelf. It is well-thumbed, its leather cover soft as flannel. She runs her finger down the long, pretty columns and thinks of Michael, how proud of her he would be. No one else's opinion has ever really mattered. Just his. And then Jamie's, of course—Jamie who seemed to accept her exactly as she was.

It's a shock when Sarah bursts into the kitchen brandishing a newspaper. Her face is over-bright, her eyes burning with excitement. Her landscape paintings are in Chicago with Craig Murray, the exhibit well underway.

"The critical reviews are very good, Ena. Listen to what the Chicago papers say: Craig is written about as 'coolly intellectual, the images, muscular and forceful, an utterly modern painter.' And they make mention of Georgina Fells. They call her a post-impressionist, and they describe the work as 'truthful,' 'stunning,' and they say it shows 'great promise.' The two painters, they say, 'are different faces of a bold new age.'"

Listening to her, Ena is proud of what Sarah's managed to do, but she wonders what part of her life she will have to surrender.

"You'll want to do more," she says. "It won't be enough."

"I suppose." Sarah is openly admiring the colourful jars that line the worktop like a small army. "You want to rebuild, don't you Ena? You haven't let go of the farm."

Ena puts the last entry into the ledger, her mind going to the alphabetized arranging of the jars. There is a cold room in the cellar of the inn, a place that Robert uses for keeping secret stores of liquor and fine wine. Ena has taken over one wall, cleaning and whitewashing the shelves, laying down newspaper. She will bring the jars down in a crate, starting with *apple,* and then move on to *blueberries, cherries* ... it is going to take several trips.

"No," she says, looking up, laying the pen down carefully. "I haven't let it go."

THE WORK IS EXHIBITED for a month and then it's over. Many pieces are sold. When Craig returns, he's preoccupied with what is next: exhibitions for them in Montreal, and Detroit, and Chicago again. Robert Piper has invited Craig to give a lecture to some of the guests, a group of naturalists, wealthy people wearing canvas coats, wide-brimmed hats and tall leather boots. Each autumn, they make the Owen Sound Inn their base, wander the shores of Georgian Bay, write poetry, paint. Ena doesn't understand them. They shift themselves from place to place in untidy chattering, groups. Nevertheless, she and the inn's chef pack elaborate lunches and suppers for them, taking great care to include linens and silverware, flasks and thermoses. Along with roast beef sandwiches made with her fresh bread, Ena sends pumpkin loaves and apple tarts.

Craig is asked to give a lecture at the inn on the subject of art and modernism. With the recent success in Chicago, guests are eager to hear him speak. Sarah remains in the background, never making herself known, although already one or two of the more informed guests have asked Craig, "And who is Georgina Fells? Where can we see more of her work?" Craig answers vaguely, implying that she's from another part of the country and they had chanced to work together in New York.

Two young women linger at the end of the lecture. They perch side by side on a rose-coloured settee, sipping tea and nibbling Ena's vanilla sponge cake. Craig casually sits on the leather top of a long narrow table. They talk with him in earnest tones about modernism, Paris, the changes sweeping the art world in the wake of the war. He hungrily draws on his pipe, his lips like a trout opening and closing on the stem. "I'm not sorry that the old conventions have been shattered," he says with a hint of brashness. "They *had* to be broken, to clear a path."

He can't mean that the war was worth it. Ena stares at him in disbelief, trying to take his full measure, the ambition of the man bright and blinding.

While she clears away the tea things, Craig's leg swings from the table like a pendulum, his eyes hard and eager as they follow the women now trailing reluctantly out of the room.

37.

ON NOVEMBER ELEVENTH, it is announced that the war is over. Ena stands on the street in Owen Sound. She wears her long navy-blue coat and she stamps her feet for warmth. Around her leaves are taken up in whirlwinds and then dashed against the road. There is a ruckus of honking. Flocks of geese have formed great Vs from which they now stray, reforming, and storming across the leaden sky.

Although Owen Sound acknowledges the end with flags and early store closings, the revelry is muted. As for Ena, the loss she feels lies outside of the war, separate from it, her grief a thrum of sorrow that ebbs and flows, a private tidal sea. She moves forward carrying it inside, a great watery absence. Only the thought of the farm reaches for her. The long, sure reach of the land.

CRAIG MURRAY HAS LEFT. "With the war over, he wants to be in Europe. He wants to see what will happen there. All the changes. This is just a backwater for him." Sarah stands in the doorway of the inn's kitchen and speaks about Craig's Murray's flight from Owen Sound. There is no hint of heartbreak in her voice. Surprising, given what Ena thought was between Sarah and Craig—a bright flare of passion. Perhaps even love.

Sarah seems tired, large dark circles like bruises blooming beneath her eyes; strain pulls at her skin, making it almost translucent. She is wearing a pair of woollen trousers and a linen shirt, the outfit that she often wears when going to paint with Craig. Her hair, which she has grown long again, is wrapped, turban-style, inside a colourful scarf. Despite the obvious fatigue, she's an impressive figure, the strong broad architecture of her body filling out the straight cut of her clothes. "I want to go up to the cabin, get the rest of the paintings. I'd like you to come, Ena."

It is very early in the morning, the sky still black. Ena wonders what Sarah says to Hugh about keeping such strange hours. "You don't need me—"

Sarah gives her a look, both piqued and pleading. "I'm steadier with you. Stronger."

The paintings, Sarah's smoking relationship with Craig Murray, the secret cabin suddenly seem too much for Ena. She has just made several batches of breakfast rolls, and three batches of buttermilk scones. She would have liked to stay, to prepare her bread and watch the loaves rise reliably on the worktop. She has orders to fill.

Sarah chews on the edge of a fingernail, her teeth bearing down, a nervous hunger in the gesture. The thrust of Sarah's energy, when turned inward, is a sort of violence that Ena can't endure. She takes Sarah's long fingers in her own and squeezes.

"All right. I can spare a few hours."

AS THEY CLIMB THE ROAD away from town, the light creeps in from the east and strikes the bay, shattering its surface into silvery shards. The road dips and rises, serpentine; it is impossible to see what is coming, but they meet no one else.

Sarah clutches the wheel of the car, her fingers straining. "So it's over," she says. It's unclear what she means—the war, the exhibition, Craig Murray. Ena frowns into the windscreen that is splattered with bits of things—bugs, leaves, the collateral handiwork of Sarah's driving.

When they arrive, the sun has barely broken the horizon and the cabin and the trees remain in deep shadow. No smoke comes from the chimney and Craig's truck is gone. They sit for a moment with the engine still running and then Sarah turns off the car. "Come, Ena. Let's go see," she says, her voice tight.

Inside, the coffee pot is partly full and sitting on the cold wood stove, a fry pan next to it bearing the remains of Craig's fried fish meal of the night before. His clothes are gone, the trunk he uses to carry his things no longer at the foot of his bunk.

Most striking of all is the absence of his work. All of his canvases and hardboards have been removed along with the easels, the brushes, the palettes—all the tools of his trade. A faint smell of turpentine hangs in the air, a remnant of the care he'd taken with his brushes. Still stacked along the perimeters of the cabin are Sarah's paintings, the canvases stretched, supported, placed thoughtfully as though he has concerned himself with what position shows each to its best advantage. Many of her more recent works have been done on hardboards, and these he has grouped neatly together along one wall.

Sarah wanders through the cabin, indifferent and listless, avoiding handling the paintings, instead walking past them. Occasionally she frowns, opens the front door and peers outside into the broadening morning, her arms folded, and Ena wonders if Sarah expects Craig to come striding in from the bush or up from the rocky beach.

"Most of these are junk," she says. "I haven't a clue what I should do with them."

A pointed light creeps in through the east-facing windows, touching particular pieces, illuminating the contrasts in them, the bursts of intense colour. Ena picks up a piece on hardboard—a pink sky over marsh, shocks of yellow-green rising up from a multi-hued brown. Not a landscape at all. Life reaching, ugly and beautiful all at once. Ena's breath catches and she stares. "Your gift is greater than Craig's, Sarah."

"I'm just an amateur."

Ena shakes her head. "It was always about what was inside

of you. That *life* inside. These haven't got anything to do with Craig Murray."

Sitting on Craig Murray's bunk now, Sarah slumps, her head in her hands. Whatever fire is inside of her, it seems too much. "I wasn't in love with him—Craig's not a man for love. Too selfish. You saw it too, Ena. I know you did. But he understood my art in a way I didn't have words for. He pushed me."

Ena thinks of herself, drowning at the Swords, absorbed by a diffuse grey. She would have stopped living if she had stayed in that place. Her eyes go to Sarah's paintings, the fierceness, the unwillingness to paint in any other way but from the inside out.

"You have to live your life, Sarah. All of it. The painting, Hugh, if that's what you want. "

"I *want* too much."

Ena considers this. Perhaps she also wants too much but it makes no difference. None at all. "You only want what's yours."

There is quiet between them.

"You'll have to tell Hugh," Ena says finally. "You'll have to tell him what you want."

W HEN ELLEN HAD WRITTEN and invited Ena to come to Toronto for Christmas, Ena wanted to say no. Her customers were already placing their seasonal orders for mincemeat tarts and gingerbread, and for the fruitcake she'd wisely begun in November. And there were the regular weekly orders to manage. She was eager for the extra income the season promised, and frankly exhilarated by the prospect of losing herself—or rather finding herself—in the work.

And besides, Robert would need her. She imagined that at Christmas, the kitchen at the inn would be busier than ever, with festive teas to prepare each afternoon and parties for the guests in the evenings. (Over the last months, special events at the inn have given Ena an appetite for producing ever more elaborate creations: chocolate eclairs, fairy creams, chocolate rulle cake, lemon meringues.)

But when she spoke to Robert, he told her that he planned to close the inn over Christmas. He would be travelling to Chicago, to spend the holidays with his friend.

"I could stay, keep an eye on things," she said hopefully. "You don't need to turn paying guests away—"

"Go to the city, Ena," he prodded gently. "Have tea at the King Edward Hotel and when you come back, tell me what you think of it."

Ena shook her head. "I'll have too many orders to fill."

"You can do all of that before. Distribute everything and

then go down by train." He was smiling generously but there was recollection in his eyes, sad and private—past journeys he'd taken and the inevitable returns he'd made.

EMERGING FROM THE STATION, the sounds are what strike her first. The city is blanketed in a dense fog, the damp air strangely hollow, and voices, horns, the clatter of hooves, are distinct and lonely. A paperboy calls out. Motorcars and horses approach and vanish in a vapoury grey, buildings stand ghostly and shrouded. The air is clammy and it carries a heady mix of horses and cars and the unfamiliar smells of industry.

Until the moment the train had pulled away from the platform in Owen Sound, Ena looked for a reason to stay. Throughout the trip down, it was as if she were being torn apart. She had missed people before, been stunned by loss, but this was different—a sickening tug, a kind of illness.

Ellen waits in the front of the station, a sullen horse and cab behind her. She seems smaller, here on the city street, but the cut of Ellen's gaze is still razor-sharp. With her rounded shoulders and her feet turned out in low brown boots, Ellen is like a little bird. To come to the station she has worn her best coat, an old herringbone tweed, raglan sleeved, a coat she's owned as long as Ena can remember. She clutches at the top button as if to make certain it stays closed.

They stand for a long while looking at one another, Ellen finally reaching and cautiously plucking Ena's sleeve. "You survived the journey."

Ena is dazed, with nothing familiar around her but Ellen, and Ellen spears her with a bright and unsparing look. "City's a bit much at first. But you get used to it. "

Ellen's third-floor room at the Ogden's turns out to be large, with twin beds and a window overlooking the garden. The walls are papered with cabbage roses, and pink satin quilts are folded neatly at the foot of each bed. The room smells of floor wax and lavender soap. Ellen has a photograph of Michael on the nightstand, one Ena remembers from the parlour on 7th Street. It is an old-fashioned picture set on thick backing, the tones silver and black. Michael is very young, his face full on to the camera, his dark eyes gazing past the lens, his expression shining, confident, a hint of playfulness around the mouth.

"Your father the year we were married," says Ellen. There is tenderness and pride in her tone, and it takes Ena by surprise.

"He looks a bit of a rascal."

Ellen laughed. "If you asked me then, Ena, would I follow him to the ends of the earth, I'd have told you yes in a heartbeat. I can't blame him for that, can I—just fancy."

"He must have been convincing when he talked you into coming over."

Ellen nodded. "He was *very* persuasive. But coming here was what he was always going to do, even after we were married, with or without me. Never a question." Ena picks up the framed picture and frowns down into Michael Connelly's gleaming eyes so faithfully fixed on his own dreams. "I didn't want to be without him," Ellen goes on.

Ena blinks, seeing for the first time that her mother had loved Michael Connelly, and that she had suffered for it. Ena's thoughts about her parents stop there, as though she closes a door, her own affection for her father too strong, too dear for her to be disappointed in him now.

For the holidays, the Ogden family has gone to Ottawa, to where Dr. Ogden's brother lives, and Ena and Ellen have the tall, elegant house to themselves. On the afternoon of Christmas Eve, Ena asks if they can go to the King Edward Hotel for tea. They take the streetcar and walk through a crowd of people, many of whom carry bags and brightly wrapped packages. Some of the people wear fur coats while others wear cloth. There are women and old men. Young girls in hats. A man about Ena's age stands smoking on a corner, his shoulders hunched, his face sharply angled, his hooded eyes warily focused on the street. Further along, a Salvation Army band plays Christmas carols, people stopping only briefly to toss money into a large glass jar. A tented sign set on the sidewalk admonishes: "Be Generous and Give To The Less Fortunate."

For a brief moment, Ena wonders if Blain is alive, here, in the lonely-seeming city. She tries but she can't conjure him up; the place, for all the people in it, is strangely flat and colourless. Of course, he'd always wanted to go west. Ena had never believed the descriptions in *The Virginian*—the silly over-sized moon, the toothy mountains, coyotes howling mindlessly in the night. Make-believe. Now, she wants the place to be true. She *wants* him to be there, his long legs stretched out on sweet-smelling pine boughs, his head pillowed by rock, an old horse blanket for warmth. She thinks of him smiling up at a night sky that is littered with stars, and it doesn't matter, really, if she doesn't see him again. Just to know where he is would be enough.

The tea at the King Edward Hotel turns out to be very good, the petit-fours precisely squared and thinly layered, the eclairs like biting into sweetened air. They each have a small slice of a high, white cake, its icing as elaborate as Irish lace, the details perfect. *I could make this with some practice*, she thinks. As she takes a nibble from a cucumber sandwich, she frowns thoughtfully into her plate.

Ellen is keenly watching her. "You're very able with baked goods yourself, Ena. There are loads of households in this city who would pay you dearly for the skill." Ena believes that this might be true, seeing the patrons in the King Edward in their pearls, their fine kid gloves, how they relish their pretty cakes and pastries. Another life is possible.

On the way back to the Ogdens, Ellen buys everything they need to prepare for their Christmas lunch, but it's Ena who bakes for them—a rich mincemeat pie with suet and raisins, sultanas, citrus, walnut and almond—Belfast scones with cinnamon for a festive breakfast, and shortbreads for their tea.

On Christmas day, after their lunch, Ellen again suggests that Ena stay. "You have to leave your ideas of home behind and make the best," she says, some of the old grimness there in the pull of her mouth. "You have to make your peace with it, the way your life is now."

Ena stirs milk into her tea. "I have made peace, and I want to rebuild the farm. I want to live my life there."

Ellen sighs, strokes her own cheeks as if to bring some blood into them. "Well, there's no stopping you from trying."

Ena is glad they don't talk anymore about her remaining in the city. They spend the afternoon by a fire that Ellen specially makes up for them in the large front room. She tells Ena about her life in Ireland, the life she left behind; her parents and their farm, her brothers and sisters, the town called Drogheda where she went to school.

"I wanted to go home, after it was clear the store was failing. I asked Michael over and over to sell. I knew, for all his dreams, he couldn't hold on to it. He was so sick, Ena. He was so stubborn. He kept the place too long and there were debts to pay off by then."

"Why didn't you go back, after he died?"

Ellen looks down and deftly brushes the crumbs from her lap. "My mother is gone, and my brothers both work in Manchester now. There isn't a home left in Ireland, and probably no positions open, at least not in Drogheda."

They are looking into the fire, each of them pulled down in thoughts of their own. "This is a good enough place for me, Ena. This is fine."

At least, thinks Ena, a place of her choosing.

Ena goes home on December 27th. The few days spent in the city have been enough, Toronto like a great mouth, toothy and voracious. Ellen hires a cab to take them to the station. After they say goodbye on the platform, Ellen's hand stays raised for a long while, grave and faithful. As the train pulls away, Ena sees her, a small plain figure, proud in her way, and Ena finds that she is sad to leave her.

The trip begins with snow. Nothing but a frenzied blur of

grey outside the carriage's window, and then a demure winter sun breaks through, the passing woodlots casting neat shadows across the tracks. She closes her eyes and lets the sway of the train take her, the play of light and shadow staying in her mind, an after-image that radiates and pulses like one of Sarah's pictures.

SIX DAYS AFTER SHE ARRIVES HOME is the first day of 1919, the New Year slipping in, modest and quiet. Ena has stopped in to the McFarland farm with two apple pies—Russet apples and Hugh's favourite. Wrapped in a plaid rug, Sarah sits on the wide front porch of McFarland farmhouse, an easel in front of her, her eyes on the hard line of a grey winter sky. She looks older in the flat light, the colour of her hair a shock against her white skin.

Perching herself on the railing, Ena tucks her gloved hands under her thighs and looks at the easel. "So, still at it."

Sarah tilts her head. "Yes."

Ena nods, showing no surprise.

"I told Hugh. I told him about the exhibition, about Georgina Fells, the cabin. I told him about Craig Murray. I think he'd figured most of it out anyway. Not Georgina Fells, though," she says laughing. "That came as a surprise."

Ena looks toward the barn where she imagines Hugh is working, his boot on the back of a shovel, his arms braced to lift a heavy load. Work setting his world straight again. Sarah had hurt him, Ena is sure of it. He would have wanted to strain against her, to pull her back to what he thought was best. Even a strong man like Hugh can't tether the world to a rail.

"I told him I was going to paint, no matter what he felt about it. And that I want to use my own name. Sarah Lawrence McFarland."

A far better name, thinks Ena, her eyes narrowing.

"Staying with Hugh, painting as much as I can—that's what I see for myself now."

They sit silently together and listen to the sound of an engine starting up, Hugh and his truck or some other machine; men tinkering behind the barn. Both women turn and search for the source of the sound.

Sarah suddenly looks at Ena. "I have something for you, a late Christmas present. Wait here." When she steps onto the porch again, she is carrying a brown-papered package under her arm. "I wasn't sure if I should give it to you." She taps the packaged canvas twice with her curled fingertips as if considering whether to say more and then tears off the packaging with resolve. "But you already *know* this, Ena."

When Ena sees the painting she freezes. Jamie's face looks back at her, his head bowed, his expression veiled and drawn down as it was when he came back from the fighting, his body a fluid stream of colours, an extension of the fields and wood behind. The most recognizable feature are his eyes, eerily alive, but distracted, consumed. She has managed to keep the gentleness in him, in the slope of the shoulders, the open hands. Ena can only stare. No words. After a few moments, Sarah puts her arm around her and bites her lip. "It wasn't part of the exhibition and I won't ever put it into a show. I'm giving this to you, Ena, only if you want it of course. Hugh can hardly stand to look at it."

"I wasn't expecting this."

"No." A small, quick shake of her head. "Of course, I don't know how Jamie really felt, coming back. I can only imagine."

TWO WEEKS LATER THERE IS A RAP on the door of kitchen at the inn. Ena has just pulled down a flour sifter from the shelf, and is readying a bowl; yeast bubbles and froths promisingly in a cup beside the stove.

Hugh stands at the threshold, his town coat on, his good felt hat on his head. He takes the hat off and holds it to the lapel of his coat—an old-fashioned gesture—his eyes on Ena.

"Mind if I step in?"

Ena motions to him to sit and pours water into the teapot. She sets out cups, milk and a bowl of sugar. They sit across from one another at the small kitchen table, Hugh awkward and oversized, his hands folded in front of him, the exposed knuckles red and scarred, boyish and impulsive.

"You're doin' good here, eh, Ena." Not a question. The inn has kept her busy, between the wedding receptions, the cultural lectures, the regular daily fare. Her baking has become part of the inn's excellent reputation.

"The work's paid off," she said. "And besides, I like it."

He nods, understanding what it is to work hard, to do well.

"You knew all along about Sarah's painting, her time with that Murray fella."

Ena doesn't answer.

"I'll have to get used to things being what they are, with her spending most of her time at her pictures. Either that or lose her," he says simply, shaking his head, "and that would be too much." He opens up his coat and pulls out a long cream-coloured envelope. When he holds the envelope out to her, it trembles, and Ena takes it from him, rising from her chair and opening a drawer for a knife. The blade slices the envelope cleanly.

Hugh watches her, the one eye struggling gamely to stay on her face. Inside of the envelope, there is a letter from the land registrar stating that the farm had been deeded to Ena McFarland on January 14, 1919. The deed itself shows Hugh's name; her own name is written below.

"You just have to go with me to the courthouse and we'll each sign in front of a witness."

Ena smooths the thick creamy paper with the flat of her hands and rereads it, determined to fully understand.

"You mean to give it to me," she says. "The farm."

Hugh rolls his shoulder in what might be a shrug. "I always meant it to be yours and Jamie's. It's land and it needs caring for. That's what I've been doin'." He takes in a deep breath and then shakes his head. "And I never knew no one to work as hard as you, Ena McFarland. You got iron in that back of yours. You *can* farm the place. Course, I'd like to give you help, if you'll take it. "

She puts the document down, her words caught and her eyes filling. They won't let Jamie go, not completely, not either one of them, and they are together in this.

"That old kitchen of yours isn't well suited for business. You got enough saved to make changes?"

"Not enough," she says. So much had gone to Blain over the months that Jamie was gone.

Hugh shrugs. "I'll get the work going. I can scare up the labour, lend you the money for materials and so on. Then, once you get yourself up and runnin', we can talk terms of repayment." There is no sentiment in his tone now, no softness or pity.

They sit in silence, Ena reluctant to move, unwilling to disturb the moment. After what seems a long time, her words—usually so forced—finally come in a rush. She reaches for Hugh, her fingers looping around his broad wrist. "Thank you. I will take your help. Of course I will."

He grunts a little, and then gives her sideways look. "And now, before we go to that office, I got somethin' to tell you about the farm. If that place is gonna be yours, you'll want to know the truth. All of it."

H UGH DOESN'T BEGIN THE STORY until she mixes the dough for the bread, forms the loaves and covers the pans with clean cloths. While the loaves rise, they bundle up in their coats and pull their chairs onto the side porch. Outside, the air is cool and damp. A wet snow has fallen overnight leaving a sodden blanket of white. "We won't be bothered by anyone here."

Sitting awkwardly, Hugh nods and frowns into the hushed street. "This has to do with what happened to Jamie," he says, a twinge of regret playing in his face.

She waits through a hum of stillness.

"Around the time his mother died, Blain started with us at the farm. Favour to Clem because Annie was Margaret Carter's sister. Still don't know what really happened to Margaret Carter. Only Blain knew. Annie was sure that it was somethin' bad, said she'd seen bruises on her sister before. Clem, Jamie, and me talked about getting the police to look into it. Course, we had no proof and Blain wasn't sayin' nothin'. In the end, we just let it drop."

Hugh pauses as a car drives past. Slush hits the snow banks the sound dull and weighted. "Blain was kind of a useless kid, his head all over the place. Aimless. Once or twice, he'd get frustrated and smash things up. I probably should've sacked him. Jamie talked me out of lettin' him go—you know Jamie. Said we ought to give him a chance and Clem agreed he'd train him."

"A few months later, when Blain ended up all bloodied at your place, Clem told me more about what was goin' on over at Jack Carter's. He told me that Carter was into his own hooch somethin' awful. I don't go in for sticking my nose in where it don't belong, Ena. But we should'a stopped Carter there and then, when we still had the chance."

Something drops inside of Ena, an orb, dense and hard, the start of recognition.

"That cash that Blain dumped at Clem's had a note in it. I think the boy wanted to make right what he could. He wrote it himself. Pretty good too for a kid who hadn't been in school for a while." Ena thought of the times she read to Blain, the way he'd closed his eyes, a secret smile on his face. He'd taken the book to his room because he'd read it again himself. Probably over and over.

"He talked about the night Jamie died. It's real bad."

"Go on," she urges. She knows what she wants: to look into the truth of things. To really see. .. She wraps her arms around herself, feeling the chill dense air begin to settle.

"Carter showed up that night lookin' for Blain and his money, and Jamie tangled with him." A vision of Jack Carter comes. A man blinded by some terrible want and made stronger by desperation. Jamie would have been unprepared, and he was exhausted from the nights they'd spent with the animals.

"I left Jamie on the Chesterfield," she says quietly. "He was going to check on the animals before midnight, and then come to bed."

Hugh solemnly nods, his wrist moving to his face, his nose beginning to drip in the cold. "Blain heard them fighting and I guess he had the brains to get Jamie's gun. Sounds in his note like he just planned on scaring Carter with it." The story drives into her. She imagines Blain as he was the morning he shot the wild dogs, his face bursting with triumph. He might have intended more than simply scaring Carter off but she won't say this now to Hugh.

"He said in the letter he'd taken Carter's money weeks before, for Owen, for the two of 'em to take off and settle someplace. Something delayed him, maybe the weather. Anyway, it was the money Carter was after. There was some sort of scuffle and Jamie got knocked down. Carter had the gun by then, took the boy out to the barn. Something happened there, a struggle between them. All the boy said in the note was he shot his father but that it was the bull that killed him."

"The bull—" She is trying to make sense of it.

"Boy said we'd find the body in the bullpen under some straw. I didn't know about the note 'til Clem showed it to me, later the same day you found Jamie."

Ena thinks of Hugh that first morning in the barn, angry and full of suspicions. Clem had been there too, quietly working around the stalls. All the while, Carter's body had been there. Neither she nor Hugh had known but Clem had.

"Clem didn't tell you right away, Hugh. Why?"

"This note might just as well have been a confession and Clem felt bad for the boy. He thought I would go to the police, and he wanted the boy to have some time to get far away." He paused, looking down into his hands.

"But you didn't talk to the police," she says softly.

Hugh takes his fingers to his forehead, roughly chafing the skin. "Me and Clem went to the police later, just to say that Owen had been abandoned and there was no sign of his father. As long as Owen had a home with Clem and Annie, the police weren't much concerned. Everyone figured Carter had taken off up north with his cash. And Blain—he was always yabberin' about going someplace. A damn mess. A bloody mess, all of it, Ena. And us: you, me, Jamie, we got caught in it. That boy, Blain most of all. And for what? Well, I'm tired of it."

"And Carter? What happened?"

Hugh shrugs. "Doesn't say how Jack Carter got into that bullpen but sure enough, Ena, when Clem and me saw Carter's body, he'd been crushed. The boy couldn't have done that.

There was a gunshot wound in the shoulder but that alone wouldn't have killed him."

"And Jamie?"

"Blain wrote he wasn't sorry for what happened to Carter. Said his father deserved it and more, but he felt awful bad for Jamie gettin' hurt. But I don't think he knew Jamie was dead. Called him the Captain. Hoped you got him in to the house all right."

A string of urgent questions form. Why hadn't Blain gone back to the house before he left, woken her up, told her what had happened? There might have been time. She might have found Jamie, brought him inside. "We'll never really know, but as far as I'm concerned, Carter killed Jamie. I think Jamie might have been going to help Blain. But he was probably confused, not knowing exactly where he was because of the beatin' he took from Carter. Probably started off in the wrong direction, thinking Blain was out there, in that field. If he was sick, his lungs probably couldn't take that cold for long."

The violence with Carter, perhaps the sound of the gun, would have devastated Jamie. He would have been back there again, in France. A moment of quiet falls between them, Hugh's eye careening back and forth like a swinging lantern.

"You probably wonder why the little bugger didn't find you. Why he left Jamie like that and ran off."

The sky is leaden, the air damp with more incoming snow. A column of slow moving trucks rattle past on their way out of town. "It was a lot for a boy," she says finally. The brutality, the loss, the weight of Blain's love for Owen. "It was too much. Too much for him to handle."

Hugh sighs and looks up at the porch ceiling, his face fixed in a frown. "After me and Clem found Carter's body, we loaded it onto a cart, cleaned up anythin' we could find that pointed to what happened, and we got rid of him." His chin shifts forward, obstinacy and pride in his expression. She knows not to ask where the body is. Hugh had taken care of that.

"And later, you took all the livestock from the barn—"

"Couldn't stand the thought of you goin' in and out of there, knowing what had happened."

Her lips press together in the semblance of a smile. "And Blain? He enlisted then?"

"He did, Ena. His pay was goin' to Clem, to care for Owen. But then somethin' happened there, in the last few weeks, before the armistice. Services sent Clem word."

"He's gone," she says.

Hugh looks away and frowns fiercely into the wintery grey. "I guess. Some kind of blast. They don't know what happened. They don't always find men after—"

She is stunned, thinking of Blain leaving not a trace of himself, not a scrap of cloth, not a button. It is an impossible idea, too far a stretch, even for her who has had to accept so much. Of course he always intended to leave *this* place. And he had done it. But that he would be blasted from the world, erased from it? A terrible fierceness gathers inside. "Well," she says, her eyes narrowing. "Well." She heaves in a breath, steadying herself. She thinks of Blain, how he has driven her mad with worry. How his sweetness has made her want to cry. She lifts her eyes to Hugh's. "Blain can surprise you. You can never know with Blain."

Hugh puffs out a bit of air and rubs his hands on his thighs for warmth. "You gave him too much damn credit. It wasn't deserved."

AT HOME, LATER THAT EVENING, Ena climbs the stairs to her room and then lies down on her bed. She keeps her eyes open, her gaze fixed on the ceiling while she listens to the sounds of icy-sleet that now clatters at her window. She thinks of herself, looking into Michael Connelly's hollowed face, the cool wind coming in from the bay tapping her on her shoulder, warning her.

"Right, then. Off to school. And back to tell me what you've learned," he'd said.

Ena had been worried as she walked the short distance to the small school, her satchel hanging across her shoulders, her woollen stockings scratchy on her legs. It was a long dull day and when she got home, Ellen was not back from the McLaren's. Ena fixed Michael's supper and then carried it up to him on a tray, careful on the stairs, her long skirt getting under foot.

The room was as Ena left it that morning, the window gaping, the curtain seeming to breathe in and out on its own. The air was chilled and only the faintest scent of the mustard from the plasters remained. She sat with him, on the edge of the bed, waiting, not wanting to leave him. Some part of her believed he would open his eyes and speak.

But there was not a whisper of movement in him. No sound.

40. SPRING 1918

L ATE MARCH, BIRDS RISING from broken fields, a great, un-stoppable stirring. Ena is driving home from Owen Sound. She's spent the afternoon at the Owen Sound Inn constructing a wedding cake for a young couple from Boston, the recipe taken from one of Robert's Chicago newspapers. A raspberry-flavoured cake with a hazelnut buttercream filling, the frosting a white meringue. She built the cake in four tiers, the result an ornate white tower with rosette piping and lacework in the frosting. "Tall cakes are the rage now, like great buildings that reach toward the sky," Robert told Ena confidently, his arms held in a column over his head, his great body as broad as a tree. She had to laugh at the sight of him.

The inn will host several wedding receptions over the summer and there will be many more elaborate cakes for her to produce. Ena isn't entirely happy with her first effort, thinking that the piping is slightly uneven—she will have to practise. But Robert beamed seeing it sitting on the worktop. "Perfection," he crooned. "And very modern." (She had to admit, at least to herself, that the cake she had created was at once monumental and beautiful. Looking at it, she had been surprised, even slightly impressed that she had managed that kind of boldness.)

She has some lemon loaf for Hugh and Sarah, left over from afternoon tea at the inn. Pulling Ted into their lane, she sees that Sarah is on the lawn at the corner of the house and sitting in front of her easel. She wears her painting smock, her red hair loosely pinned, the skin on her hands and forearms speckled with colour. She is dabbing paint onto a canvas—huge stocks of vibrant green—oversized leeks perhaps, and above the green are slashes of unwavering indigo blue.

"I've been offered a place at the Ontario College of Art in the fall," Sarah frowns into the painting, "with a scholarship. One of the teachers saw my work in Chicago and recommended me. Of course, they thought I was Georgina Fells. When they asked the gallery owner how to contact me, he got in touch with Craig, and Craig told them my real name and that I lived here. The letter just came."

"Will you go?"

She doesn't answer at first. Hugh is clambering over patches of snow on his way to the truck. Stopping behind Sarah, he squints bemused at the picture. "Can't make head nor tail of that. Cornfield is it?" He is grumbling, teasing, but Ena hears a hint of admiration.

"You know nothing of paintng, Hugh," Sarah's tone is unsparing. She cocks her head and carefully considers the canvas. "College will mean going to the city for eight months." Her features gather new tension, a light coming into her eyes. "But it will be worth it, to get better."

Suddenly, she reaches back, her hands catching on Hugh's coat, her head resting on his chest. He grins, looks away from the painting and toward the truck waiting in the lane. "Annie will help around here some," he says. "And you'll make sure I don't starve, Ena."

"I'll make sure," she says.

AS SOON AS THE WEATHER TURNED in April, Hugh put a crew on the remodelling of Ena's kitchen, two men and a wagon clattering up her lane each morning with lumber and tools. The detailed plan for the enlargement had been completely Ena's own. Now, in late-May, the work is done.

Inside the kitchen door, Ena puts down a basket of freshly-harvested rhubarb and surveys the changes. A modern Hoosier sits where once a cramped jam cupboard had been. There is a new gleaming white porcelain sink, and a worktop that is much longer than the old one and made from a single slab of maple. The scarred pine floor has been torn-up and replaced with waxed oak boards which Hugh tells her (with satisfaction), will last and last.

A wall separating the kitchen from a cramped pantry has been taken down and the kitchen stretches from the front of the house to the back, and windows on both ends allow the light to pour in. She has two vistas now: the barn and the yard to the south, the spreading fields to the north. From her kitchen, deep in the quiet of work, she will look in either direction and take in the changing seasons. She has no one with whom to share these views, and so they will hold a particular poignancy for her, a weight.

What intrigues her most is the modern woodstove. Hugh had it specially shipped for her from Toronto. He's been wonderful, helping her with the remodel. It would have taken her years and years to accomplish such a thing on her own.

The stove is magnificent, the range broad enough to accommodate six kettles. "A professional model," Hugh called it, his arms crossed, his great chin sprung forward in satisfaction. The double sized oven has sliding racks and four levers for moderating heat, a temperature gauge and a generous warming hood. She is anxious to experiment with it—tea biscuits first, and then perhaps pastry. Less can go wrong when yeast isn't involved. (She won't tell Hugh, but she will miss the old woodstove. She knows the oven so well, how too much heat pushes at her hand. When the heat is just right, she can almost taste it, mellow and woody, and slightly dry.)

Eventually, she will master this new one.

JUNE HAS BEEN DRY and there are few bugs. Ena is in the

bush where the air is cool under the canopy of maple, ash, and oak trees. She hunts for wild strawberries but doesn't find any. The slanted sunlight catches on the etched tips of ferns, the mossy skulls of rocks. Billie roots energetically beneath a pile of rotting logs. Not far off, the stream makes its way through the cedar valley, a vapour of insects rising from the grey-green foliage. The air in the bush is rich and loamy, and laced with the sharper, drier scent of dust blown in from the fields. Hugh uses a tractor now, and today she can hear the rumble of it. But for all of his talk of progress and mechanization, he keeps his team of horses, lavishing them with renewed care.

Around her, in the bush, the dappled light dances and shifts, each stone and log changed, transformed into something alive. Amongst the solemn trees, Jamie appears, his body a long narrow column, shades of graduating grey. His eyes are the only point of colour—bluer than she remembers them—and they stretch and hold the whole of her, every last small part. He draws her gently, not only to him, but to everything that now shines out from his eyes. There is no separation, no space between. From somewhere far away, comes a shout, a laugh, the strange protestations of a saw. Ena smiles at the sound and watches as Jamie becomes a tree, his arms wide and generous. Her heels scrape trenches into the soft earth and she tips her face upward, her heart radiant, open.

Billie has abandoned the logs and now she sits beside Ena, her nose pointed toward the farm. Her eyes suddenly widen and Ena follows her gaze to the bottom of the lane where a black motorcar has stopped. For a few seconds a cloud of road dust obscures the view and when it settles she sees a man step out. He leans in to the driver, says something, and then turns toward the house. He doesn't hurry. He stands looking, his hand at his cap, his other hand gripping his bag which he then hikes to his shoulder. He is tall and lean and she doesn't know him until he walks. And then it's there, the slight sinking-in at the hips, the recognizable gait—Billie knows him right away and she shoots from the bush and down to the lane.

It can't be him. It isn't possible, and yet some part of her had always known. Ena emerges from the bush and walks beside the stone fence and down the field where her cows are grazing. She grips herself, arms clenched across her chest. The grade of the land forces her feet; she is powerless to resist the possibility.

Seeing her, he takes off his cap and rubs at his head with his wrist. He's grinning, standing straight and tall, so much older than she'd last seen him. And then she is holding him, too tight, but it's all right because he feels solid beneath her hands. Whole.

Blain stands back from her, his eyes searching her face. "Owen told me about the Captain, Ena. I'm awful sorry."

Ena nods. "Come in and sit with me. We can talk. I'll give you something to eat." He follows her down to the house, Ena swinging open the door to the new woodshed and then leading him through to the kitchen. When he steps in he takes his hat in his hands and looks around, gawking. "This is real nice, Ena. Dandy."

She pulls out a chair and motions him to sit, sets out lemonade for them in a big glass pitcher, a basket of her sliced bread, some butter and cheese. "You're still pretty scrawny."

Blain laughs, then he looks at her, his eyes keen, a sharpness in them that she hasn't seen before. "I owe you, Ena. You know I do."

She says nothing.

"I want to tell you what happened. I came back for that. And Owen." He doesn't look afraid, just determined.

"The truth," she says and his eyes stay on hers.

"That's what I'll aim for," he says. "You won't settle for less."

He pours himself out some lemonade but doesn't drink it. "The night the Captain got killed, my father came 'round here. I heard him hollerin' for me and when I went to the window,

I seen him standing in the snow, his shoulders hanging down like a sad-sack. Captain must have heard him too.

"Next thing I know, Captain's out there trying to get the old man to push off, but the bastard started walloping him—Captain coughing and struggling. You know how he got so winded, Ena." Blain takes in a deep draw of air, as if remembering has caused him to lose some measure of confidence. "Anyway, I went down and told the old man to quit, that I'd get him the money if he'd leave after he got it, and never bother any of us again. Sure, he said. Nothing left in him but greed, Ena. He stayed out in the snow, with Jamie, and I *did* get the money.

"Your room," she says. "You'd put it there." Blain nods

"A few days before, I'd taken the money from where I'd hid it in the barn rafters—the money you'd given me—and I put it with the money in the rucksack in my room, the money I *took* from him." His eyes spark with the mention of his father's cash. "I just wish I got Owen out sooner. I was set on leaving, Ena, as soon as the Captain got better. But while I was inside, I also got Jamie's gun."

A vision of the gun propped against the barn wall comes; she'd thought maybe Blain had been worried about the wild dogs again.

"I *had* the gun on him," Blain goes on, his words racing now, "but he kicked me. He'd worked on the log booms as a pike poler before, and even oiled he was quicker on his feet than you'd think." She thinks back. Long ago, she'd watched Blain play the fool, clowning with the logs on Hugh's wagon, his legs waggling ridiculously at Clem. He had been mocking his father then.

"Next thing I knew, my arse was on the ice. Easy for him to get the gun off me while I was sprawled out like that. I tried to get up but he hit me with the gun, took the rucksack, and he marched me out behind the barn."

"He had the money," she said. "Why didn't he just go?"

He shrugged. "Me and Owen were the only people who knew

how low he'd sunk. Maybe he hated us for it." He looked at her, his gaze scrubbed clean and open.

"The dog was locked in and once we got close, she was making a racket. I managed to get the bolt off the door and let her slip out. She started goin' crazy and when Carter took a swipe at her with the gun, I jumped him. Can't say how long we struggled before the gun went off, the old man hit in his shoulder, swinging at me and raging. I was scared of the old bastard, Ena. Not gonna claim otherwise. What I did next was to protect myself, but I'm not sorry for it. Not this part."

"It came to me that he didn't know the barn like I did. Working here for all that time, there was no place on earth I knew better."

Ena's eyes bear down on the barn and find the certainty of it—gaped and worn, settled on fieldstone.

"I lured him inside, scuffling and wrestling with him. Then I jumped the gate of the bullpen, bull in there all riled, likely because of the dog and all the commotion. Old man never lost a second. He swung himself over the rail and got in there with me—stupid bugger—and the bull, maybe because of the blood, started going out of its mind. And then I was back over the rail and safe. Carter didn't know that bull like I did. Watched the bull put him up against the wall, choke 'im. Once it settled down, it moved off and I could see right away that Jack Carter was crushed and dead. So I got a beat-up blanket from the loft—the bloodstained one me and the Captain had used for the calf, Ena, you remember—and I tossed it over the bull's gate and over Carter. I heaped forkfuls of loose straw over him. Bull was quiet by then. You know bulls. Like nothing happened. I tied it to the rail, just so the body would stay hidden under the straw.

"There were blood smears here and there so I put straw over anything I could see. I left the gun standing against the far wall, locked Billie in the barn, and got the rucksack with the money from the yard where the old man dropped it. I was almost to his truck when I saw you and Billie moving around the yard. I figured you'd gotten Jamie, that you'd help him inside." His eyes are glistening. "I was terrified of going back, being caught for what I done."

The house seems to hold on to every breath, every heartbeat, and there is too much anguish in it. "Let's go outside," she says quietly, drawing herself up from the chair, her hand on the door, their cups and plates abandoned on the table. Stepping out, the sudden rush of light fills her. They've been talking for a long time; they had spent an age together, during Jamie's sojourn in France. Blain had helped her bear the work, the loneliness. Now, they sit side-by-side on the flat rock in the field.

Standing in the yard, his shoulders set, his fist around the handle of his spade, Hugh is watching them. She wonders if he will rage at Blain. Demand that he make amends. Instead, he raises his hand and then lets it fall.

Ena answers Hugh's wave, her eyes lingering on him. "You enlisted right after."

"Was always going to do that."

"They said you were gone."

Blain shifts and then eases back on the rock, and for a moment he closes his eyes. "Got buried in a shell blast and after I crawled out, I didn't know where I was. Walked a long way — miles and miles—and you'll laugh: I found myself a farm!" He grins at her. "They were a nice family," he goes on. "An old lady, and a younger one. A man without a leg. The little boy was real sweet. Reminded me of Owen." The old delight has returned to his expression. "Strange coloured ducks, and cows with horns, fresh milk. Cheese—all sorts, Ena. And bread. Almost as good as yours."

He might be telling her a story now, she thinks, but it's all right if he is. "How did you get home?"

"When I was well enough, they brought me to a Jerry field hospital and they told the doctors there that I didn't know my name. At first, after the shelling, I didn't, but by then I did."

A sly look comes into his face. "But I pretended for a while not to."

"You'd be good at pretending," she smiles.

Blain laughs. "My mum taught me that. I think because she couldn't hear right, she made pictures in her head. Stories. She shared them with me and Owen."

Ena can see Margaret Carter quite clearly now: Margaret in a world that was wrapped in quiet. She'd thrust herself into its noisy heart, wringing from it all of its boisterous possibilities. Blain rubs his ear into his shoulder and then shoos away a bug.

"What happened in that swamp, Blain?" Her voice is clear, blameless.

He squints toward the west, in the direction of the peninsula and Jack Carter's forlorn scrap of bush, the abandoned still, the tumble-down house.

"Everything started with my mum."

"I know." She keeps her eyes on him. She had always known that the beginning was there in the black water, a frantic violence that was bent on reproducing itself.

"The night she died, Carter came home well-oiled from The Queens and they started to quarrel. Mum had enough of it by then. She told him she was going to take us boys and move into town. Annie had helped her get a permanent job and Mum was set on takin' it. She'd told me about it—she was proud of herself for making up her mind, for finally doing what she wanted. Told me to keep quiet about it. When she told the old man, he went crazy on her, and not for the first time. I was in the kitchen when it happened, watching the whole thing, all the while, Mum trying not to catch my eye, wanting to keep me out of it."

Blain looks up at the sky, a hand cupped over his eyes; for a moment his expression reflects the swiftly moving cloud, some of the old dreamer in him, but when his eyes travel back to hers, he is all there, not an inch of him restless or trying to run. "When the fighting was over, Mum went looking for

Owen. He'd been in his room, listening to all the yelling, so she looked there first. When she couldn't find him, she walked straight out of the door. She was pretty bloodied-up, and woozy, tipping this way and that. She went straight past the old man and disappeared into the bush. She was way over being scared by then.

"It was getting' dark when I went after her, but then Carter got in my way, told me to mind my business, to load some pallets into his truck. I was scared of him, even if Mum wasn't, and so I didn't follow her. Not right away."

His eyes travel over her face, looking for some signal, but she only waits for him to go on. "When I finally got done the loading, I followed the track to the swamp. Owen was down there. I could see him, even though it was real black by then. I didn't know, but I guess he'd gone there before, to get away from the quarrelling. This time, he was out on the ice, his arms wrapped around a log, cracks spidering out all around."

Blain is lost to memory, his head tilted.

"Mum must have spotted him. She'd tried to go to him and then lost her balance. Anyway, by the time I got there, she was face-down in the swamp, and not much I could do. Owen was perched there, on the ice, like a little half-frozen owl."

Ena puts her hand close to where his rests on the rock, as if to encourage him to draw strength up through it, from the land itself, as she has done.

"Owen told me later he'd called to her. Told her not to go across where she did. Told her he could see water. But she couldn't hear him." He stops, his eyes filling. "I picked my way across the solid part, down at the far end and got him."

Ena's mind goes to Blain standing at the side of the swamp, peering into the black water, not a thing left for him to do but to get to Owen. And that is just what he did.

From the shadowed bush, a fox barks—three bursts followed by a rich and unfolding quiet. The two of them sit while the sky turns pink in the west, and then darkens to violet.

"If you need to turn me in because of the old man, Ena, I'll understand."

She looks at him—this boy who wanted to leave, who should be gone. She draws all of his secrets to her.

"You said you owed me. You ready to do some work?"

His head lifts, surprise and astonishment in his eyes, and then he laughs. "Now? But it's almost night, Ena—" He whoops, affection in the sound.

She smiles. The fields are taken up by shadows until Ena can no longer make out the edges of things—the snaking stone fence, the line of bush, the angled barn.

"Tomorrow will do. Tomorrow will be just fine."

They are together at the centre of it, this bit of ground, Ena shaking out her skirt and offering Blain her hand.

ACKNOWLEDGEMENTS

IN THE LONG, HOT SUMMER OF 1914, Canada was still largely rural in character and had known peace for several generations. Few Canadians could have anticipated the impact the Great War would have; Canadian nationhood coalesced during this time, shaped by fervent change and heart-rending loss, at once socially far-reaching and profoundly and exquisitely personal.

Some important observations about land ownership and the transfer of property that might have affected a woman such as Ena McFarland: although women had been entitled to own property for decades, well into the 1940s farm women had a tenuous relationship to their farm businesses. Traditionally the transfer of farmland occurred within the tight web of family clanship and tended to follow male bloodlines. These transactions were not always formalized and relied greatly on family loyalty. To complicate matters, many rural wartime recruits failed to prepare a last will and testament before embarking for France. No doubt, particularly at the beginning of the war, volunteers were naive about what horrors awaited them. But as the war went on and casualties mounted, the reality eventually took hold; officials urged recruits to make sure their affairs were in order but the truth was that farm people had great faith in their families to take up their work, to give care in their absence, short or permanent as the case might be.

Writing historical fiction is a risky undertaking and any errors in the novel are entirely my own. The Grey Roots Museum and the Billy Bishop Museum, both in Owen Sound, were tremendously helpful in researching the era.

Several books were essential to the writing of *The Land's Long Reach*. These include, in no particular order: *The Selected Journals of L.M. Montgomery Volume II, 1919-1921*, editors Mary Rubio and Elizabeth Waterson (Toronto Oxford University Press 1987); *Soldiers of the Soil*, George Scott Auer (Ginger Press, 2016); *Inheritance Interrupted: Estate Files during WWI*, Jane E. McNamara (from lecture notes, the meeting of the Ontario Genealogical Society, Ottawa); *Marching to Armageddon, Canadians and the Great War 1914-1918*, Desmond Morton and J.L. Granatsein (Lester & Orpen Dennys Limited, 1989); *Vimy*, Pierre Berton (McClelland and Stewart, 1986); *Canada's Great War Album*, editor Mark Collin Reid (Harper Collins Publishers Ltd, 2014); *The First World War*, John Keegan (Vintage Canada, 2000); *Intimate Voices From the First World War*, editors Svetlana Palmer and Sarah Wallis (HarperCollins Publishers, 2014); *Northern Light, The Enduring Mystery of Tom Thomson and the Woman Who Loved Him*, Roy Mac-Gregor (Vintage Canada, 2011); *A Terrible Beauty, The Art of Canada At War*, Heather Robertson (James Lorrimer & Co. with The Robert McLaughlin Gallery, Oshawa, National Museum of Man, National Museums of Canada, 1977); *Five Roses Cook Book, Bread and Pastry* (Lake of the Woods Milling Company, 1915); *The Great War as I Saw It*, Canon Frederick George Scott (F.D. Goodchild Company Publishers, 1922).

The Virginian, by Owen Wister (MacMillan Publishers, 1902), is a real work of fiction that took North American readers (particularly young readers) by storm in the early 1900s. Through the power of imagination, a boy such as Blain Carter might well have been transported by it.

Many people were helpful to me in writing *The Land's Long Reach,* too many to do justice here. My special gratitude goes to Donna Mills, who generously shared her experiences of rural life in Grey County, and warmly conveyed her great love for the people who have for generations called it their home. My thanks and abiding admiration to the late Mary Lou Jones for her insights into women and art, and for her brilliant thoughts about technical solutions that might have been available to rural women artists, like Sarah, painting in 1914. I am deeply grateful to Margaret Pelz who read an early draft and lent her intense love of baking and preserving to the novel's next incarnation—her reflections were invaluable to the writing of this book.

It was my great fortune to meet George Auer who provided both resources and keen insights concerning the Grey 147th. Most important was his empathy for the recruits and their families, which was infectious and profoundly affecting.

My ongoing appreciation to Bethany Gibson for her astute guidance in all matters connected to writing. I am very thankful to Dr. Peter Neary for remarking on historical detail and to Hilary Neary for her help. My thanks to Margaret Milde for her careful and dedicated reading, and to Luciana Ricciutelli at Inanna Publications, who is an endlessly supportive and thoughtful editor.

I make special mention of my late father-in-law, Michael Milde Senior, who demonstrated a rare dedication to work while keeping great faith with his family. You have been an inspiration.

Finally, I am deeply grateful to friends and family for their encouragement, most particularly to Michael Milde, my north star.

Photo: Ruthless Images

Valerie Mills-Milde lives, works, and writes in London Ontario. She is the author of the novel *After Drowning* (2016), which won the IPPY Silver Medal for Contemporary Fiction. Her short fiction has appeared in numerous Canadian literary magazines. When she is not writing, she is a clinical social worker in private practice.